ROB RUSSELL

RACING TO "US"

RECRUITMENT IS A PRIVILEGE ***BORN IN BLOOD***

R.P. FORBES

Copyright © 2020 by R.P. Forbes.

ISBN: Paperback 9798483822059
Hardcover 9798484210060
eBook 9780578300238

All rights reserved. No part of this publication may be reproduced, distributed, or transmitted in any form or by any means, including photocopying, recording, or other electronic or mechanical methods, without the prior written permission of the publisher, except in the case of brief quotations embodied in critical reviews and certain other noncommercial uses permitted by copyright law.

Published in the United States of America.

Dedication

This book is dedicated to the strong women in my family, and to one other person—the best friend a guy could have, Mike Bowes of Steamboat Springs, Colorado. Mike left this Earth much too soon, but will never be forgotten.

Acknowledgments

Unequivocally, I would like to thank some very special people who indulged me in this writing adventure. Without the reminders of my enduring and lovely wife, Lisa, over many years, to "write that book," this novel would never have come to pass. Indeed, Lisa was my inspiration. Without my Aunt Nancy, well into her 90s, the most voracious reader of thrillers and viewer of action movies who ever existed, and her encouragement after reading my early chapters, my pen surely would have returned to its practical usage in non-imaginative endeavors. Without the amazingly strong and talented women in my family, from my grandmother, Marion, and my late mom, Jerre, to my own amazing daughters, Jessica and Susannah, and my cousin, Amy, and sister, Sandy, there would have been no motivation for this novel.

Without the heroism and bravery on the battlefield of two true American heroes, Navy Corpsman Alejandro "Alex" Salabarria, and Army Ranger Sgt. Enslin Dewitt, the exploits of the main character would have been pure fantasy. These two men embody the definition of "warrior." Thank you, Enslin, for entertaining my questions about what it means to be one of the best, an Army Ranger. I would like to thank Capt. Kelly Galvin for his expertise in all things military. His generous advice greatly helped all aspects of military movement in the novel. Look for his upcoming book, *PowerPoint Ranger: My Iraq War Logs,* due out in 2020.

My brother, USMC Lt. Col. Allen Forbes (retired), provided great insight into military life, as well as admonishment for making Rob a Ranger. I want to express my deep thanks to him, and these three other men, for their service to our country. We owe them and our other men and women in uniform, past and present, at the least a huge debt of gratitude, but much more as well.

I would also like to thank Rick Guthery for his invaluable insight and advice regarding helicopter flight and controls. By definition, Rick is also a hero. As a marine rescue helicopter pilot for Miami-Dade County, he survived a helicopter crash during a severe storm when attempting an open-ocean rescue operation, spending 17 hours in the deep blue before being rescued himself.

Without my cousin, Kay Forbes, a beta reader for the great Gerry Riddle, author of the incredible *Atlantis* series, I would never have found my editor, Michael Waitz. Mike's edits were more than helpful, and his careful eye caught things that propelled the book forward. My thanks to Jake Muelle for his formatting work, and Sean Strong for an amazing book cover. Thank you to my beta readers Kay Forbes, Miriam King, Bruce Brockhouse, Stefanus "Fani" Dewitt, Cissy Peters, Kate Garvy and Ed "Unc" Brigham. You are deeply appreciated.

My ski racing buddies growing up, Heidi Bowes, Billy Ward, Doug Finney, Tim Magill, Jack Miller, Coach Jon Leffler and the late Mike Bowes, provided rich memories and the raw materials for my book. I am in awe of your talent and fearlessness. To the late Carl Rammuno, my wrestling coach, and his son Tony, thanks for giving me the skills and confidence to stand my ground with anyone—or run like hell! Regarding the other parts of the story, suffice it to say I grew up in Steamboat Springs, Colorado, and loved every minute of it.

Thank you for reading my novel.

Chapter 1

Certain death lay before him. He looked down from his tenuous perch atop a monstrous, frozen cornice of snow at the tip of the Zugspitze, the highest peak in Germany. The cornice itself looked like a huge, white, thick-as-a-train flash-frozen wave that had curled into its most ominous and angry fist right before it smashes the smooth water just below. Eerily illuminated by the pink dawn of an azure cloudless sky, the vast, nearly vertical snow field below the peak stretched all the way to the valley far below still twinkling with streetlights.

He nodded to himself. It could happen in so many ways. A ski could come off, causing him to fall on jagged, unforgiving rocks. An unexpected avalanche, or maybe two. Like what killed his childhood hero, Buddy Werner. Buddy could easily outrun one, for God's sake, being a world-class downhill ski racer. But another one coming from the opposite direction? Not so much. But hell, that was just freakin' destiny, you know? And to die like that making a movie with the hottest female racer in the world? Frickin' poetic.

Immediately dismissing this thought, Army Ranger, Sergeant Robert "Rob" Russell, looked to his right, making eye contact with Jim and Danny, then to his left with Mike and Ricky, gave a big nod with his stealth-gray ski helmet, and all five simultaneously launched off the edge of the cornice. Just like they were at the top of a race course, they instantly accelerated to well over ninety miles per hour, free-falling through the air, not yet even contacting the very steep snow field a good seventy yards below, which was zooming up really fast to meet them.

The second his skis lifted off the cornice, without warning or willpower, Rob's life flashed before his eyes, or at least a part of it did.

Chapter 2

Just like dozens of other times, it was as if reality turned into slow motion, Rob's mind started a flashback in full, high definition color.

This time, Rob's mind flashed to two boys, Mike the racer with an Olympic skier dad, leading wannabe racer "Robbie" Russell to the Avalanche Chutes for the first time. Known to the locals simply as "the Mountain," they rode the towering gondola to mid-mountain, then flew down Central Park, catching some air on the catwalk halfway down to Four Points lift line, then up to the top of Storm Peak on the infamous Poma. This crazy lift was a single pole with a Frisbee-like disc on the very bottom that you were not supposed to sit on. Instead, you stuck it between your legs, let it rest on your butt, and let it pull you up while you stood upright on your skis. If you were like most racers, you could make that thing stretch like a rubber band, compressing the internal Poma springs. At its most stretched point, it would launch you like a giant frog for about fifty feet before your skis hit the ground again. The lift operators would yell but didn't really care unless you fell on the actual track, requiring them to stop the lift. If that wasn't enough to keep most intermediate skiers away from the top of Storm Peak, the imposing and very steep bald face of the mountain would.

Now at the highest point of Mt. Werner, at 10,500 feet, Robbie took a moment and gazed at the incredible view of the valley below. There was "Old-Town," Steamboat Springs, far down below, a little to the right. From that vantage point, he could look as far west, north and south as he wanted. For a kid from hot, humid and flat Miami, Florida, this view never ceased to take Robbie's breath away. Mike, who was born here, had already started to ski off towards Buddy's Run.

"Russell!" he yelled, "C'mon!"

Robbie jump-turned around and tried his best to catch up. Instead of taking Buddy's Run straight down, Mike traversed to the far side of Buddy's, trying to get as much speed as he could. They ducked under the out-of-bounds rope through some evergreen pines, trying to keep their momentum. If caught, they could lose their season passes and be banned from the Steamboat Ski Area for the rest of the ski season. But this was a special day. After a fresh dump of powder the night before, Mike knew the conditions were perfect. If they were lucky, and early enough, it could even be champagne powder, the ultra-fluffy stuff so unique to Steamboat. Mike had already persuaded Robbie to follow him. Sensing major excitement, he was eager to take the risk.

About 30 yards beyond the boundary, Mike stopped for Robbie. "It's just a little hike from here," he said, and started cross-stepping, with his skis on, up the hill and through the fresh snow. For about twenty-five minutes, they climbed on, exhaustingly sidestepping to another peak. Unknown, except to the crazies like Mike and the ski team, this peak was out of sight by about a mile from the in-bounds trails.

That same morning, Mike had told Robbie, "You're ready," and "you're coming." Matter of fact. No discussion. No arguing. No fear. By Mike that is. They were best friends since they met as sixth graders. Mike was a freakin' genius. He was also crazy. Absolutely insane. And had no fear.

At sixteen, Mike was already one of the top ski racers in the West. Which of course made sense. His dad, Stanley Burns, had been in the Olympics 30 years prior competing in his favorite race, the downhill. The downhill is the fastest race with the fewest turns. There is no room for fear. Some of the best slalom racers suck at the downhill, though. Why? It's a totally different race and favors different skills. The biggest difference is raw speed. Racers reach mind-bending speeds well over ninety miles per hour on a downhill course, on the razor's edge of control every second. The winners often admit they actually were out of control many times in a race, but somehow stayed on their skis. To truly excel at the downhill, the racer can have no fear of death. That is a rare person.

Thirty years earlier, in his first Olympics, Stanley was in the race of his life. He may have even won the gold if he had kept it up. Flying down The Streif at Hahnenkamm, Austria, home of the fastest downhill race course on the planet, he had just recorded the lowest time on the most difficult and steep section when the binding on his right ski released in some washboards at ninety miles an hour. He definitely won the dubious honor for the most hellacious crash ever survived on that mountain in the little town of Kitzbuhel. Barely escaping alive to tell about it, he ended his quarter-mile crash-slide less than five feet away from a 2,000-foot cliff and an ugly death. His Olympic aspirations, due to a severely sprained knee in the crash and only a crutch for a trophy, were over. But at least he was alive.

Although sabotage was clearly suspected—after all, how dare an American potentially beat the famed Europeans at their own sport—nothing could be proven, and the will to investigate died out rather quickly. Almost immediately, actually. But Stanley would never forget. He vowed to himself he would find out who sabotaged his bindings, ended his Olympic dreams, and nearly killed him.

But that did not end his love of skiing and ski racing. In fact, Stanley loved it so much he and his wife bought a property in Steamboat Springs with a nice hill and twenty acres, found the steepest section, chopped down some trees, cleared some brush, made a ski run and installed a rope-tow ski lift. The kind where you hang for dear life on a big knot on the rope as it drags you up the near-vertical slope for about half a football field long. At the top, you let go, turn around and look down on your very own private ski-racing training run. At the bottom, he built a three-story, Swiss-style chalet. He now had his dream home and dream property, all in one place.

Since Mike was sandwiched between two older brothers and two younger sisters, learning to ski before he could walk was just a normal thing. He was running gates before he was five. Gates are the poles that ski racers make turns around at crazy-fast speeds, where the winner only medals by fractions of a second. Mike didn't quite start off that fast, but by high school, he was bad-ass fast.

If it sounds easy, all anyone needs to do is try it sometime. There are few things in life more humbling than running gates on a slalom course, especially for the "expert" recreational skier. It is one thing to make beautiful turns down a steep run, even on a double black diamond run. It's another thing entirely to have to make a turn around a gate when your body and skis say, "No way!" Ninety percent of so-called expert skiers suddenly realize they are not nearly as great as they thought. The other ten percent think they just need better equipment. That ratio is about in line with the axiom that ten percent of the population are narcissistic delusionals, and who cares what they think anyway.

With years of dedication, starting before age four, combined with the proper physical training, expert coaching, incredible athleticism, and quite frankly huge balls, one may become an "A" racer. It's a well-known but understated fact, but many girls have bigger "balls" than many guys. In terms of ski racing, it's a combination of courage and overcoming fear, just like other endeavors in life. Since the beginning ski racer starts at "F," the climb is not easy, and progress is granted only by winning races in your grade.

World Cup skiers, on the other hand, the members of a nation's national ski team, are in a category beyond the best "A" racers. Beyond the athletic prowess and training, which of course they possess in abundance, they have reached that deepest level in their minds where they find peace in the face of terror and near-certain death. The winners are the ones who combine the physical with the mental better than any other racer on that particular day of the race.

Except for Downhill and Super G, every racer gets two runs. The lowest combined time wins. Everything matters. To say every second counts is a gross misunderstanding of ski racing. Many times, the winner is determined by mere hundredths of a second. Without the electronic eye keeping the time, it would be literally impossible to determine the winner.

Chapter 3

When Robbie was 12, he and his family moved to Steamboat and he began to ski in the sixth grade. At 12, he was already eleven years behind Mike in skiing. And when he finally decided to stop wrestling and start ski racing in the eleventh grade, no matter how gifted an athlete he was, he would never make up the skill gap between him and elite racers like Mike, Ricky, Danny and Jim. Even after two years of intense racing training and competition, he was just beginning to get to their level of casual skiing.

Not to say that wasn't impressive. Like the A racers, when faced with a double diamond, deep mogul run, instead of basically asking permission of each mogul to carefully negotiate a turn, Robbie basically made a straight line down the run, decapitating each mogul, if he really had to contact it at all. Most of the run was spent in the air, as the bumps and traversing "cat-walk" roads made for nice launch pads for ample flight. For the rare fall, the culprit usually was an unfortunate binding release.

The remedy for the binding release problem was to get the experimental "black" bindings. These bindings were only specially made for elite A racers, the national ski team members and professional racers. Since they were all prototypes, they were not even sold. Ski binding companies supplied elite racers with new stuff every season, for free. The idea was fairly simple. The bindings just did not release.

The reasoning was uncomplicated. When a racer gets to a certain level in skiing, the skis are really just an extension of his physical body. Losing a ski for such a skier is like a leg falling off a runner mid-race. It doesn't make sense. Ninety-nine-point-nine percent of the time, a good racer can recover from a mistake when skiing recreationally, without exaggeration. In a race, good racers can usually recover without falling and at least make it to the finish line, and may even make it onto the podium. Falling is so rare for elite racers, it often makes international headlines. Because of the speed and steepness of the race course, these rare falls are often truly spectacular. At the insane speeds and cliff-like runs these races are held on, these falls can be catastrophic and tragically, even fatal.

Somehow, over the years of training, coaching, free-skiing and just plain craziness, these elite few have learned to lock their fear of death into a vault more secure than Fort Knox. That doesn't mean they are fools taking foolish risks. It's the same way a successful hedge fund manager makes a hundred-million-dollar investment no ordinary investor could ever imagine making, for the reasonable fear of losing everything. But for him, it is not a gamble. It is not foolish. His training, experience, knowledge and instinct guide him. The failure for him is not in losing the money, but rather in not making the investment due to fear.

For the racer, failure is not pushing himself to his fastest speeds and tightest turns on an extraordinarily dangerous race course.

But if part of his body falls off, like his ski, he is out of luck. Even if he doesn't fall. Many times, he stays upright and skis out of the course on just one ski, and then skids to a normal stop. But no time is recorded next to his name. Just DNF. "Did Not Finish." The worst three words in a racer's vocabulary.

The binding companies cannot sell these "black" bindings to the public. Ever. Even to the "expert" level recreational skiers. They would soon be forced out of business with all the lawsuits. The lawyers would easily win by proving the obvious: "design flaw: binding did not release after fall." Knees would be wrecked and legs broken by the non-releasing binding. Before that, the negative publicity would have dealt a critical blow to the company anyway. So the only way to get them would be to impress the national ski team's scouts and ski club coaches.

It would be a long while before Robbie would impress anyone, if ever. Mike, however, had long ago impressed everyone at the national level, and had several of the prototype bindings. But Mike knew Robbie needed his first year of ski racing in regular bindings, like training wheels. But that would change, if he could stick it out.

With Mike as a best friend, Robbie's success was inevitable. Like a great chess player, Mike always had his eyes on "the fall-line," the fastest way down the race-course, thinking two turns ahead at all times. It was just a matter of time before he got Robbie to think that way too. From there, his natural athletic talent would kick in and he would belong with the best, anywhere on the planet.

Mike really believed it when he witnessed Robbie's first race. Robbie recorded the worst time of any racer in his first slalom race, falling two times, but getting up and finishing the damn run. But it actually showed the kind of person he was. Nobody does that. Maybe Robbie didn't know you were supposed to just ski off the course and hope people didn't notice your fall. Mike's dad even got a kick out of it.

"Well, he finished the race," he chuckled wryly.

That's what Mike believed, anyway.

"Way to go, Russell!" Mike told Robbie at the finish line, slapping him on the back. "You got your worst one over with!" he said, laughing.

With that little bit of pick-me-up from his friend, on his next run, Robbie not only had no falls but had one of the fastest runs in his class.

Hell, yeah.

That's the kind of friend everyone wants, but very few have. Sadder still, the lucky ones who have that friend often don't recognize it until they're gone.

Chapter 4

Back on the Zugspitze, while his body was rapidly descending at close to a hundred miles per hour, his mind in flashback mode was moving even faster. More like at the speed of light. Simultaneously concentrating on his aerial descent off the insane pinnacle high atop the German peak, Rob's mind continued to flash to the next part of the mental movie, back in Steamboat.

....

Of course, there is the training. No one can be good at anything without it, including ski racing. The answer to that problem is about three months of intense, gut-wrenching, ridiculous physical preparation. At the high school level, any athlete, well, at least any coach, will tell you that if their players are in fantastic shape, having spent months in intense training, like running, sprinting, lifting weights, stretching and eating right, combined with the best technical skills training, the athlete has a chance to be the best he or she can be for that particular sport. Without it, the only real chance they have is mediocrity at best, or serious injury.

For ski racing, it's called dry-land training. Those three words spoken together create an immediate and sharp response deep inside a true ski racer. The muscle memory itself produces an instant flush to the head, remembering the first two weeks of training after a summer of fun and adventure, perhaps physically strenuous, but nothing like what awaits them. Many people can relate to starting a new exercise program, or going for a run after a couple months off. All high school athletes remember the first couple weeks of training in the next sport's pre-season training. The soreness was inevitable. At times it was excruciating.

The pain of muscles full of lactic acid cannot be denied, and must be felt and overcome. Most pretenders will drop out at that point, plainly neither expecting nor willing to fight through this difficult time. Some of the most talented, God-gifted natural athletes will drop out at this point, or may not even start a sport, given that their fear of pain is so great that this first brush with physical discomfort is all their imagination can contemplate. Everybody knows a few of these people. How ironic it is that less-talented and less-gifted athletes go so much further and experience so much more satisfaction, in life itself, just by making it through the first three weeks of training.

For the ski racer, it is not about becoming massive in the weight room or having a perfect physique. Strength is very important, vital really, especially leg strength. But reinforcing wolf-like quickness and cat-like balance is what the best coaches work to develop. No two great coaches train exactly alike. Each one will draw from his own experience and past mistakes. One coach may have learned by having two vertebrae crushed while "successfully" hitting his max squat lift of 630 pounds, essentially ending his racing career. This coach knows to not over-train his racers in the weight room, to put it mildly.

Then there is the truly talented former-successful-racer coach, who mistakenly expects his racers to learn like he did, with little coaching and only a few key words. This coach gravitates to the one or two most talented on the team, and basically gives no coaching to the others. When mistakes or injuries happen, or the talented ones just don't do well, the coach doesn't really care. Maybe next year he'll find someone like he was. A star. Coaching optional.

Somebody like Ricky.

Ricky was just a kid, coming up in the program at the Steamboat Springs Winter Sports Club, or SSWSC. Kind of a funny little guy, with a raspy voice. Like some of the A racers, he was about two years old when he started skiing. By the time he was five, he was one of those crazy little bastards on the Mountain who would fly down the blue runs, always in groups of four or five, all screaming with delight, dangerously passing all the intermediate skiers and terrifying the beginners. Even at that early age, they loved speed, and were becoming very comfortable with it. With their low center of gravity and short skis, a fall was almost as fun as going fast, and certainly didn't hurt.

But Ricky was different. Ricky was already skiing with kids much older than him. On the recommendation of his pre-school ski instructor, a local girl with a passion for teaching her favorite sport, Ricky's parents took him one day to the SSWSC training facility and asked if he could join the club. They somehow persuaded the coaches to let him join, even though he was two years younger than the first age class at the club. The racing practice hill is just across the Yampa River on the south side of town, named Howelson Hill. Carl Howelson, a Norwegian Nordic racer and jumper, singlehandedly and enthusiastically introduced the European sport of skiing to Steamboat Springs in the first half of the 1900s.

Carl flatly couldn't imagine living in the winter wonderland of Steamboat Springs without any of its residents knowing the sheer joy of skiing and ski jumping. Without Carl, the sleepy little town never would have earned its title of Ski Town, USA.

Rob's mind moved back to Ricky.

Ricky took to ski racing like a polar bear takes to snow. It was so natural, so right. Ricky quickly beat out that first age class and moved up to the next age class, and the next, and the next. It was becoming obvious he would soon need to enter the same pool of junior racers the middle school and high school kids were in, or else have no competition. His parents were afraid he would get bored by being the winner all the time. But they were more afraid that after winning all the time, he would be devasted by a defeat once he finally entered into real competition, and would quit altogether.

But he was not even in the fifth grade. The decision was made that Ricky could move up to the junior levels in the sixth grade. He would have to wait two years. That meant Ricky would win every single race he entered for the next two years, unless he fell. And he never fell. The only races he didn't win were the ones he didn't enter, because of the flu one time and a scheduling conflict another.

One reason Ricky won all those races was that he trained on the same training course as the junior racers. Coach wasn't stupid. He knew Ricky could handle it. Train on the longer, steeper junior runs, with much tougher turns, and race in the pre-junior races. Just think of Andre Agassi. Before he entered high school, he could already beat any high school player and most college players. Superstars are like that. Of course, Andre went to the premier tennis program in the country for high school age exceptional tennis players, becoming Nick Bollettieri's favorite student. Except for the first semester, Andre never paid a dime to attend Nick's school, and never gave a dime after he became a superstar. As is always the case, there are two sides to every story, so Rob made no judgments. As every athlete knows, coaches who give a lot, expect a lot. Sometimes too much.

In sixth grade, Ricky finally was able to join the big boys. For the first time in his life, Ricky didn't win, even at the lowest Junior level, Class F. Such a horrible name for the last Class. F. Everyone the world over knows F means fail. It was hard on Ricky. To not be in first place. Or even to place in the first three spots. He would look at his recorded times, and he was not last, but far from first. It was so disheartening that he said to his mom, "I quit!" Not skiing, but going to races. His parents made a decision that kept him in the game …of life. They didn't force him to keep going, to push through it, to suck it up and act older than he was. It was a wise moment of taking one step back before taking two steps forward.

Ricky would continue to train, but would take a year off from competition, maybe two. In reality, about the only thing holding him back was that he was 30 pounds lighter than the top 10 finishers in Class F in any given race. He literally couldn't make himself go faster, by sheer laws of gravity. His parents knew they needed to give him a few years just to grow up physically. And emotionally.

By eighth grade, Ricky was ready to reenter the competitive field. That happened to coincide with Robbie's first year of ski racing in the eleventh grade. Mike told Robbie that Ricky was special. With awe in his voice, he told him he had never before seen a racer take a technical word from a coach after a run, and implement it perfectly on the next run. Ricky would be entered in Class F for the second time, as would Robbie, but for the first time.

Mike was all-encouraging to Robbie, telling him he could beat Ricky. After all, he was just an eighth grader. Mike reminded Robbie how they both were just cocky punks in the eighth grade, so he shouldn't worry, too much. For Robbie, that first season was about getting better times than Ricky. On the speed races, the giant slalom and downhill, Robbie had the weight advantage by a good twenty-five or thirty pounds. He would beat Ricky by several seconds. He would even win a few. Only in ski racing and a very few other sports could a high school athlete be so pleased to edge out a middle schooler.

Ricky, however, would edge Robbie out on the skill race, the slalom. Tight, fast, difficult turns are what this short but thrilling race is all about. This is where a truly talented racer will shine. By far the most technical race, the slightest of errors, undetectable except by the most experienced and trained eye of a seasoned coach or racer, will add the fraction of a second that separates gold from gravel, podium from also-ran, winner from "competitor." Robbie made more than one of those errors, on every turn. Ricky made none, on any turn. Ricky's weight after his two-year hiatus was such that weight didn't matter. Skill did.

By the end of that year, Robbie and Ricky advanced to Class C. There were just too few slalom races in the season for Ricky to win, so he could only advance to C by the end of his first season back. Although it was impressive that Robbie went from an "expert" recreational skier to Class C racer that season, by winning downhill and giant slalom races in his class, it was far more impressive that Ricky did it in slalom races only.

The A racers knew it, too. Next year, this little whippersnapper could challenge even them. The elite members of the club. The A racers. The best of the best of Ski Town, USA. The celebrated future of American ski racing on the world stage. From professional ski racers to Olympians, no other town in the nation has produced more champions and medalists than Steamboat Springs. As much as they noticed him, aside from Mike, it was funny how much they underestimated Ricky, and his talent. After all, he was just an eighth grader.

Once Robbie graduated from high school, he was unaware of Ricky's progress. He didn't really care anyway.

But that would change in several years, more to Rob's surprise than Ricky's.

Chapter 5

Directly behind Howelson Hill was Emerald Mountain. Dry-land training season ends with the grueling seven-mile round-trip run all the way up to the radio towers at the very top of the mountain, and all the way down. But that was 60 days away.

Each training began with two laps around the gravel baseball field, followed by stretching, then push-ups and sit-ups. Lots of them. Always to fatigue. For some, this meant 15 reps. For others, it meant 80. At the end of dry-land season, even the least athletic racers could do 100 sit-ups. The best athletes could do six times that.

Then there was stretching. Not just warm-up stuff, like before a run. Stretching was so important that the coach brought in professional stretching coaches and a local orthopedic surgeon to show proper techniques. The surgeon told the racers that properly stretched-out muscles can perform 20 percent better than unstretched ones. Robbie immediately committed to becoming the most flexible one on the team. He knew he needed any advantage he could get.

The stretching coaches, an ultra-laid-back husband and wife team from California, traveled the country giving stretching lessons. Coach found a poster they put together while he was visiting his parents near

Mammoth Mountain, in the central California Sierras. He reached out and invited them to come to Steamboat during dry-land training to teach his racers. Robbie was pretty sure when they weren't teaching stretching, they just pulled chairs out of their VW van and sat out in the sun, lit up their bongs, and worked on their tans. What a life.

After stretching came running. And more running. Not too much long distance, but uphill and downhill, sprints and sidestepping, all were essential. The most fun training was running down nearly dry mountain creek beds, hopping from boulder to boulder, rock to rock, barely keeping from falling but always moving and never hesitating. By late fall, these once-raging little creeks were slowed down to a trickle, exposing the huge boulders and giant rocks, worn smooth by eons of grinding under the long-extinct glaciers dragging them down from the mountains far upstream. Looking back, Rob realized how dangerous even this was, but no one complained. And no one wore helmets, or even thought to. In fact, Rob could not remember anyone getting hurt, boy or girl.

Coach knew if you had good balance to begin with, this training would bring it to a whole new level. And there was something about being out in nature, breathing cool, fresh mountain air, honing your balancing and quickness skills and testing your instincts. It was just much more fun than wrestling in a hot, stuffy basement with 50 of your fellow hygiene-challenged teammates.

The wrestling coach, the ultimate take-no-shit Italian boss man, who doubled as the drafting teacher, encouraged his devoted wrestlers, with a wry smile, to use any and all weapons they had, including stink warfare. Many took him literally.

Although his respect for his fellow wrestlers was unquestioned, Robbie thanked God for his broken foot right before his sophomore wrestling season, ending his season before it began. The week before, Robbie and a couple other buddies were doing something a little different during their lunch hour. The track coach had temporarily moved the massive pole-vaulting porta-pits, which were just huge, soft foam blocks in nylon mesh, into the basement wrestling room. Directly above the porta-pits were the floor-to-ceiling ropes used by the wrestlers for strength-training. But Robbie and his friends discovered a new use for them that day.

The long flight of stairs that led down to the wrestling floor were open on one side except for a metal railing. The pits were just below. The ropes could be walked up to a launching point above and behind the porta-pits. If one was brave and stupid enough, one could grab the end of that rope and Tarzan-launch himself, swing through the entire arc, and right at the highest point, let go, then free-fall down into the soft porta-pit, bounce up, roll off and do it again, over and over.

Robbie learned that day why pole-vaulters are taught to land on their backs instead of their feet. Those huge, thick blocks of foam easily let go of larger, wider objects. They do not let go of small objects very well, like feet when landing feet-first. When Robbie landed on his feet from his free-fall, he twisted slightly to get a faster exit toward the stairs for another jump. His feet did not twist with him. Instead, when his left leg was twisting, his foot, completely immobilized in the foam, did not, and the extreme torque from the ligament connected to the outside of his foot caused the tip of the bone to break off. Several painful days later, a visit to the doctor with x-rays resulted in a six-week cast to immobilize the foot so the bone would re-attach—he hoped.

Disappointed at first with the forced interruption in his wrestling career, Robbie's perspective on things took an interesting and positive turn. Next year, he would finally choose a sport he loved, rather than what he felt pressured to do.

As his mind continued its flashback at lightspeed, Rob now understood why he had felt so obligated to wrestle instead of ski race. Other things would also become clear in this flashback.

Apparently, winning the district championship in the eighth grade did not go unnoticed by the high school wrestling team. It didn't seem like that big a deal, but it kind of was. Not everyone who wrestled won championships. Actually, very few did. In a small town with a cowboy tradition, football and wrestling were the tough guy sports. Even basketball, according to our demi-god wrestling coach, was for "sissies who want to bounce balls."

Hell, ski racing wasn't even a school sport. How ironic, especially for "Ski Town, USA." It was a club sport, outside the school. There were no cheerleaders and pep rallies for ski racers. Until Robbie's senior year, you couldn't even stand up at the end of the season and get your letter, like the other school sports. Your coach wasn't even part of the school.

Only ski racers cared about ski racing. Like every other high school in America, the only sports that mattered to Robbie's school were the classic school sports. Robbie couldn't say to the upper classmen wrestlers he was ski racing this year. They would have assumed he was just turning his back on the team, and didn't want to train that hard. So along with the championship, there would have been pressure. Along with the pressure would come the threat. He would go out for wrestling or be hazed, harassed and bullied. Not that he was afraid to fight, but that might not be the best way to start high school.

It was no surprise then, that Robbie went out for wrestling his freshman year, hating every moment of it. Even if you are pretty good at something, but you hate it, and you still do it, it's like voluntarily going to prison and pretending you enjoy the food every day. And the company. If hell is a place void of joy and fun, then he found a little pocket of it in the high school basement where the team practiced every day. Realizing most of his teammates were there because they actually loved it, Robbie was beginning to think this sport may not be for him.

The problem was that he couldn't quit. He would be despised by the team and the coach. That mattered to him. He would be labeled a pussy, which would no doubt make him fight for his reputation. To say that the broken foot was a life-saver was not exaggerating, even though Robbie didn't realize it at first.

The silver lining to breaking the bone in his foot was that no one could argue with the former district champ to try another sport after missing a season. Although it was too late to join the ski team for his sophomore year, especially without dry-land training, Mike said he should go for it next year. No one had been allowed to race without doing dry-land training. Ever. Without this intense training, it was just too dangerous.

The final day of dry-land training occurred in late October, right before Halloween. Every year, without fail, Steamboat got a huge dump of snow on Halloween, two feet or more of the heavy stuff. It was Mother Nature's way of telling us that fall was history and winter was now reality. Deal with it. Coach knew he had to get this run in before that snow, or the run couldn't happen. Even though most of the first big snow would melt, it would still be around in the shady parts of the road near the top of Emerald Mountain. Coach did not want this mandatory run cancelled or unnecessarily complicated. It was the culmination of his carefully crafted training season. He knew if his athletes could make this run, they were ready for racing.

After the final run, there would not be enough snow to ski on for a few weeks or more, but the team could do many other little things, like play soccer, run wind sprints and hundred-yard dashes, and do sitz against the wall. Sitz are where you lean with your back against the wall, slide down like you're sitting in a chair, and then hold it for one minute. Rest for one minute. Then repeat. Twenty times.

The agony of that exercise, as thighs burn with oxygen deprivation and extreme exhaustion, is barely outweighed by the screams of the coach – "You have only one hundred yards to the finish line in your downhill race! Giving up is not an option!" he yelled. "Every second counts! The longer you hold this, the faster your time in the race!" The amazing thing about Coach was that he was doing it with the team, and still could yell at everyone. The moaning and screaming as they fought through the pain sounded like a medieval torture chamber.

••••••••••••••••••••••••

But today, Saturday morning at nine, the last day of official dry-land training, the run up to the radio towers at the top of Emerald Mountain loomed large over each racer.

As Robbie prepared himself to attack the run up Emerald Mountain, getting his mind wrapped around this crazy final day of dry-land training, he looked around to see if everyone was there. Mike was there. So was Ricky. All the girls were there. Only two racers were missing. Two A racers. Two absolutely fearless racers. Jim and Danny. Extremely skilled, with a good dose of natural talent, they were usually within the top ten finishers in their ski races. Jim had even won two downhill races last year. Also, they were two of the hardest partying guys Robbie had ever met. He guessed they didn't feel quite well enough for this run, after a particularly fun Friday night.

But just as the group was about to run off, Jim's tricked-out Chevy Blazer came flying down the road, skidding to a power-slide stop at the base of Howelson, throwing up a huge cloud of dust from the gravel parking lot. Jim jumped out, leaned over, and puked a good five seconds, then jogged over to Coach and said, "What are we waiting for?" and started jogging up the hill. The team just stood there, mouths open in disbelief, disgust, and strange admiration for a full three seconds.

For the first time, Robbie looked at Coach and saw his bare feet. "Coach, where are your shoes?" he asked incredulously. "Forgot 'em. Let's go." And he ran the entire run barefoot.

Rob had no recollection of anyone complaining that their feet hurt on that run.

The first part and last part of the run would be the toughest by far. The first part started at the parking lot at the bottom of

Howelson, next to the 90-meter jump, then to the right to a steep road that four-wheelers couldn't even get up. That was the first and shortest section. The next mile was straight with increasing grades of steepness. There was no way to run fast. Most normal, non-racer people had difficulty walking any part of it.

For the racers, it was just one foot in front of the other, on the balls of the feet, running style. The next section was full of steep switchbacks, followed by some long stretches. Finally, after a last turn and a dense aspen thicket, the road opened up to a beautiful overlook of the entire Yampa Valley in three directions. One quarter of the run was left.

Looking due east about three miles as the crow flies, the massive Mt. Werner rose up from the valley far below. Looking due north, one could see Hahn's Peak far in the distance, a long-extinct volcano, forming a perfectly pointed cone. Looking west lay the Sleeping Giant, the last mountain as one heads out of town on Highway 40, still peacefully asleep in the mid-morning light.

The overlook was a fairly famous spot to locals. It was a bend in the road and a natural place to take a break, if one were walking or mountain biking. At the elbow of the bend, one could stand and look down a shear two-thousand-foot cliff. You could throw a rock over the ledge and count a full six seconds before hearing the crash below. Rocks were not the only thing to go over the edge. No fewer than three crashed cars could be made out from the top of the cliff, lying in mangled heaps on the jagged boulders far below, rumored to still have the bones of the drivers and their passengers. The stories of the late-night keg parties ending in a joyride gone wrong circulated far and wide in the county.

As Robbie was just getting to the edge of the cliff, one of the older and more vulgar racers was finishing a story on one of the crashes. He was saying "… and he closed his eyes right then and went flying off the cliff. They found them that way the next morning!" he laughed, as if he had just told the funniest story ever.

“Kent, you are so full of shit your eyes are brown!” said Jim, who couldn’t stand him.

“Why do you hate me so much?” whined Kent.

“Because you’re such a dipshit,” Jim laughed, as if that was the most obvious thing in the world.

Jim and Danny, the two other seniors on the team, were seriously cool dudes. They could talk the talk and walk the walk. They were fearless speed junkies who had no pretense.

Kent was the opposite. Actually only a B racer, he nevertheless told everyone at school he was an A racer, and one of the best. He often wore his racing stuff to school, loudly bragging that he was entering another, highly dangerous and elite race in some other ski town, like Aspen. What he left out was that only the A racers were allowed to run the downhill on the most difficult run on Aspen Mountain. The B through F racers were on the Racer’s Edge on the nearby but totally different mountain, called Buttermilk. The Aspen Mountain run, called “America’s Downhill,” is actually not one single run, but three strung together. Only the best racers in the world were allowed, which included high school age A racers.

Kent was a B racer, so he did not qualify. But Kent never let truth get in the way of a good story, especially about himself. Because of his big bragging mouth, he occasionally was quoted in the school newspaper, as “the” authority for the SSWSC, making sure they misrepresented his skill level as one of the top A racers. The guys despised him for all this.

So Kent, the weasel that he was, became the butt of every joke on the team, and subject to merciless teasing and practical jokes. He was lucky Danny wasn’t there today. Compared to Danny, Jim’s comments to Kent were glowing compliments.

Amazingly undaunted, Kent was launching into telling everyone about the supposed police report, but stopped short when he looked at who was just now coming up the road.

This was clearly not the time for Kent's gross storytelling. Keeping pace with the slowest runner up to this point, Coach was not at all happy when he saw the seniors stopped and loudly demonstrating how fast the crashed cars had to be moving to land so far away from the cliff's edge. Coach knew they were just hoping he would decide to end the run there and start back down. He was barefoot after all, and surely ready to quit. Fat chance of that.

As Coach turned the corner without breaking stride, he called out, "I'll be at the second tower." Everyone knew, especially the A racers, that if Coach didn't see them touch the second tower, they would be running this again. So off they went.

That was the three-quarter mark of the run. The last section was an extremely steep road cutting diagonally up the thick evergreens covering the steep north slope of the mountain. This steep section was where the name "Emerald Mountain" came from. From the valley below, it looked like the giant gemstone was glistening in a perfect setting. At one time, the mountain proudly held the world's longest chairlift, spanning from the parking lot at the bottom all the way to the top of the mountain.

But once the first ski runs were cut on the new ski hill called Steamboat, the writing was on the wall, and the chairlift was disassembled and moved down and across the valley. What was left on Howelson Hill was a world-class 90-meter Nordic ski jump, and a fast T-bar to the top of an ideal though small ski-racing training hill. And Emerald Mountain could get back to simply being the jewel of the Yampa Valley.

The only way up this super-steep section was one small step in front of the other, but in our case, a running step up on the toes, not a walking step. The top of the mountain had huge radio towers, visible for miles around, sticking up like needles scraping the sky. All they had to do was touch the towers, high-five Coach, turn around and run back down. It felt so good to finally get to Coach and slap hands. It was no small feat to make it to the top. Then it would be so nice running down. Piece of cake.

Hardly.

Anyone who thought the run back down would be easy had some nasty surprises in store. Your legs, exhausted by the three and one-half mile run *up* the smaller mountain, were not at all stable coming down the same road. Maintaining balance on exhausted legs in loose gravel on a steep road was anything but easy, and took a great deal of concentration. Then thirst became a huge factor.

No one brought water on this formidable run. There were no water fountains along the way. Now they had to run all the way down to get their first drop in what would be almost seven miles round-trip. Even worse, without having to breathe super hard like the uphill part, the inexperienced runner would start taking shallow, short breaths going down. That is, until the excruciating cramps seized their sides and stomachs, and thighs started burning like an acetylene torch was taking aim on them. The only remedy was to slow down and immediately start breathing deeply, hoping more oxygen in the lungs would make its way to the cramped areas. Within a couple hard and long minutes, the cramps eased up. The rubber legs were still a big problem, though.

To Coach, the downhill part of this run was just as or even more important as the uphill part. For the rest of the racing season, all the racers did was ski down a hill, never walk up it. The lesson to learn was how to breathe to feed the oxygen-starved and on-fire muscles going down a run, not up it.

And the A racer who wasn't there for the run? Two days later, Coach ran all the way with Danny to the top and back down. This time he even had his shoes. Danny was nearly as fit as Coach, and had no trouble with the run.

Chapter 6

Still only a second later from his launch off the cornice at the top of the Zugspitze, seeming like extreme slow motion in the physical realm, Rob's mind continued its flashback, bringing to life the next subject his subconscious wanted to expose.

The untrainable factors, which no coach can instill, are something else entirely. Like talent. And heart. Talent and training will take an athlete very far in any sport, especially in high school. Depending on the depth of the program, it may get him on the A squad, the first team, and if it is an individual sport, like ski racing, in the upper half of finishers in a race. Depending on the level of talent, he may even medal in a few races.

Heart, with training, but without talent, will get an athlete to a certain level of competence and strength, and maybe on the B squad, or a perennial alternate in an individual sport. He may be just above average, and may really get to know the sport, but just not quite good enough to play with the best. He will stick around and be reliable, at least more so than a talent without heart. These athletes will not be able to play at the highest levels. But that will not stop them from becoming good or even great coaches.

But then, if he has the training, the talent, and the heart, he can become an elite at his chosen sport. Chosen by whom is usually the question. If he starts at a very young age, then the parents will have made an indelible impression on his choices that carries him into his peak years as an athlete, devoting a huge amount of time and money to his development. In ski racing, the technical training is what separates these incredible athletes and the five best finishing times in a race. At that level, they have dealt with the fear, and have found that they are capable of existing on the razor edge of control and chaos, life and death, alternating between the two and pushing through without reservation or hesitation.

Like every other sport, the equipment is crucial. And more important than that is the technology of the equipment. Take the evolution of skis, for example. They used to be long, straight, and made of wood, with leather strap bindings. Then they progressed to laminated wood with steel edges, reinforced with layers of fiberglass and other strengthening layers, but still very long and skinny. Thanks to Bode Miller, who certainly does not get enough credit, and no royalties, all skis are now parabolic, meaning fat on either end and skinny in the middle, and much shorter than they were years back.

In 1996, Bode was the first racer to successfully use the new parabolic skis in any major race. It just so happened that he used them in the 1996 Junior National Championships, and won gold in three of four events, and silver in the fourth. By the next year, the long, less parabolic skis were practically given away, and skiing made a monumental leap forward. The reign of the long straight skis was over. Every racer on the planet either had the new design or was just not competitive anymore.

However, if Bode had done poorly, no one would have noticed the strange skis he was using, and the long, skinny skis would have ruled for another year or more. Fortunately for skiers worldwide, and certainly the ski manufacturers, Bode was an exceptional talent who used the revolutionary new ski design. Since copying is the sincerest form of flattery, especially in a competitive setting like ski racing, the ski design revolution had officially begun.

In real time, barely another second had elapsed during Rob's flashback.

Chapter 7

The subconscious mind is uncontrollable and unreasonable. No one can choose what she dreams about, or direct a dream's subject matter in her sleep. At that certain-death, life-flashing-before-my-eyes moment, the same is true. Even though you are fully awake and conscious, you have no control over the order of your thoughts, or whether you bounce around from topic to topic. Many subjects arise, but are never dealt with.

At this moment, Rob's subconscious chose to return to the Avalanche Chutes, that crazy-perfect day 10 years ago when Robbie and Mike were juniors in high school.

Both only 16 years old, they were at the very top of the Avalanche Chutes. Clearly, Mike was unbothered and totally relaxed. Robbie could not believe Mike was serious about this. It had to be a joke, maybe to see if Robbie really had the cojones to be a racer in this elite club his friend belonged to. He looked down, and because there was a little cornice overhang where they stood, he could not see the bottom, which was 150 yards below.

The slope itself had to be nearly vertical, almost impossible to stand on. If you could stand at all, balancing on the inside edge of one ski, you could touch the slope's wall with your hand barely reaching out past your elbow. If the inside edges of your skis were not expertly filed to a razor's cut edge, you would not have a chance to turn on a slope this steep, or even stand on it. The only skiers in existence who would take care of their skis like that on a daily basis were the racers, and then not even all of them. That's one reason a piste, or chute, like this is so very hard to ski.

The other reason is that it is insane.

All he could see far below was the flat bottom, expanding into a large open area, and then the trees. The open area had been formed by being the place for the avalanche of snow to finally come to a rest. There were no trees for the obvious reason that the tons of snow in motion had long before mowed them down. It had to be a joke.

Mike then said, "Back up a little." Robbie exhaled a huge sigh of relief. Actually, he almost cried with relief, believing this test was over and they could go back to the "normal" double diamonds they used to fly down. Then he saw Mike pull out a little round M80 firecracker from inside his ski jacket, light it, then throw it six feet from the edge of the cornice, where it sank several feet into the snow. He said,

"Watch this."

When he heard the muffled explosion of the firecracker, a massive chunk of the cornice itself broke off and disappeared, unleashing an avalanche with a huge upward rush of a snow cloud.

Falling 50 feet in the air, the detached cornice crash-landed on the insanely steep slope and rushed down the chute all the way to the bottom before slowing down and running out of energy right in front of the trees. Now standing at the new edge of the cornice, and just as the massive snow cloud cleared, Mike said, "See you at the bottom!" and launched off the new mini-cliff he'd just created, instantly disappearing.

Within seconds, he was at the bottom of the chute, having expertly turned at impossible speeds like he was running a downhill race course. He turned and looked up at Robbie at the very top, and waved his poles in a great big "C'mon!" gesture.

"*Fuuuuck* You!" yelled Robbie. There was absolutely no way he was going to do that. He would simply retrace his steps and meet Mike back on the in-bound run somewhere. At least he would be alive. He had no doubt in that moment that he did not belong in that elite club. Turning around carefully to leave, Robbie planted his pole into the snow where he stood.

Instantly he realized he had just caused the snow under him to disappear just like the first cornice had mere minutes ago, and without conscious intent, he was now flying down the nearly vertical slope at ungodly speeds, doing anything not to fall and be buried by the new mini-avalanche just behind him. Although the real avalanche danger was gone with the first one, even a little avalanche could cause some real problems if he got caught under one.

If fear is one of the greatest motivators, then abject fear must be life's ultimate motivator.

Making crazy jump-turns, each one feeling like it would be his last, losing and gaining his balance simultaneously, barely feeling the snow beneath his skis, sensing death behind him and in front of him, only animal instincts kept him from falling to either death or catastrophic injury, at least in his mind.

Seconds later, at the bottom of the run, heart pumping and adrenalin still coursing through his veins like lightning, Robbie made sure he sprayed as much snow on Mike as he could. Robbie stopped inches from his best friend, laughing, crying, spitting, yelling, screaming at the top of his lungs, and also ready to kill him.

"You are a fucking asshole! Are you trying to kill me or something?" Robbie said breathlessly.

Mike grinned widely, leaning his chest on top of his ski poles as he stood, giving Robbie a chance to catch his breath. "You liked it, huh?" asked Mike. "Feel good now, dontcha?" Mike asked. "You're the fucker," he taunted, as he jump-turned around and started skiing down through the trees in untracked powder to get back in-bounds.

Robbie turned around again and stared up at what looked more like a cliff than a ski run, barely believing he'd not only survived, but didn't even fall. He then pushed off and raced after Mike, who was already gone except for his tracks, hoping he would catch up with him. He could already sense the increased confidence in his skiing.

Up to that point, that was the most terrifying and awesome feeling he'd ever had in his life. Nothing at all compared to it. He didn't know this yet, but nothing ever would. He would later realize that in that moment of indecision and near death, just before his skis touched the vertical slope and before he made his first turn, his whole life flashed before his eyes. Many things became clear to him, although he was not entirely sure why.

What he would find out was that even though he would later face many near-death experiences, and each time his whole life would flash before his eyes, there was nothing like the first time.

That in no way minimized his enjoyment of other things, as if there was nothing better to live for. On the contrary, when one has experienced and survived a death-defying event, one is now able to appreciate the simple, or even the great things in life, like relationships and accomplishments, and not fear he is missing anything, wondering if there is anything better, more fulfilling, more ultimate. He can enjoy life for what it is, with a sense of contentment even. He can now relax and be even more in-the-moment with his experiences and adventures, not trying to outdo the last thrill, but not shying away from it either.

What Robbie had just done, thanks to his best friend Mike, placed him in that truly elite category of humans who have conquered fear, and can rise above their legitimate fear and perform, expertly. Robbie had no idea at the time how this one insanely dangerous ski run would impact his life, and all his choices. But time has a way of explaining things, sometimes sooner, sometimes later. Some people wait a lifetime for clarity.

In Robbie's case, it was now.

Chapter 8

As abruptly as it started, Rob's flashback ended. Rob was completely back to full speed reality on the Zugspitze, acutely aware that he and his buddies were about two seconds to impact.

As they simultaneously hit the fresh, untracked powder on the near-vertical slope at 90-plus miles an hour, Rob and his four friends made two turns before they funneled into a narrow chute between two bare and jagged rocky formations. Without slowing, they made another 60-or-so-yard flight through the air off a mini cliff into another beautiful unmarked snowfield. Skiing like hawks diving to seize their prey, they missed deadly rocks on one turn, then floated through knee-deep dry powder on another. It looked like the run of a lifetime.

As Rob's GoPro-drone began to elevate to about a hundred feet above the group, the incredible natural beauty of the Zugspitze came into clear focus. The five skiers were nearly in tandem in their long, nearly straight turns. Impossible to see were the critical micro-adjustments made each second, which kept the formation nearly perfect at breakneck speeds. The fresh powder sprayed billowy white plumes on each turn, leaving perfectly carved tracks behind them. The mountain peak was treeless on the top two thousand feet. About three quarters of a mile west of the five, the in-bounds terrain of the ski resort came into view.

As the drone continued its vertical climb, one could see that this out-of-bounds run actually took a hard left to what looked like a feeder path leading down to rejoin the main ski area. In two more seconds of vertical climb, the drone revealed why.

The Zugspitze ran out of mountain.

A half-mile below the five skiers, the slope disappeared into a sheer five-thousand-foot cliff. The group showed no signs of slowing down or making a move to the feeder path. From the individual GoPros, it was plain to see the absolute rapturous joy and zeal these skiers were experiencing. Seeing each skier's view down the slope, turn for turn, missing killer rocks by inches, flying over steep sections and landing on the soft, dry powder made it look easy. Like anybody could do it. Nothing could be further from the truth.

This was exactly why they were recruited. They made the impossible look easy.

Without the years of race training, fear breakthroughs, learned technique, Ironman-like fitness, physical strength, and of course, "prototype" equipment, this would be a suicide run, impossible to survive. Even with all that, the risks were insane, the danger well beyond unreasonable. And they were not even halfway through their run.

Their helmets were not run-of-the-mill. Built for skull protection, they were also aerodynamic and warm. The mirrored goggles fit perfectly on them and the strap was locked in place by a special snap on the back of the helmet. Each skier had special but unobtrusive earpieces, that not only allowed them to communicate with each other, but allowed near-perfect musical fidelity to be pumping in their ears, simultaneously.

Jim and Danny had similar musical tastes. They could listen to Zach Taylor and Florida Georgia Line all day, and fairly often did just that. Mike had listened to every kind of Top 40 music growing up and little had changed. He currently liked Maroon 5, Marc Anthony and Bruno Mars. Ricky was switching between classical string orchestra and The Dixie Chicks. Rob's favorite was classic rock, like seventies stuff. Regardless of their tastes, for this truly radical run, they all agreed to the first three songs; Lynyrd Skynyrd's "Sweet Home Alabama," Aerosmith's "Sweet Emotion," and Rolling Stones' "Start Me Up," in that order. Rob was very happy. "Freebird" was his first choice, for the whole run, but this line-up was a stellar compromise.

Although each skier could not have cared less if they did not have music pumping in their ears during this insane run, they were quite pleased that Mike had provided the yet-to-be-released version of the dual earpiece and microphone. Mike always had a line into the pre-releases of the most advanced audio devices, ever since his granddad got his first Walkman tape player back in the Stone Age. For this run, the military didn't require the use of their earpieces and mics.

Coming up fast was the two-hundred-foot radio tower, which height did not include the nearly 50 feet buried in a concrete foundation deep in the granite mountain.

Aside from radio transmitting devices securely attached to the tower in several places, there was a large rectangular warning sign. Rob eyed the sign and read "ACHTUNG!" A large orange skull and crossbones was below the warning. Below that, in German, read, "Do Not Advance! Death Beyond This Sign!"

"Only German?" Rob thought as he and the group executed an almost invisible move to sail past the warning sign heading straight to the cliff and certain death, at close to 100 miles an hour.

As Rob's drone elevated to 600 feet above the five guys, showing their epic run from the top of the Zugspitze, the final 200 yards to the cliff's edge came into alarming clarity.

When will they stop? Aren't they going to stop? And then, 100 yards above the cliff, the five skiers dropped their poles and got into a tuck position, like sitting in a chair, leaned over with the head close to the knees, arms straight back and to the sides, increasing their speed to well over 100 miles per hour, and aimed straight for the edge of the abyss that lay in front of them.

With impeccable timing, "Sweet Emotion" began just as Rob and the other four guys, in near-perfect formation, in defiance of all reason and ignoring overwhelming survival instincts, flew off the edge of the cliff, instantly looking down 5,000 feet of sheer rock cliff to a snow-covered valley miles and miles in the distance.

At that instant, as Rob's heart nearly dropped out of his chest, he realized he and these four friends had just made an irrevocable choice, with no turning back, no do-overs, no trial runs, no second chances. And then he screamed, for joy! The absolute absurdity of this choice and the harsh reality that he had less than 10 seconds to live hit him square on.

"Ten seconds? That much time?" he said to himself. Hell, his F-16 pilot buddy only had eight seconds to eject safely when his jet went into an uncorrectable stall spin, and his whole life flashed before his eyes as he also executed every single corrective measure to regain control, all the while knowing that not one of the last three airmen who'd experienced this exact same event had survived.

"Ten seconds? That's like an eternity in comparison," Rob thought, as his second life-flash of the run began.

In this one, his childhood flashed up – scenes of his Mom and Dad and two brothers and sister and all his cousins playing in a North Carolina river with Granddad and Grandmom on the bank, just watching and laughing at their grandkids. And then to his first girlfriend and what she showed him that night, before he dropped her off at her home. And then to that firefight in Afghanistan, where he was in a life or death shootout with a Taliban mole. He and the other Rangers had just trained this guy to be an expert soldier in the Afghan army. As thanks, the vermin shot a bullet through Rob's best buddy's neck, which would have killed him had Rob not been there.

The Army calls it "green on blue." They could call it whatever they wanted. It was a whitewash. It was *sanitized.* They did not want the American public to really *know* the very Afghans we train are the ones turning around and killing us.

Eight seconds left. So much time left! "Well, this wasn't war, and no pressure really, so it's ok to have all this time," Rob's mind told him.

Almost unconsciously, two seconds into the flight from the edge of the cliff, simultaneously with Rob's life flashing before him, Rob yelled, "Boots!" into the microphone. All five guys reached down for their boots. Each skier, consciously thankful for his lithium-ion heated gloves, popped a snap and opened the boot-shell just enough for the wind, at over one hundred miles per hour in the free-fall, to strip the shell from the inner boot. Both the boot-shells and the skis came off with ease, instantly creating distance between the falling skier and his skis.

Six seconds left! "Jackets!" yelled Rob. The last item was the outer jacket shell, which, with two opposite snaps, flew off instantly.

Four seconds left. Rob looked around to see the other five guys. All five were side to side, having also shed the now-unnecessary equipment, freefalling to certain death in less than two seconds. With three seconds before certain death, Rob yelled his last order, "Wings!" And the five guys extended their arms straight out to their sides and spread their legs wide, filling the little air pockets of their human wing suits and leveling off.

And off they flew.

Now flying through the air at about 160 miles per hour, they had roughly 30 seconds before they had to deploy their parachutes for the final landing close to five miles away in the lower valley. If all went well, they would land almost 8,000 vertical feet and nine miles from where they started not even 10 minutes before.

Chapter 9

Twenty-four years *before* the crazy run on the Zugspitze, Rob was taking his very first steps in life deep in the mountains of western North Carolina. Over the years, he and his cousins had spent many summers at Granddad and Grandmom's place up there.

They bought the place from a spring-steel coil-making company nearly going out of business that desperately needed money. For many years, mountain land was cheap and plentiful, especially during a national real estate downturn. No local mountain people could think to afford buying the property, and the company didn't have the imagination to market it. After all, who in their right mind would buy one thousand acres on the side of the second-highest mountain east of the Mississippi?

Rob's Granddad would. Tired of all the changes, the heat and the traffic in Miami, where he'd lived since he was six, he decided he would find his ultimate retirement project. He made the company a low-ball offer he thought they would surely refuse. Instead, they accepted it. Not one to look a gift horse in the mouth, he bought the property and immediately started clearing trees, making meadows and planting fruit trees. Apples and pears were his tree of choice, so he planted 50 of each. On one meadow, he started a blueberry patch. On another, he told his wife, Mirium, she could plant as big a garden as she wanted and grow anything she liked. "Mir-e-uhm!" he would say in his booming voice, "This is your garden. Do whatever you want."

He had no idea how this diminutive, full-blooded German girl would take those words to heart. Before he knew it, she had cultivated and planted, with the help of their new caretaker, a garden big enough to feed a small army. It was a good thing, as they would eventually have 13 grandchildren who loved to spend the summers with them. Besides teaching them how to work a tree farm, they never lacked a home-grown meal from the best of the land, grown right there on his dream property.

Right after the closing, he drove up the mile-long logging road into the property to the small log cabin near the top of the meadow before the mountain began its steep rise. He would begin there. That would become his staging office and first get-away cabin. His new caretaker, a local World War II veteran, was mountain-skilled in just about everything. From operating and fixing a backhoe or bulldozer, building a road, or a house from the foundation up, there was nothing he couldn't do.

With his new man in place, he started building his dream. First, he built a caretaker's home 50 yards away and around the bend above an enormous, cavernous, three-car garage. He then added six more garages next to it for a tractor, front-end loader, dump truck, two pickups, and even a full-size bulldozer. He figured he might want to build some new roads up the mountain fairly soon.

While all that building was going on, he drove around the county, looking for an old log home that was obviously unoccupied. After four or five attempts, he struck gold. Late one afternoon, he pulled his Fleetwood Cadillac into the driveway of a newer home next to the old log home. He then got out of his car, in his khaki long pants and matching long-sleeve shirt, with suspenders and a belt, just in case one or the other broke, put on his canvas fedora, and slowly made his way to the front door.

When he was seven, he had just finished chopping down a tree and was ready to quit, so he swung the big ax behind him to make an underhand throw toward the barn. As the ax was making its way down the arc of the swing, he slipped slightly to the right and moved his leg directly in the path of the ax blade, severing his Achilles tendon clean through. In those days, there was no doctor to reconnect a severed Achilles tendon, so he was forced to adjust to living with a brace, which attached to his custom-made shoe and circled around his calf, just to keep his right foot from dropping and tripping him up.

Even with the handicap, he was an amazing athlete, growing to an impressive six feet four inches and strong as an ox. Although his real passion was baseball, he realized his true potential as a successful attorney and real estate investor. In his mid-fifties, he had enough money to take a step back from his successful law practice. Now he could travel to North Carolina and build out his grand plan on his new mountain property.

As he walked up to the front door, up the steps to the wrap-around porch, the residents inside saw him well before he knocked on their door. There was just something about a big black Cadillac, and a hulking, dapper gentleman with a fedora and limp coming to visit.

"Pardon the intrusion, ma'am," he began in his deep booming bass. "Would you and your husband be willing to sell me the wood from that cabin over there?" he asked, pointing to the abandoned cabin.

"Why, that place ain't had nobody in it for twenty years or more. Besides, it's a good seventy years old. What you want it for?" she asked.

"Well ma'am, I like old wood, and I think I can use it on my property, and I'd be willing to pay two hundred dollars cash for it," he stated matter-of-factly, along with his pleasant smile.

Hearing "two hundred dollars," the man of the house came from the kitchen to the front porch and said to his wife, "What's going on here? What does this here fellow want for two hundred dollars?"

When he heard what Granddad was asking about, the abandoned, ancient log cabin on their property, he was shocked at first, then amused.

"This city slicker wants to pay me to take that old eye-sore off my property?" he whispered to his wife. "Watch this…" He winked to his wife and turned slowly back to the stranger on his porch.

"Well, I might be able to part with it, even though I am rightly attached to it, seeing's how I was born there, and my kids, too. I could see fit to let it go for two-fifty though," he said to Granddad.

As Granddad pulled out his wallet and began counting out the cash, he asked, "How about we split the difference and make it two-twenty-five?"

The wizened old farmer, eying the wad of cash, already spending it in his mind on a brand-new lawnmower, said with a sad face, "Well, sir, it breaks my heart to sell it, but if it's all right with Momma," referring to his wife, "then we have a deal."

Momma looked like she was about to cry, but valiantly nodded, excused herself and went back inside, letting the men finish up their business.

That night, they would laugh and brag to their friends how this "outsider" paid good money for something they would have gladly let rot or burn. Either one or both.

Granddad would then have his new full-time tree farm caretaker come over to the seller's cabin, mark each log and piece of lumber, then carefully transport it, piece by piece, back to the new foundation he had just laid for the new old log cabin on his property. Then he would recreate it on the new site, replacing any wood if needed. He would not have to replace more than five percent of it, as the wood was cured hardwood, and would last several more generations if minimally cared for. For 225 dollars and keeping his caretaker busy, he built himself a classic vintage cabin.

He knew he would love it here in North Carolina.

With great appreciation, Granddad inspected his "new" log cabin after each day's progress by John the caretaker and skilled handyman.

After building two other apartments over two adjacent garages, it was time to start getting all the grandkids up for the summers.

....

Grandmom was just as unique as her husband. The only child of two German immigrants, she was as fierce as she was short. At four-foot eleven and one-half inches, she was mighty short. It always amazed everyone how she looked half the size of her huge husband. But after all, love is blind. And she had plenty going for her.

Her parents had immigrated to America prior to World War I and settled near Detroit, Michigan. There her father became a very successful business owner and inventor with several valuable patents. After many years of hard work and great success, he sold his business and took his fortune to the land of sunshine, beautiful beaches and palm trees. Fort Lauderdale, Florida.

As an only child of wealthy parents, she wanted for nothing. At 12 years old, her father bought her a Steinway grand piano, which she played her entire life thereafter. He sent her to the finest women's college in the country, all the way back East in Boston. She was not spoiled, however. Her German instincts of hard work, precision, and sheer willpower, coupled with her mother's strict discipline, would not allow for that. She was definitely not one to trifle with.

It was her mother who told her the real reason they moved away from Germany. But her stories were not the subjects of dinner table conversation with all the cousins. The dining room table was where Granddad held the grandkids spellbound, both with his booming voice and huge laugh, and with the fascinating stories of his law practice and life. He told about an accused murderer he kept from the electric chair, believing in his innocence, as well as police officers he represented for free, when they occasionally got sideways with the law.

His grandchildren loved his life stories the best. One of the best was, as a young married man, he went to find gold in the jungles of

Ecuador, where he found no gold but did find hepatitis and nearly died. He returned to his wife three months later, 60 pounds lighter and about as broke as he looked in his sagging clothes. He decided he would buckle down and practice law, and give up this dream of finding gold in the wild jungles of Central and South America. After his near-death experience in Ecuador, he realized just how nice it was to have world-class hospitals and doctors within mere miles of his home in Coral Gables. That would be the first and last time he would explore the deep muddy rivers and dense jungles filled with malaria, hepatitis, and who knew what else in that third-world country, or any other for that matter.

He talked about how Miami was a sleepy little town near the Everglades, when the Miami River was clean enough to drink from, and certainly swim in. He talked about the fresh water bubbling up in the middle of Biscayne Bay, where they would dip their buckets and take a cool drink while they were out fishing for snapper.

Grandmom, on the other hand, preferred to talk one on one. She loved to play cards, especially gin rummy, crazy eights and double solitaire. It was during those times that if Rob asked the right questions, she would tell stories about her relatives. The most interesting ones were about her mother and her sisters. She said she didn't know very much about her aunts, since she wasn't born in Germany and never visited them. She did say they were very special women who did very important things. Secret things. Her mother told her about them.

Since Rob was one of her "unofficial" favorites (what kind of a Grandmom would have "official" favorites?), she filled in more details of her German family. She mentioned that these women in her family did amazing things to save the world from evil people. It was kind of funny to hear her talk like that. Rob would laugh and tease her a bit about it, but she would never even crack a smile in response. She was dead serious. She said their missions were usually highly dangerous, so much so that her parents decided to emigrate to America. They did not want their future children, especially daughters, to get involved with her mother's sisters and their covert operations, no matter how noble they were.

Rob was clearly intrigued by these stories. Over many years at the card table in the family room next to the upright piano at the "place" in North Carolina, Rob learned a little more each time. He was never fully sure it was nothing more than great fiction, but he mentally logged every detail she ever told him.

Finally, one summer, she divulged more details than she had before. Only blood family, and a very select few at that, were qualified to join this very secret group. Only the women of the family could join. Men were always being called to be soldiers and fight the wars that the ruling class declared. Women, on the other hand, were left behind and could be very effective and largely unsuspected, especially German women. She once showed Rob an old picture of her mother with her sisters. It was one of those very old black and whites where they were all dressed up and looked surprised.

According to her, they were active but behind the scenes during World Wars I and II, and helped bring down the evil in Germany during World War II. She did not offer further details, but since then, they had continued on against evil wherever it reared its head, in terrorist groups and rogue governments around the world.

She made it sound like they still existed and were doing secret things even today. Having learned from more than a few stern German stares to not be too flippant, Rob gently pointed out that they must not have been around in the Second World War with all the horrendous atrocities committed by the Nazis. Without missing a beat, said answered matter-of-factly, "Imagine how bad it would have been had they not been there." Rob had no trouble imagining most anything. But he would sure like to find out if it was really true.

It sounded beyond intriguing.

Chapter 10

Eight years later, at 25 and just finishing his final tour as an Army Ranger, Rob Russell knew he may just find out. Four tours in Afghanistan and two covert ops in Syria had shown Rob all he needed to see as a United States soldier. Enough was enough. He would miss his team, but he knew the bonds he formed there were forged in the furnace of life and death, and could not be broken. He knew he would see his Ranger brothers many more times in his life.

Rob knew there was no finer and better-equipped military in the world than the USA's. But he also realized pure politics must have reared its ugly head on more than one occasion, where absolute victory was certain, only to be called off at the last minute with orders to disengage and withdraw, leaving blood-gained ground to be reclaimed by terrorists. Like cockroaches, they always returned en masse once the danger was gone.

Burned out, suffering a mild case of PTSD, from all the horrors he witnessed, and frankly, took part in, he was not yet ready to return home to the States. Although his family was anxious for him to return home, safe and sound, at last, he knew he needed some decompression time. How long, he had no idea. Maybe a couple months. Maybe longer. He had a little money saved up. He'd see when that started to get low. Then he'd decide.

As a two-time recipient of the Silver Star, the Army knew the special brand of soldier Rob was. They were not ready to let him go. As a highly decorated Ranger, he proved he had the mettle of the finest soldiers in existence, past and present. In his earlier Afghan deployments, Rob had earned the reputation of a "high-speed, low-drag operator." By his third year, he had been promoted to E-4, Corporal.

Rob had more than prov.ed himself as a leader who could inspire men and accomplish the mission, without supervision. In the third year of his four-year enlistment contract, he was one of only a dozen Rangers from the entire 75th Ranger Regiment handpicked by the ultra-elite Delta Force to join a Top Secret covert insertion into Raqqa, Syria. In this new age of war, the war on terrorism, new methods of engaging and defeating the enemy were required. Battlefield improvisation and keen instincts were vital to staying alive. Especially when the enemy looked like every other civilian. Earning his second Silver Star and a battlefield promotion to Sergeant, Rob clearly proved he had those qualities.

The last stronghold of the ISIS caliphate was well-armed and highly complex. The enemy learned early on in their terroristic pursuit of a caliphate, or their own new sovereign country, that wearing a uniform made them an easy target. They learned to blend in with the population. Being the brutal, merciless butchers they had become, they even took it one step further. They surrounded themselves and their command centers with freshly captured women and children, now widows and orphans as the ISIS thugs had just murdered their husbands and fathers, ensuring that any attack on the terrorists would result in innocent deaths.

When a US or Allied attack eventually came, in purely evil and cynical recruiting videos, they would loudly gnash their teeth and lament that the Great Satan, America, was murdering their women and children, mercilessly targeting them in their highly precise air-strikes.

••••••••••••••••••••••••

A fatal mistake of previously victorious countries throughout history has been to fight the present war using the previous war's tactics. After all, that was how they won the last one. That was how the current generals earned their stars.

Changing tactics and methods meant going against the conventional, the proven, the accepted and unquestionable path to victory. A new idea was fraught with unequaled risk and danger. That is, not so much for the country, or the soldiers on the battlefield, but to the career of the officer who dared advance a new idea or method. Each and every step would be criticized, scrutinized and potentially sabotaged to prove the old methods still ruled. A misstep or mission failure could have easily ended a career, or at the least, derailed any further promotions.

Even when the maverick idea succeeded, and the new method was successful, the maverick officer may have been blocked from further career advancement. The current leaders had no intention of letting this kind of person become a power challenge to them. In the military, there has only been so much room at the top. Ascending to the top levels has been about as difficult as being elected POTUS, minus the nearly three years of campaigning. The filtering process is so extreme and competitive, and within a relatively small community of potentials. Having a spotless record always was just the beginning.

But the war on terror changed everything. Instead of a challenge from another superpower, since the USSR had gone bankrupt and the Eastern Bloc was reborn into a form of democracy, warfare was no longer from an enemy nation-state, at least not with army against army. Of course, rogue nations developing nuclear capabilities were still an existential threat to American security, but the war on terrorism had blossomed into the only real war in the world that affected all freedom-loving democratic nations. But no country was more impacted than the USA. September 11, 2001 proved this.

Revenge for that attack was ferocious and overwhelming. Americans and the world watching live coverage on CNN witnessed the shock and awe of military destruction that only America, the world's only superpower, could deliver against an enemy. Victory in Iraq was achieved in less than a month, though it took over three years to find Saddam Hussein. Too bad for him, it only took a couple months for the new Iraqi courts to convict him of gassing his own people and to hang him. With Saddam gone, the most wanted man in the world remained Osama bin Laden. But that capture or kill sentence would have to wait eight long years.

Turned out, no matter how much Saddam deserved to be deposed, removed or killed for his various crimes against humanity and abuses of power, the pretext for the war was unable to be proven. Some think he was just bluffing. But no WMDs were found when US forces entered Iraq following the 9/11 terror attacks. None. Perhaps he had smuggled them out of his own country, to some empathetic fellow Middle East dictator. Maybe he had used them all up on his own people and his enemy, Iran. As much as anything else, Saddam was a provocateur. And such a big one that it cost him his country and his life.

One of the pitfalls of being the absolute ruler of a country is that he will kill or imprison the owner of any voice that disagrees with him. The dictator with extreme wealth, absolute political and military power becomes blind to his weaknesses and vulnerabilities. With no one left to tell Saddam to shut the hell up, he continued to taunt the lion that is America until it finally woke up with a roar and inflicted a vicious and killing swat of its paw.

The final straw had to be Saddam's sanctioned attempted "hit" on the first President Bush during a fishing trip. Who knows, that might have been the reason the USA did not officially discover there were no remaining WMDs until *after* we destroyed Baghdad and sent Saddam running and hiding like the sewer rat he was.

With Saddam's just but gruesome death by hanging, the world could celebrate the end of a vicious dictator, and look forward to a new era of democratic freedom in the Middle East.

Right.

Evidently, thousands of years of tribalism and strongman-rule does not transform that easily into democratic rule. Evidently, sole supremacy over the divisions in the world's largest religion, Islam, and lust for power are far more compelling than an elected structure with separation of powers amongst three co-equal branches of government, like on the other side of the world. America.

Consequently, the newly disenfranchised of the wrong division of the faith, the Sunni Muslims, blackballed from any job with the new holders of power, the Shiite Muslims, decided their only future was in creating their own nation. Rapturously unaware of their total adoption of Machiavelli's advice from centuries before, perhaps taken to a new extreme, their modern version of "the ends justify the means" would be proudly displayed to the whole world.

Live-streamed beheadings, ethnic and religious "cleansing," drug and human trafficking, sex slaves, claiming credit for cowardly and deadly mass-casualty suicide bombings and other not-so-lovely things were all to be thoroughly celebrated and used as worldwide recruiting tools for new soldiers. Whatever it took to create the caliphate, the new country, and to make their god proud of them, was fine. After their success, they could sort things out, like the definition of murder. And their recruiting tool? The internet, of course.

Among the wonderful things that the World Wide Web, or the internet, created was instant transmission of recruiting videos of the atrocities of this group known as ISIS, or Daesh. In a way, the internet follows a Machiavellian trajectory. More than any other industry, the web and the technological revolution owes its massive acceptance and trillion-dollar industry to the lawless, seamy, filthy and dirty underbelly of human evil. More than any other product, pornography has funded and provided the greatest growth and advances of the web since its inception in 1991. Even today, porn accounts for about a third of all internet traffic. It should not be a surprise that the web has also become the instrument of terrorists, not to be confused with cyber warfare.

In fact, it would be hard, if not impossible, for either to exist without the internet. Certainly true for cyber warfare, a little less so for terrorism. But not much. Without the internet, bitcoin and other cryptocurrencies, or altcoins, would not exist. Without altcoins and their user anonymity, like with Monero, terrorist groups would be unable to get funding for their nefarious activities. Or at least be greatly impaired.

For all the great things the internet age has ushered in, like providing access to knowledge and education, eliminating intellectual borders and removing language barriers when its best use is allowed, its early hostile takeover by pornography and current use by terrorists and the new warfare of choice by anti-American nations like Russia, China, North Korea, Iran and Cuba, is very much Machiavellian. "The ends justify the means" rings true here too.

Perhaps the price the free world pays for a free internet is to die very slowly from a thousand cuts. Some cuts, like September 11, 2001, are more brutal, deep and shocking, but not fatal for a nation-state, especially the United States. But, an ever-increasing occurrence of wounds to our society, and the country as we know it could be on its deathbed in less than a generation.

Especially true if the people of the country become desensitized to immorality, and right and wrong. If good and evil become relative, then it becomes a country without a soul, and subject to destruction from within. A country without a vision is a country not for long. How can evil be challenged and defeated if evil is just a preference that should be protected and celebrated like any other preference?

All it takes for a visionless free country to be willingly defeated is a person with a vision to give it one. And that vision might be completely different than the country's original founding principles. How ironic is it that a free people would themselves vote away their freedoms one by one, until they finally open their eyes and find themselves the next Venezuela of the world?

On the very day of America's creation, wise old Benjamin Franklin knew how elusive true freedom was for mankind. Immediately after emerging from signing the brand-new US Constitution, a savvy woman asked him, "Well Doctor, what have we got, a republic or a monarchy?" He replied, "A republic, if you can keep it."

A pure democracy, or "mobocracy," leads quickly to a dictatorship. Only a republic guarantees individual rights, given by the Creator. A republic protects those inalienable rights, even if the majority wants to steal them. In a democracy, the majority defines what rights the individual has, whenever it wants to, and can change them anytime it wants. The fact that the vast majority of Americans do not understand this difference is an epic failure of our schools. The time is ripe for our country to be swept away voluntarily by a personality of great charisma and vision down the path toward dictatorship, if our gross negligence in educating our citizens continues.

To develop the internet, a blind eye was turned on the proliferation and accessibility of pornography, with its unimaginable exploitation of women and children, as long as the money rolls in to the ISPs, the Internet Service Providers, and builds search companies like Netscape, Yahoo and Google. The tradeoff for the evil? Great technical leaps and bounds achieved as companies perfect and expand their transmission, speed and content for the good, legitimate uses. So just like the lawless Wild West, with its open brothels and wanton murders, abuses are being tolerated until the internet is fully developed. By then, it could be too late to reverse the damage caused by a thousand cuts, as moral relativism takes hold.

The new global war, WWIII, although not so named, is about fighting terrorism anywhere on the planet. To make it easier and less personal, it is called the Global War on Terrorism. Iran and North Korea either sponsor terrorist activities directly or assist in them indirectly. And along with Russia and China, they also actively conduct cyberwarfare against the USA and its freedom-loving allies. Without fail, Russia actively supports any dictatorship on the planet, in either hemisphere. A poke in America's eye is its goal, and causing it embarrassment is its game. Another civil war in America would suit Russia just fine, as well.

....

In terms of wars, the US is always the last one to the party. Having endured attacks for years, it was not until 2006 that the USA began taking cyberwarfare seriously. It took three more years, after very costly and damaging cyber-attacks, until USCYBERCOM was installed in the NSA Headquarters at Fort Meade, Maryland. A couple years later, each and every branch of the military now has its own cyberwarfare division.

The realities of this new type of warfare did not have the effect of reducing the number of real, trained soldiers needed for the five military branches. Quite the opposite. More soldiers were needed. Additional new, highly trained cyberwarfare soldiers may never fire a weapon with a bullet, but make no mistake, the trigger they pull affects thousands, if not millions, at a time.

But cyberwarfare wasn't what the Army Ranger brass had in mind for Rob. At least not for now. Rob's skills and usefulness to the military were to test new insertion strategies. In fact, Rob's next mission had everything to do with getting real up close and personal with the new enemy, on their own turf, without them having a clue.

It so happened that his unique skill was in an area the military wanted to develop, with urgency. When Rob informed his superiors of his intent to retire after his four-year enlistment contract, and the fact that he requested permission to be discharged in Garmish, Germany so he could pursue his passion of extreme skiing, they realized they had an opportunity that could make both parties happy.

For Rob and a few of his friends, extremely happy.

As his bosses described his new, and last mission, even though it would require an extra year commitment, Rob could not stop the slow burn of excitement building from his toes upward. His skin was tingling with goosebumps, and the hair on the back of his neck was up. He knew he had to do this. There was actually nothing he'd rather do.

Leaving his fellow infantrymen-warriors at the front lines for this new and last mission would be the toughest thing. But he knew bonds formed in blood do not break. They were stronger than titanium and steel. "Never shall I fail my comrades… I will never leave a fallen comrade to fall into the hands of the enemy…" He knew the whole Ranger creed by heart, but those two parts as if they were seared into his mind with a red-hot poker.

After an intensive month-long planning of the new mission, Rob was ready to make a side-trip back to his hometown of Steamboat Springs, with the blessing of his immediate brass. He was looking forward to the rest. But that wasn't the reason he was going back.

He needed a few good men. Thankfully, Steamboat had a few of those. One more requirement: they needed to be damn good skiers.

He had just the right guys in mind.

Chapter 11

Nothing truly satisfied his soul more than driving into Steamboat from Rabbit Ears Pass. Rounding that last corner, overlooking Stagecoach Reservoir, and then the big 'ole Yampa Valley, it was like no other place on Earth. Just plain home. The Ute and Arapahoe Indians, the first known itinerant residents of the valley, reportedly had said that you could depart the valley anytime you wanted, but your soul would never leave.

Returning home to the valley from the horrors of war, exhausted, traumatized, jaded and spiritually bankrupt, Rob could well relate to those Indians. In fact, he hoped it was true. He hoped he still had a soul and it was in the valley somewhere. He just needed to find it. He had to put that thought to rest, though, and concentrate on his next, and final mission.

Three months prior, not even knowing about his new mission, he group-messaged two of his buddies that he would be coming back on leave and wanted to get together with them. It was pretty easy to arrange that these days, in the age of social media. Even if he hadn't been in touch with these guys for a couple years, he could reach back out, leave a message, and reconnect. He let them know when and they agreed to meet for dinner at the Riverbend Inn, just west of town.

Now fully briefed on his final assignment with the military, with the late addition of Danny and Jim, he was even more excited to meet with his friends.

And it damn straight wasn't a surprise Amway meeting.

Little did they know, but Rob wanted these guys on the mission, and "No" would not be an acceptable answer. After spending a great afternoon and night with his parents at their "house on the hill" west of Steamboat, Rob was ready to get on with the Army's business. About 4 o'clock the next day, he headed down to the lower Yampa Valley to one of his favorite restaurants.

The Riverbend was well-known for thick, juicy, local pasture-fed ranch steaks, killer mashed potatoes, and other rancher fare. *Cowboy* was more of a marketing term that the Ski Corp gave the Ski Town. Ranchers were the real thing. Hell, anyone could be a cowboy. Just dress the part with the boots, a cowboy hat from F.M. Light & Sons, a snap-button shirt, and some boot-cut jeans, and Voila! You're a cowboy! The ranchers called those phonies "drug-store cowboys."

Maybe they called them that because Lyon Drugs was right next door to F.M. Light's, or maybe it was John Travolta's character in *Urban Cowboy*, Rob didn't know. But a fake is always a fake.

One way to tell a rancher from a drugstore cowboy if you saw one at a bar, was to slap a five on the counter, and place a quarter on it. Tell him, "Five bucks says you can't bend that quarter with one hand."

The rancher, with hands strengthened to nearly superhuman levels, growing up throwing hay bales from the field to the truck, would take that quarter between his thumb and two first fingers and actually start to bend the damn thing. The fake cowboy wouldn't even try. He could barely bend a beer-bottle cap.

Back to dinner: add ample bowls of buttered peas, string beans, roasted carrots and Brussels sprouts, finished with the best flaky-crust apple pie west of the Mississippi, and it would be a feast indeed. This would do just fine for what he wanted to talk to them about. Rob would make sure there was an abundance of Rocky Mountain Piss Water on tap, more widely known as Coors Light.

Coors was the go-to beer for their frequently busted high school parties. But no one drank it for the taste back then; after all, they just wanted to get shit-faced as fast as possible. It was different now. Now the taste reminded them of being rebellious and living dangerously, just outside the law, especially mom and dad's law. And there was something kind of sweet about that, mixed in with the hops and barley. Like the first taste of growing up.

Back in high school, smoking pot and snorting cocaine were clearly crossing the line of legality, but both drugs seemed to be always available. My, how things have changed in the Rocky Mountain state since then. Since then, John Denver's "Rocky Mountain High" has taken on a whole new meaning. It would not be surprising to find out more than 50 percent of all high school students regularly used weed, like every day.

Along with the disgusting spike in meth use, and the resurgence of the once-forgotten drug, heroin, the current youth in Colorado and the entire USA face some serious temptations and lethal consequences.

But they still liked the taste of their Coors beer. Only now it was Coors Light. Theoretically, you could drink and not get the dreaded beer belly. It was a great excuse to drink more, anyway.

Within minutes of each other, the guys arrived at the Riverbend and skidded to a stop in the gravel lot in front of the restaurant. One by one, they walked up the porch steps, opened the big pine double doors and walked right up to the big bar past the main dining room.

The place lit up with all the commotion and back-slapping and hugs all around as the friends saw each other for the first time in years. The laughter and banter grew so loud that the young and hot-looking hostess came over to Rob and very persuasively asked,

"Would you gentlemen like to move to your private room? It's all set for you."

All the guys got the hint and began moving toward the room except Danny, who was still making a loud joke to the bartender. Danny finally got it when the hostess approached him and said, smiling through clenched teeth,

"There's either this door, where your friends are going, or the front door. Which one are you going through, Mister?"

"That one, missy," said Danny, smiling widely and pointing to his friends. Danny hurried to catch up with the group.

"Ohhhhuh. Danny just got his ass handed to him by the hostess!" said Jim, arguably Danny's best friend.

"Not hardly," said Danny. "She just wants me is all."

"Will you listen to bullshit speak," laughed Jim, with just a hint of admiration mixed with jealousy. The others laughed and started finding their seats.

Being that Danny was over six feet, smart, good-looking, had a full head of wavy brown hair, and was just plain crazy by all standards, he was more often right about that subject than wrong. Jim knew that only too well. But Danny would give it a rest for now. At least until after dinner and when it was time to go home.

It was one of the best dinners Rob could remember, with all the old stories that only school buddies can relate to, and much more importantly, ski racers. After finishing the two-inch-thick, medium rare T-bone steak seasoned and grilled to perfection, with the all-you-can-eat fixins and sides, he took a gulp of ice-cold Coors Light, pushed his plate back and stood up. Clinking his mug with his antler-handled steak knife, Rob launched into his pitch.

"Ok, you misfits, one and all, I want to make a toast. For all the good days, fast races, and faster women we've had in the past, here's to a thousand more even better!"

"Hear, hear!" the boys answered loudly, raising their thick glass-handled beer mugs and slapping the huge, rectangular, dark-lacquered lodgepole pine table with their open palms a couple times. Whether it was true or not, they really liked the part about the faster women.

"And I mean that, in a big way. Let me elaborate. Why did I put this little dinner together, you may be thinking? Was it just because I missed you so badly and can't live without your smart-ass jokes about how I was the slowest racer ever to come through the Club?"

At this the boys had a good laugh, knowing what Rob said was true, but the teasing was always in good fun, because they respected him for finally going for it and actually getting pretty decent.

"Not exactly," continued Rob. "I'm going to be done with the Army after my next tour, I mean, if I make it out, God willing..." The guys immediately stopped making any noise.

"You'll make it, Rob, man. For sure," said Danny.

"I'll drink to that," added Jim, dead-serious, as mugs were raised and slammed back down on the table again, including Rob's.

"From your lips to God's ears, brother," answered Rob, continuing. "And by the way, you'd better freakin' hope so, but we'll save that for later," Rob interjected, but continued quickly. "Well guess what. I've been getting into some pretty cool stuff as a Ranger, and some of it I can even tell you about without having to kill you right afterwards." The guys chuckled a little as he continued.

"Any of you guys ever flown before? And I don't mean on an airplane. I mean by yourself." They all looked around as they were shaking their heads in confusion.

"You've probably seen some videos of crazy mothers in wing suits, right?" They nodded. All had seen that.

"Yeah, that's pretty radical. Serious bad-ass shit," said Ricky, the most accomplished racer in the small group of friends.

....

This was the same Ricky from Rob's first year of ski racing. Ricky was an eighth grader and Rob was in eleventh grade. After Rob's senior year, he lost track of Ricky and his skiing career. But it was extraordinary.

Just two years later, Ricky became the dominant junior ski racer in all of North America. Winning the Junior National Championships an unprecedented three years in a row, he was named to the US Ski Team immediately after his senior year in high school.

But early athletic success does not guarantee Olympic or professional sport greatness. As in every sport, the most talented are not always the most successful at the highest levels of a sport. In no way does this take away from their amazing talent; it just reflects the incredible demands of mental and physical discipline needed to achieve greatness.

Not to mention single-minded desire to achieve your dream, no matter how naturally talented you are. You have to do so many things right—sacrifice good for best, clear out doubt and grow in confidence. All this while having the freedom to make your own decisions. That's freaking hard.

So for a million reasons and for none, Ricky didn't continue his winning streak straight to the top. As everyone expected, Ricky earned a spot on the US Ski Team, just in time for the Winter Olympics. But, his shot at the Olympics was a disappointment. He fell in his two events in the first run and was disqualified. DNF.

After another year, the Ski Team decided to part ways with Ricky, and give his spot to another up-and-comer. Although very disappointed, Ricky decided to continue his racing career and entered the World Pro Skiing Tour. For whatever reason, he just couldn't crack into the top 10 racers on the Tour. After he'd spent five years of world travel to the coolest ski areas in the world, having more fun than he'd ever had in his life, his sponsors decided not to renew his endorsements. He flat out couldn't afford that incredible lifestyle anymore.

With the little bit of savings left from his endorsement deals, he took his dad's advice and went to college. There he got a marketing degree and started working for an advertising company in Denver.

Still, that little voice inside him told him he still had some adventure left in him.

And he really did miss the action on the World Pro Tour.

Funny how dreams become realities sometimes. And funnier still is the people you never imagined would help you fulfill them.

••••••••••••••••••••••••

Knowing he had captured their imagination, Rob continued in a hushed but intense tone about wing suit flying.

"I'm here to tell you nothing else comes close to it."

Rob paused for a second and let that sink in. Each of the guys was leaning in, mentally drooling on those words. He continued more matter-of-factly.

"Of course, it's beyond dangerous and all that, but everything you guys did in high school, college, and the pros, in all the downhills, all the crazy out-of-bounds skiing, the avalanche chutes, was dangerous as hell," Rob explained with a somewhat dismissive smirk.

"Yeah, but it wasn't dangerous for us, really," said Mike, and continued, "I mean, we're racers. We've skied all our lives. Hell, I mean raced all our lives. None of that was crazy for us, except a couple of the downhills and out-of-bounds shit, I guess."

"Exactly," said Rob. "Not dangerous for us guys. Correction: *you* guys," Rob said, smiling, "But death for anyone else, right?"

"Yup," Mike answered. "I would agree with that." The other guys grunted their agreement.

Rob looked down at the table for a second then looked up at the guys. He put both palms on the table as he continued.

"And that's one reason I'm here with you, besides being reminded what a lame-ass racer I was," he said as he stood up straight again.

"I'm here to recruit you guys to combine what you did better than most anybody on the planet with some new stuff that you'll have to learn. It's pretty crazy shit, and as far as danger goes, it's off the charts. Not even measured. At a certain level, they just don't bother to measure things anymore," he continued.

"So, if you're done with that kind of action, that's fine. This isn't for you and that's totally cool."

Rob paused for a second, and looked around at each of the guys. They were still munching on the last delicious morsels of steak and mashed potatoes on their plates, having emptied all the ample Western-style bowls of food in the middle of the table.

"I'm still listening," said Danny, chewing enthusiastically.

"Yeah, so am I," said Mike.

"Me too," added Ricky.

"Yup. Me too," Jim chimed in, incoherently as it was with a mouth full of his last big bite of choice, perfectly prepared T-bone steak.

"Good," said Rob. "I thought you would be. Here's the deal. My bosses are aware of my racing days. Also, I've done some crazy stuff over the last five years as a Ranger. I've done three hundred and twenty-three jumps with a parachute. Believe me, that's not that many.

"But at a hundred and fifty, they asked me if I wanted to do the wing suit thing, and I said, 'Hell, yes!'"

"So now I have a hundred and seventy-three more jumps, all wing suit followed by parachute. Let me tell you, when you fall out of a plane or helicopter at ten thousand feet, or jump off a twelve-thousand-foot base cliff, the rush you get on the hundred and fiftieth one is the same as the first one."

Mike lifted both hands, elbows down. "Rob, what exactly are you recruiting us to do? Wing suit jumps or whatever you call it?"

"Sort of," Rob answered. "I mean, we could get lots of great parachute guys, and maybe some girls, too, but you guys have some skills that take way too much time to teach, even if it could be taught, which it can't. I've already told them to forget trying to teach soldiers to ski like you guys."

The guys liked that, and the looks exchanged across the big pine-slab table were confirmation enough that the guys knew Rob was right.

"No. What they want is to combine everything we've got so far, and do it all at once. See if it can be done. Test the equipment. Helmets, gloves, jackets, pants, boots, bindings, skis, poles, wing suits, you get the idea.

"We're doing this in Europe to stay as far away as possible from the news in the States. Possibly South America too. The Alps and Andes. Starting with the Alps. We're working out terrain, slopes, cliffs, altitudes, ski routes, fly routes and landings as we speak.

"The ski equipment will be state of the art. We pick it. Skis, bindings and poles, that is. The other stuff is being custom-made. Boots, jackets, helmets, gloves, wing suits, parachutes. Everything's got to be made to military specs," Rob finished. "Questions?"

"So what do you guys need us for?" asked Danny. "I mean, isn't it a little overkill to have racers like us doing this? I'll bet you've got some other Rangers who are pretty good skiers."

"That's just the point, Danny," said Rob. "Yeah, we've got some pretty serious, bad-ass hombres in Spec Ops, like Rangers, Delta Force, SEALs, DEVGRU, Recon, PJs and FAST guys," he said, listing the elite units of the five military branches. "Even 10th Mountain, who have some good skiers. But guys who can really ski this mission calls for are nearly impossible to come by. It's like one in a million.

"So, they asked me if I knew any guys," continued Rob, looking down as he started to smile. "I said I know some guys that *used* to be good. I'll see if they think they're still worth a shit," he teased. The guys let out a collective laugh, looking at each other, knowing they were among the best skiers on the planet. Smiling knowingly, they looked back at Rob.

"What do you think so far?" asked Rob, slightly smiling.

"We haven't had dessert yet, so I'm still listening," said Jim, and the rest chuckled in agreement.

Rob motioned for the waitress to bring in the warm apple pie with melt-in-your-mouth crust, topped with two scoops of home-made vanilla bean ice cream. He had never been close friends with anyone but Mike, but he could tell these guys weren't just drooling for the dessert. He had awakened the adventure-lust that lurked just below the surface of who these guys really were.

Rob had done some research on all the guys before tonight. Not just Rob, but ARMINT, Army Intelligence, too. They had done a little more in-depth research than he had, to put it mildly. In fact, Rob had an exhaustive dossier on each of the guys, compliments of the Army. In each file, Rob was mildly surprised by some of the details, while some of the facts were pretty shocking. Five other guys and two girls Rob wanted to be here were rejected by ARMINT. Two were outright rejects.

It was not that they were bad people, it's just that a few situations they had experienced had indicated they might be liabilities down the road. Like skirmishes with the law, for instance, and excessive traffic tickets, like reckless driving or speeding, even a "Driving While Impaired," or honesty issues on applications, were considered mild but telling. The two immediately rejected were for outright fraud and a domestic violence conviction, resulting in jail time in the former and a suspended sentence in the latter.

The four guys at this dinner had already been vetted and approved, however, and it was up to Rob to pitch the opportunity and get these guys on board. Rob had especially hoped one of the girls he had on the list would be available, but unfortunately for him, she was married and pregnant with her second child.

The other girl was the domestic violence conviction.

Chapter 12

It's funny how that domestic violence conviction caught Rob by complete surprise. When he verbally heard the reasons for the outright rejections, he naturally assumed the domestic charge was one of the guys. Only when he read it did he realize his mistake. He then thought about it for a few moments and remembered that this chick never took any shit from any of the guys, on the team or in school. He guessed the poor bastard probably thought he was free to go a little further than she wanted, and paid the price. He was probably lucky to be still walking. As deserving as it may have been, it still reached the definition of the crime, and the jury returned a guilty verdict.

The lady judge did her best by handing down a suspended sentence, just short of dismissing the verdict. Doing the right thing and dismissing the verdict would be too high a political price to pay for the judge. Being accused of not meting out equal justice for the sexes, kind of a reverse backlash of the Me-Too movement, would have been just as bad as dismissing the case. She did her best to divide King Solomon's baby, and make everyone happy. The saddest thing was that this charge would forever be on the girl's record, and would negatively impact her entire life.

If one of these guys dropped out, Rob would really go to bat for this girl. In Rob's mind, she would be perfect for the job, and none of the guys would even try anything on her. He didn't know for sure, but he doubted she deserved to be tainted with this rap for the rest of her life.

As Rob looked at each of the guys laughing and telling stories, there was now a different feel in the room. There was excitement. There was loud talking and new claims of greatness and exploits. Aside from Mike and Rob, the other three guys were talking about some of their runs down the steepest and most dangerous mountains on the continent, frequently and excitedly talking over the others for best bragging rights.

With three loud taps on his beer mug with his knife, the guys all settled down after a final shout and laugh by Danny. Rob moved to the door of their private room and closed it.

"This will not be easy on you guys. But the government will pay you pretty decently as outside contractors. It's going to take eight months to get ready for this season. Obviously, you have to be in the best shape of your life. That means some pretty stiff training. Kind of like our dry-land training, but trust me, ten times harder."

At that, Jim let out a not-too-subtle moan and an "Aw.... shit." Rob continued as if he didn't hear anything.

"Hold on a fucking second, Rob," said Ricky. "Are we fighting, or shooting people? Or shit, being shot at?"

Silverware dropping on plates made loud clinking sounds as all the guys stopped mid-bite and looked up at Rob.

"No. Hell, no," said Rob. "This is not a combat mission. There is no battlefield assignment. Although, for those outside this room, this would be way more dangerous than getting shot at," Rob said, smiling.

Satisfied, the guys hungrily returned to their food. Their faces showed they agreed with that assessment. Rob continued.

"There's a helluva lot of parachute jumps before you can even think about wing suiting. It will take at least two months to make one hundred and fifty parachute jumps. Then, if your instructor thinks you're ready, you will start training for the flying suits. That averages four jumps a day, not counting weekends. You don't start making any jumps for the first two weeks. It's parachute and wing suit classes, land simulated jumps, and dry-land training, Ranger style," said Rob.

"Oh, by the way, you have to pass certain written and fitness tests on these subjects, so it's no walk in the park. You will have to study.

"Once you start jumping, there will be days you don't jump, and days you jump six to eight times. You will learn everything possible about the two air disciplines, including the parachute itself and the wing suit. You will be trying out the prototype equipment after your first fifty or so wing suit jumps. You always end a wing suit jump with a parachute landing, so that will also count as a parachute jump. It's a two-for-one jump.

"You will be studying the runs we intend to take, and the routes down the runs. We will use satellite images as well as closer drone and other aerial photography and video.

"This next part should be fun. Before we start with the combined ski, wing suit and parachuting runs, we will have two weeks of just ski training. After that, depending on the conditions, we will go heli-skiing in the alps. Guys, we will not be skiing at resorts. This is strictly virgin territory. As you can imagine, we will be hitting some of the toughest ski terrain in the world, in all conditions; powder, packed, and icy. Not to mention rocks. You will be filmed and evaluated. It's possible you could be cut, at any time. They are not fucking around. It's not a vacation.

"We will not be staying in five-star resorts, or be otherwise openly visible. If word leaks out to the press on our activities, the project will end and we will all go home, hopefully not before we get started.

"On that note, each of you must sign a non-disclosure agreement, an NDA, which basically says you cannot talk about this with anyone without written permission from a certain Army General's office. The project itself is considered "Secret." The geeks in intel decided it would be too hard to get you fuck-ups Top Secret clearances, so they settled for Secret and an NDA.

"Rob, hold the fuck up!" said Mike. "What the hell are we supposed to do with our jobs, man?" Mike asked with genuine anxiety. "I mean, shit! Some of us may have pretty good things going right now, you know? Fucking A, man!"

"Yeah. Fuck. Yes," said Ricky, exaggerating each word for maximum effect.

Jim and Danny stayed silent but were extremely engaged. They were the ones who could leave their jobs in a heartbeat and not blink twice. Danny already worked for a helicopter ski guide company for the uber-wealthy, based out of Aspen. But it didn't pay enough for him to do it himself. And the company would not let him ski the real crazy terrain, for their own liability reasons. For Danny, this was sounding like a dream come true. New terrain, the Alps, new equipment. He was seeing his destiny unfolding before his very eyes.

Jim was a local stone-mason who had work whenever he wanted, and at his asking price. Jim had taken river-rock masonry to an artistic level that was nearly untouchable. His past jobs had made him the go-to guy for all the huge, custom log cabin mansions being built all over the Colorado mountains these days. Seemed like the upper one percent were all building their mountain paradises in the last 10 years. At least they were making good use of some of the beetle-killed lodgepole pine that browned out nearly 90 percent of Colorado's evergreens. Even though he knew he may lose a couple jobs, Jim's inner fire had just been re-lit.

Jim and Danny were majorly tracking in their thoughts. They had not heard anything better, ever. "Get paid for doing crazy cool shit like this?" thought Danny.

"I am so in, it hurts," thought Jim.

Mike and Ricky had decent jobs, and although they were both still single, they were on again, off again with a significant other.

"I know, Mike, Ricky, guys," Rob started.

"I'm interested. Don't get me wrong, man," Mike said. "This sounds totally cool, but I don't know if I can do it. Like giving up everything else I've worked for."

"I get that, Mike," said Rob. "It's a personal sacrifice. A personal choice. Trust me though, this is an opportunity which will not come around again. I can't even believe they're willing to do this thing right now. But it fits in with the crazy immigration that's occurring in Europe, and the increase in terrorist cells on the continent.

"The military wants to have the capability of hitting the terrorists anywhere they hole up. On any mountainside, in the dead of winter, completely undetected. Our job is to prove this is one of the ways to do that.

"You can walk away from this and keep on going in your same direction, and you'll probably be just fine. You'll make a decent living and get your families started and all that. But, and this is a big 'but', you will always have that feeling in your stomach, in your soul, that you missed out on something real special in life. Something you were uniquely qualified to do and were sought after to do it. Something where you could combine your radical skiing skills with other things like wing suiting that you always dreamed of, but maybe you've given up on.

"How many companies do you think you'll work for in your life? Look at the C-suite execs and Silicon Valley dudes. Hell, look at everybody these days. They move around from company to company seems like every couple of years. Good people get downsized out a lot for no good reason. So, now *you're* choosing a new opportunity and a new direction, and something you've always dreamed about. Not somebody else choosing. *You.*

"Do you think your current bosses really give two shits about you? Really? Jim excluded, of course," Rob said, smiling.

Jim laughed and raised his mug again. Being your own boss wasn't easy, either.

Rob continued.

"The second you screw up, or the second they screw up but can blame you for it, they'd can your ass and pin it on you so fast you wouldn't know what hit you. And if the economy goes down, you think they'd hesitate to lay you off? Or do you think they would take a pay cut so you could stay?

"Look, you decide if you want to jump on this, or decide to stay with whatever you're doing. Nobody will think you're a pussy. Nobody that goes ninety plus on skis is a pussy. Either way, this dinner is still free and we'll still be friends. You can take that little concern off the table," Rob said with a grin.

"So, who wants in on this?" he asked.

"Hell, yes!" exclaimed Danny and Jim, almost in unison. Ricky looked around at the other guys, stone-faced and serious-looking. He bowed his head for a quick second, and then looked up with a huge grin on his face and said, "Yup. I'm in."

Last was Mike, and all eyes were on him. Looking down, pursing his lips and clenching his jaw at the same time, then looking up at the ceiling, obviously in decision hell, he said, "Man, I'll have to quit my job, get out of my lease, my girlfriend won't understand," as he started down his list, falling just short of whining. He slapped his hand on the table, making all the silverware jump, and said, "Oh, fuck it! I'm in." The room erupted in whoops and hollers and handshakes all around.

"Guys, guys," began Rob. "The NDA is right here, in a file with your name on it. Sign it and we can bring this little dinner to a close, and go downstairs and have a few rounds. I think dinner is over down there so they can't throw you out, Danny," he said as everybody chuckled.

"At least not yet," said Ricky.

"So Danny can see if he was right about the hostess, huh Danny?" said Jim.

"You never know..." said Danny as he flipped the pages over to the signature line, took the pen, and signed it with a flourish.

"Feel free to read it, Danny," cautioned Rob.

"Whatever, man," Danny answered. "You're not going to fuck us, are you? Besides, we know where you live," he said and smiled. "See you downstairs." He walked out with Jim, laughing and pushing him hard on the shoulders.

Jim had a pair of thighs almost like the running back Earl Campbell of the Dallas Cowboys, and nearly as strong. Danny's push would have knocked an ordinary man off balance, and maybe right to the floor. Jim barely noticed it. If Danny got too rambunctious, Jim would settle him down. He'd done it many times before.

After Jim and Danny, Ricky and Mike both signed. Mike stayed back as Ricky went down the stairs for a few more drinks and some good stories. Not a big drinker, and we knew he might just stick with water. With lemon. He was probably the most naturally fit guy of all five guys, and liked to keep it that way.

"You know, Rob," started Mike. "This is really screwing my life up, like I had planned it."

"Then don't do it, man," said Rob. "You gotta wanna do this so bad it's like you just can't say no to it. Like you could never forgive yourself for not doing it," said Rob.

"Mike, listen. It's just like when you finally got me into racing, you know? Hell, I was in eleventh grade and would never be close to your level starting that late. But you convinced me to go for it. Without a doubt, it was one of the best decisions I ever made. I finally decided to do something for the right reasons. Because I wanted to. It was for me.

"Now I'm returning the favor. And I think you feel it too," said Rob. "What do you think the old man will say? he asked.

“Oh. He’d say, ‘Do whatever you want, Mike. Just be prepared to live with the consequences.’ That’s what he’d say,” Mike said emphatically.

“So, what do you want to do?” asked Rob.

After a long second, he’d made up his mind. “We’re doing this, Rob,” said Mike, smiling for the first time since dessert. “*Hell*, yes!” Mike laughed as they shook hands and slapped backs like the brothers they were, grabbed their stuff, and headed downstairs.

As Rob was headed down for more rounds of Coors Light and tall tales, he knew he’d accomplished what he came for. He had his dream team. He was feeling pretty damn good, actually. He was a little surprised that right now his mind went to another matter, and made him sad but just for a few seconds.

Rob thought he would have no time to look into his grandmother’s stories about her sisters and their covert exploits in saving the world.

But Rob wasn’t giving Providence its due. And Providence laughs when we mortals think we determine our own future.

Chapter 13

Little did Rob know, those stories his grandmother told him over the many hours of playing gin rummy, war, double solitaire and crazy eights, were actually real. But they didn't even scratch the surface of how clandestinely successful the group was.

The current leader of the ultra-secret society, known simply to the members as "Us," was Rasha Walther. A stunningly beautiful woman in her late forties, with raven hair and emerald green eyes, she could easily pass for a woman a decade younger. At five foot seven she was neither tall nor short. Rasha was the youngest daughter of Ana, whose older sister was a woman named Amy Nitschke. Amy had moved to America with her German husband almost a century prior, before World War I. Despite the pleas of the emigrating couple, Ana and her other sisters decided to stay in Germany, hoping to make a difference in their beloved country. They were acutely aware there were evil men embedded within the homeland, with a thirst for power and total European dominance, by any means necessary. They would stay and try to do something about that.

Ana and her sisters had made a pact that they would remain in Germany and do whatever it took to keep their country from slipping into abject evil. They did not know at the time that although they would not waver from this goal over the next century, their activities and purpose, not to mention the realities of war, would force them to choose a different country as home. Although fully assimilated into their new home life in Zermatt, Switzerland, a large piece of their hearts still longed for their German homeland.

As difficult as it was to move from their ancestral home and country, Providence shone its light on them. Moving actually saved the families from the absolute destruction of World Wars I and II. Being such a secret group, Switzerland turned out to be the one place on the planet where the family business could continue in total secrecy. No names or faces would appear on daily newspapers. Gossip was not celebrated in Switzerland. Unlike most any other free nation, gossip and hearsay was shunned and unprofitable.

Rasha's daughter Amelia was just turning 26, was unmarried and fine with it. She was fully committed to Us. Although she had her mother's amazing looks, her hair was blond, and her eyes were a luminescent hazel-green. By 16, she had traveled the world and already spoke seven languages with native proficiency. In Europe, it was not that unusual to speak four languages. No one in Europe spoke only one language. Most spoke at least three rather fluently. But to speak seven languages like a native was exceptional. She was working on Mandarin Chinese and Japanese in her spare time.

By 26, Amelia had already been on some very dangerous missions. Lia, for short, was a highly trained warrior in covert ops. A recent op was in nearby Belgium, infiltrating and taking out an ISIS terrorist cell wreaking havoc and murder in that country. Her cover in that op was a German arms dealer, sympathetic to the new caliphate. Through back channels and impeccable bona fides, the cell's leader agreed to a meeting to take possession of rocket-propelled grenades for his next, most vulnerable target; a Christmas pageant at a large elementary school in Brussels.

Neither the Belgian police nor Interpol could figure out how the cell obtained the bomb that exploded in the rundown warehouse where the terrorists were plotting their next slaughter of innocent victims. To the police, it came as a great surprise that these terrorists were even in the country. That they supposedly detonated the bomb among themselves rather than on Belgian citizens was divine intervention, or so the authorities thought.

The police had no idea about the attacks planned on the children and the first responders. In the rubble they would find the plans outlining the school attack using RPGs and be a little confused. They would suddenly realize the terrorists weren't even planning a bomb attack, so how was it that a bomb blew up their warehouse? Certainly, the police would never publicly disclose that information, or the real target. The panic and fear it would cause Belgium's citizens meant the truth would never see the light of day.

But this kind of non-public, inside information could prove useful to Us in the future. Since WWII, Us had files on dozens of unsolved deaths and mysterious disappearances of some very bad people, mostly men, some in very high government positions, in first-person multi-colored detail. The information extracted from these individuals had saved so many thousands of lives over the years with key intel leaks, Us had quit keeping track. Getting key information to the right persons in law enforcement was difficult, and even ignored sometimes. But it was enough for Us that good was overcoming evil at times and innocent lives were not destroyed.

But Lia didn't care what the Belgian police thought. She was already on to another mission. One she and Us had been working on for years. This mission was both long-range and long-term. It was as large as it was dangerous, and the personal risks were extraordinary. Failure was not an option, but success was far off, and quite complex. It could be the operation of a lifetime, but had the high potential to be a short one, given the danger. The dirty money in it was richer than even the narcotics trade. In fact, some former narco-traders were switching to this:

Human trafficking.

Chapter 14

It started slowly. Immigration to the USA from the USSR was closely monitored and strictly limited for national security reasons. This all changed in the 1990s when our most formidable enemy and fellow superpower collapsed economically and the Eastern Bloc nations immediately asserted their independence. Most of the emigration of the newly rich from Russia headed to the city that never sleeps; New York City. Long Island, Queens, and Brooklyn to be exact. Manhattan and New York City proper were too tight a circle of power.

Having ample warning of the nature and impenetrability of the Wall Street banks and major law firm network, the newly emancipated Russians picked greener pastures. Having successfully looted Russia of billions of dollars in the 1990s under President Boris Yeltsin, Boris Berezofsky and other self-exiled oligarchs, including high-ranking managers of state-owned enterprises and their families, got the hell out of Russia. They could never return to their homeland, due entirely to their manipulative and cynical fleecing of Russian state assets during the privatization rush. These former government managers of state-owned industries became billionaires practically overnight through Yeltsin's critically misguided attempt to change Russia into a market economy, and to win reelection.

Why would these nouveau riche even want to go back to a bankrupt Russia? What kind of enjoyment of their wealth would that be? Some were happy to start up and live normal lives, as much like Americans as possible. Although living among other Russians would be nice. Having to explain to new American friends how all they and their Russian friends were able to live better than them, have nicer homes, faster cars and flashier clothes, fresh from the Communist homeland, might be a little uncomfortable. Their new neighbors might be a bit jealous. Or indignant. Maybe it would be best to keep to themselves for several years.

Lucky for these immigrating Russians, CNN was not that interested and the internet was barely in use. So very little focus was directed toward this disruptive event.

Imagine what would happen now, if, with the instant news coverage, the US allowed Nicolas Maduro, his high-ranking military officers, all his cabinet members and heads of state institutions, his upper managers of all the state-owned industries, their entire extended families, and all the wealth of Venezuela they collectively looted from that country, in the multi-billions of dollars, to immigrate to America and face no retribution or accountability. And then these people became your new neighbors, with their new mansions, luxury cars and items, and flashy clothes. All with the blessing of the US president, senators and congresspersons.

It just might go down like this:

Venezuelan exiles and refugees already living in the USA would organize and show up on the doorsteps of these very people who so viciously raped, robbed and pillaged their own country. These freedom-loving Venezuelan refugees and asylum grantees would surround the new homes of Maduro's thugs and burn these people out to get some semblance of justice. It would take the entire National Guard to try and keep them from doing this. In the very next election, American voters would throw out the elected officials and the immigration services who let Maduro's thugs in.

But this is not what happened when the Russians were let into America *en masse* in the late 1990s and early 2000s.

The big difference from the Venezuela scenario is that the Russian government officially did it to itself, by ignorance and greed. Specifically, it was Boris Yeltsin's successful but economically devasting strategy for re-election as the president of the USSR. Only years later did they realize what catastrophic and mortal damage they had done to their country. On August 17, 1998, less than eight years after they began privatization, the country went bankrupt. The legal looters had long ago fled and Russia was a broken and abused shell. Their own President Yeltsin did it to them.

It is highly likely that Yeltsin's resignation as president, on the very eve of the new millennium, December 31, 1999, was more about avoiding execution than his stated health problems. His appointee? None other than Vladimir Putin, former head of the "new" KGB, the Federal Security Service. It would not be too long before Putin would begin to undo the damage Yeltsin's policies had wreaked on the nation. Even today, there are several oligarch billionaires rotting in Russian prisons on trumped-up tax evasion charges. The price for freedom? Just sign over all your holdings back to Putin. Well, technically to Russia, but effectively to Putin. "It's good to be king," as the old saying goes. Or the president of Russia for life.

The Russian government and the citizens who remained were broken and destitute. And that was the good news. The future looked even worse. Practically the entire wealth of Russia was owned by people who had left during privatization and were never coming back. The profits from oil and forestry and minerals were now siphoned off to the Russians who had moved all over the globe, but particularly in the Western Hemisphere. America, Argentina and Brazil had the most immigrants. None of that great wealth was being reinvested into the mother country.

The newly rich Russian immigrants to America, particularly those arriving in New York City, were ready, willing and quite able to have a great and prosperous future in their new host country. The land of the free and the home of the brave: America. Ironically, most had already achieved the American Dream before they even got here. In fact, they had already surpassed more than 95 percent of American citizens in terms of net worth before they even landed. That they had achieved it by legally looting their own communist country was an irony that would have deep repercussions on their view of the American Dream.

Not surprisingly, these new immigrants were eager to maintain and grow their considerable wealth. They identified businesses and industries that could produce high cash flow and easy profits. For many of these new immigrants, but of course not all, legality and illegality were all relative. Getting caught was only of small concern.

With their Russian-looted money and rabid American law firms, they knew that even if they were caught, most charges would be dropped, and even fewer convictions would be made. They had seen the American movies. They even watched the Trial of the Century: The People v. O.J. Simpson. They knew even the guilty get off with good lawyers. That the accused even get a trial was amazing, if not amusing to them.

By contrast, in Russia, the accused are sentenced after a quick formality of presenting the evidence. The defense lawyer's skill was in begging, or bribing the judge to keep the jail time as short as possible. To take more than two hours for both trial and sentencing would be highly unusual. A trial lasting three, four or six months? That was absurd. Laughable. With evidence so damning and incriminating, like against O.J. Simpson? Insane.

Lastly, American prisons were of little concern. Compared to Russian prisons, high on the list of the most brutal and inhumane institutions on the planet, on par with China, North Korea and Cuba, America's notorious San Quentin, Attica and Sing Sing Penitentiaries were country clubs. Prisoners in America actually had rights. They were fed, clothed and sheltered. If that was the worst America had to offer, being required to take a vacation for a couple years might not be so bad if the lawyers screwed up and didn't get them off.

To put it nicely, respect for American criminal laws was non-existent. Like a mosquito or an annoying fly, criminal laws were nothing more than a nuisance. Certainly not more than a damn nuisance, or maybe an expensive one. What worked in the mother country would no doubt work here too. A little grease on the palms, a little money under the table, into the right hands, maybe the cop, detective, the police chief, even the judge, and of course the politician, and problems seem to disappear.

The result of the Russians' understanding of America's legal system? Life was good and it was going to get better. It was time to make money any way they could, and as fast as they could. They understood that in America, money and power are conjoined twin sisters, sharing the same heart. One can't survive without the other, and two heads are better than one.

Having just come from a country that inoculates against morals and ethics—after all, no one gets rich in Russia with those vices—America was full of low-hanging fruit. Countries adjoining Russia certainly have opportunities to exploit for easy profits, but nothing like America. And far less enjoyment of their new spoils. Argentina and Brazil were nice, but in America, the rich can enjoy a lifestyle unlike any place on Earth. Every imaginable materialistic product is available, to lease or own, with easy credit and monthly payment plans. You did not need to be rich, as in loaded with cash in the bank. All you need is a good and steady cash flow.

Having figured out that reality of American life, the search for cash cow businesses became relentless and vicious.

Chapter 15

The Russians quickly discovered that Wall Street was of course dominated by the powerful banks, stock market brokerages, and huge law firms. The heart of the world's financial and legal center was run and ruled by Americans. American men, that is. The power structure was so incredibly lopsided with men, that there was rarely even opposition to it. Women were so underrepresented on the boards of directors or the executive suite anywhere on Wall Street that inroads were all but impossible.

The fact was that most women's primary goal in life wasn't just to be the richest asshole on the planet with the most toys. Sadly, outside of the medical and science professions, men's first choice was just that. Rare exceptions do occur, and a few highly motivated and smart women have made it fairly far, but never to the top of the largest flagship firms. Maybe in the next generation, if the current war against anything masculine continues its victories. Although many of the victories were overdue and warranted, a society where men were ashamed of being men was a country soon to be defeated by a society that wasn't so.

For generations, however, the best, brightest and most ambitious young men and women came to New York City from all over the

US and globally. They were drawn to the Big Apple by the common knowledge that landing a job with the biggest, most powerful banks and law firms in the world would set them up for incredible financial success and opportunity for the rest of their lives.

The promise of wealth, the intoxicating smell of luxury, and the aphrodisiac of power drew endless waves of avaricious and highly qualified contenders for scarce positions. The feeders came from the most prestigious colleges in the country. However, Harvard, Yale, Columbia, Northwestern in Chicago, Wharton at Penn State, Duke, Stanford and Berkeley were all given priority, in roughly that order. Most applicants had no idea they were fighting over just a fraction of the openings at the most powerful firms.

The networking inside these bastions of power and wealth was intense and entrenched. Close relationships of families and friends went back for decades and even generations. Friends and allies arranged marriages among their children to unify the alliances and power structures. It was a rarity, and highly frowned upon, to marry outside the network for something as trivial as love. It may very well have been cause for excommunication from the tight circles of power and prestige. Most certainly the leadership. This may well be one of the main reasons New York City was always in the top cities in the US where husbands and wives cheated on each other. Monogamy is a lesser known disease among power and wealth, and Wall Street was no exception.

That most of the positions were already to be filled by the power network was a known and accepted practice within the individual organization. The public would never know. After all, who would really care to find out? With the remaining openings, rigorous and exhaustive protocols would be meticulously followed to ensure strict compliance with anti-discrimination laws and fair hiring statutes. Some of the brightest and best minds in the world would be hired and integrated into the organization, benefitting it immensely. Little did these brilliant new hires know, but never in their lifetimes or a dozen others, would they ever reach the highest levels of the organization. Those levels were already set, drawn from a pool of the best of the inner network's alliance. Even so, no one would ever trace back that there was any discrimination or other violation of any laws.

Given this environment surrounding the hiring of American citizens, who were protected by US law, a foreigner was in an even worse position to enter this tightly knit and hyper-competitive New York City job market. However, some did. That they were brilliant was almost an insult. They were either beyond brilliant, or their family's connection to the inner network was tied by golden cords. In the same way alliances were cemented by marriage, a very rich foreigner's loyalty and revenue generation to the organization could be assured by the hiring of a son, grandson, nephew or cousin. The challenge of the organization's inner network was to stem the ever-increasing attempts to exert control or policy by the rich foreigner over the firm. It could be exponentially more difficult in the case of a foreign billionaire.

Many a small to mid-size financial firm has been ruined for lacking the wisdom, courage, and political skill it takes to control a billionaire outsider who has gained a toehold in the firm by just this kind of alliance. As in the animal kingdom, the jungle has a law that must be followed. The survival of the fittest determines the eventual outcome of just this sort of alliance.

Consider the old fairytale about the charming, warm and charismatic lion asking a friendly but small pack of hyenas to raise his young cub, his son and future heir. The cub's mother had tragically perished, and the lion must go far, far away to explore and hunt. The cub is too small to make the long journey. The hyenas eagerly agree, gleeful that they now have a lion as a friend, and will benefit greatly by not fearing constant attacks by their natural enemy. Within a few years, the cub grows into a young lion, and is easily the best hunter for the pack. Also, this pack of hyenas rules the land, since no other animal or pack of hyenas will dare attack them, with their highly unusual member.

At last, years later, the lion's father returns, and now he has a couple she-lions with him. He greets his old hyena friends with smiles and nose-kisses, and the reunion with his son is truly touching. He is so thankful to his old friends for raising his son and teaching him how to hunt that he invites them to a feast of fresh impalas that night, an all-you-can-eat buffet. Sharing the amazing story of raising a lion as a hyena, and the love they now share, brings tears to the lion's father and his two lionesses. As the hyenas gorge themselves on fresh impala, they cannot believe their good fortune. Not only do they have lions as friends, the lions themselves generously share their kills with them. No other hyenas have ever had this kind of alliance. Life is so good. Their sleep that night comes quickly and deeply. Never have they felt so safe and satisfied.

Around midnight, when deep sleep has overtaken every hyena and their snoring is as loud as a herd of stomping water buffaloes, the lions open their eyes and look at each other. With their pupils fully dilated, their night vision is as good as hyena day vision. Silently as ghosts, they tiptoe around and with powerful, savage and precise bites, they crush the windpipe and break the neck of all but one of their hyena friends. So deep is their sleep from the impala feast just a few hours ago, the hyenas don't know what is happening. Only in that last split second before death, in the jaws of the lion, right before the crush of their neck and spine, do they realize their foolishness and grave mistake.

The last hyena feels the nose of his lion-brother pushing him, rolling him from his back onto his side. As he finally jolts himself up, he distinctly smells blood, but not impala blood. It is dripping from his lion-brother's mouth. The growls and snarls just then from the other lions as they look up at him from ravishing some familiar-looking fresh kills sends him into a panic run as fast as he can to get away from that sound. As he flees, his impala-gorged stomach rejects its contents, projectile-vomiting its entire contents to each side, not even slowing down his run.

Behind him, the lions continue their feast of fresh hyena meat, only eating the largest sections of meat. Hyena meat is really disgusting to them, but they are hungry from having to watch those same hyenas eat their fresh impala just a few hours ago. They have already decided to let the last hyena go.

After all, you never know when you will need another hyena friend.

The foolish hyenas forgot the law of the jungle. The lion is the king and they are not. If you try to raise a lion to be like a hyena, he will probably eat you and your family someday when you're least expecting it.

The issue is and always has been—who is the lion and who is the hyena? Big banks and brokerages, and large, multi-national law firms are clearly lions. Even billionaires cannot bend them to their will. Some regional banks are also lions, even though their scope and influence are more limited. The gray area is the billionaire's playground. They know their sandbox. They know if they are or can be the only lion in the pride land. They love the challenge of gaining control of the bank, causing it to work in their best interests, preferably without being discovered.

This billionaire knows its prey. Over the years that his grandson was at the firm, he directed so much business and revenues to the small firm that he and his affiliates eventually accounted for over half of their profits. The firm did not appreciate how strong the relationships were that existed between the billionaire and the affiliates. They believed, erroneously, that the relationships were loyal to the firm, since their service was stellar, even Ritz Carlton-like, maybe better.

They were mistaken. They were unaware the affiliates owed their very existence and certainly their success to the billionaire. The time to take control was at hand. When half the business would walk if the billionaire coughed, the bank would have to accept 80 percent less than the market value for its business. For a fraction of what the bank was worth by market standards, the bank would have to sell to the billionaire.

They actually had to sell it for well below what it was worth even before they generously gave the grandson his very first job, years ago. The billionaire ensured that there would be no competition for the remaining half of the revenues. He made his offer contingent on the bank owners agreeing to all but token amounts being paid in 10-year non-compete agreements. All would have to leave, except for the grandson, who would now be the new president and chief executive officer.

Having to pay only 30 million dollars for a business worth 150 million meant that the billionaire's net worth had just increased by almost 120 million dollars. Actually, since the payout was over ten years, he really did not even pay for that. The revenues of the company did.

A moderately ambitious billionaire could do this scenario once every several years, all over the world. It would not take long to amass another billion to their net worth, at this rate. Imagine what a very ambitious billionaire could do.

Self-made billionaires are not wired to walk away from creating wealth. Only the inheritors of wealth can stand just spending their wealth without further attempts to increase it. The only thing that keeps self-made billionaires feeling alive, however, is the next dollar they create. Both fear and greed push them. At this level of wealth, fear is irrational but is the primary motivator. They fear that if they don't keep driving even harder, they will lose everything. Like overnight. To the outside world, it looks like greed. More, more, more. Outsiders have no idea how paranoid these people live.

Why do the best basketball players want more and more court-time? For the same reason. Fear. Fear of losing their spot. Unlike basketball, for the billionaire, the game is rigged. It is not a competition of equals. It is not a game of chance. The win was guaranteed long before the other side even knew they were playing. The win, the transfer of dollars, the change in ownership, the closing, was just a formality. It's like a brilliant, super-quick-on-his-feet player who made the Game-Show after a lifetime of preparation, going up against another player who had been surreptitiously fed all the questions months before, whose answer-button would override the other contestant's. The fix was in.

After closing one of these conquests, it is time to celebrate. After a week or two of celebration and relaxation on a billionaire's budget, the bug hits again, and the cycle repeats.

If this sounds strangely like a serial killer, it should. Or like a lion after a kill. There are two laws at play: the law of mankind, and the law of the jungle. Following the law of the jungle is breaking the law of mankind. Only the lion gets to follow the law of the jungle. The challenge in human history is to keep men from getting away with acting like lions.

Once a man becomes like the lion, he cannot be allowed to be around other humans. The danger is both terrifying and completely obvious. One is the prey, the other is the predator. Whether the lion is good and only kills for sustenance, or it is evil and kills for sport, is irrelevant. It must be neutralized. If it cannot be captured and caged, it must be hunted down and killed.

Unlike a lion in the wild or a serial killer on the loose, the lion-billionaire is well-protected by his fortress of wealth. Like a brutal dictator who controls the military, the lion-billionaire has an army of dollars, and all the lawyers, politicians and police money can buy. Most every time, that same dictator becomes a lion-billionaire, having looted all the wealth of his country along with his subservient lieutenants in the military brass. For a leader like this to be toppled, his military commanders must be absolutely convinced that it is better for them with the new guy than with the current guy. One can see how truly difficult this is when a dictator grabs power. For a population stripped of all their guns, it must be a pretty convincing argument.

Can this kind of predator be stopped? Can good really overcome evil? Is it worth dying for? Will it make a difference? Can anything be done?

Can anything really be done to stop human trafficking?

Thankfully, some people think we must try.

Chapter 16

Unfortunately, most people in any society on the planet would say "no" to those questions. As long as it doesn't affect them, they don't care. Thank God there are some who answer "Yes!" to those questions, including the last, and fight on. They are not all politicians, police and soldiers. They might have been, and some still are, but they are faced daily with an apathy toward the problem. They live beyond the sound bites of the politicians pretending to care on the election trail. They soldier on once the echoes have long died out, and the promises turn into a million pieces of dust. Blown away by the first wisp of wind before the rain, they wash into the sewer of darkness, where old promises go and are forgotten.

And forgotten they stay, until the unidentified female body is found floating in Biscayne Bay, or tangled in the mangroves on shore, or in the canals that peacefully meander around the multi-million-dollar mansions along the intracoastal waterway. On the Rivieras of the lux Gold Coast, from Palm Beach to Fort Lauderdale to Coco Plum all the way to Gables by the Sea, it is safe to assume that the poor woman's disposal was not done properly.

The official reactions are very predictable. Immediately, the outrage from the local mayor is vocal and fierce. Interviewed on breaking news, he passionately recounts the programs he has initiated, the appearances made, and the money raised to eradicate the scourge of human trafficking in their districts. "But more needs to be done," he pleads, directly into the camera. Even more police, resources and money will be directed here and there, and he will courageously lead the fight. "That is why you voted me in here in the first place," he valiantly points out.

By the next day, he has made a proposal to advance new gun control measures, as if that were part of the problem.

"If only the President would grant us the funds we requested long ago," he will say. "If he cared anything about basic human rights, he would do this," he'll say, shifting the public rage away from himself. "But we will do what we can with such limited assistance from the feds," he adds to complete the circle, lower the expectations, and get people to move on to other, more important things.

Like what the Kardashians tweeted about their latest wardrobe malfunction.

After all, it was just one body. And not even a US citizen.

"Thank God for social media, especially Twitter and Instagram," the Mayor's staff tells him, breathlessly. Even though they have existed less than five years, they already have predictive data that can show with surgical precision just how long the public outrage will last on virtually any issue. This valuable data is sold to the public relations firms in real time, allowing them even to steer public perception. The public relations firms have responses for almost anything, including timing and frequency, to help move beyond any scandal. One unidentified female corpse, probably only one night's news cycle. Many times it just appears deep in the back of the Miami Herald. Put the police spokeswoman on, and a quick shot of an anxious mayor, and it's forgotten by tomorrow.

“The mayor is on it, after all,” assures the spokeswoman, following the prepared script. “The mayor and the *entire* police force will not rest until we find who is responsible for this heinous act and bring them to justice,” she concludes.

The public rage has been acknowledged and mirrored, and thus neutralized.

Chapter 17

Realizing they could never bribe their way into the insane money of Wall Street, the Ruskies quickly regrouped and looked in an entirely different direction. Outside Manhattan, it became apparent there were multitudes of independent gas stations operating all over the place. Gasoline shipments into the area came from all over the world. The surplus not taken by the majors was eagerly sucked up by independents supplying their own little networks of gas stations. As long as people needed gas for their cars, the flow of gasoline provided an endless source of cash flow to the owners and operators. But the system was fragmented and inefficient.

It did not take very long for the Russians to buy out a few small networks, like fewer than five gas stations in total. After many years in the struggle to own and operate the small stations, owners were more than delighted in taking a cash offer of at least twice what they and their accountants knew the business was worth. They thought they had better act fast and bank the deals before the buyers either woke up and realized their stupidity, or went broke.

Before anyone really noticed, the Russian consolidation really got moving. Then they quietly made inroads into the gasoline distribution business, from the refinery to the gas stations. The new

Russian investors began to control the market. They began to both raise the prices and limit the supply to the stations they did not yet own, but not to their owned stations. The remaining independent owners were faced with the awful truth that they were screwed, and consequently their business value was now cut in half. Most clearly realized they had held out too long, and, to cut further losses in their only retirement nest egg, jumped at new cash offers by their new competitors. Selling at only a 45 percent discount seemed far better than losing their entire nest egg.

The last remaining independent holdouts, too stubborn and unwilling to sell to what they perceived to be the Russian Mafia, would just walk away from their station. They simply were unable to compete against both the competitor down the street and the supplier of their gas, which were of course owned by the Russians. In time, all the Russians had to do was buy the abandoned property for pocket change from repossession companies and banks, who were happy to unload it. The Russians figured out quickly that bankers could be bought, just like the police, judges and politicians. The bankers even had an excuse no one could argue with. No need to keep a potentially contaminated piece of property on the books. Their shareholders wouldn't like that.

In five short years of arriving from their mother country, Russian expats had cornered the market of gas stations and gasoline delivery on Long Island and large parts of Queens and Brooklyn. Now they could and did raise the prices at the pump. They had their cash flow. They wasted no time in acquiring the finest things money could buy, all on credit. Fancy new homes with gated entryways, expensive cars, especially Ferraris, furnishings, modern art, speedboats and yachts were all within reach.

It wasn't just the money made on selling gas. Actually, that was a nice piece of profits, but they also controlled the market for car repairs and maintenance. Most of the gas stations they now owned also had garages with mechanics, which local people were accustomed to patronizing. They made sure they did good work and charged what the former owner charged, for at least a year. Then they gradually raised the hourly rates, citing inflation as the main excuse. They learned fast the methods of entrepreneurship that defined their new home in America. If big business could do it, they could too.

Vladimir Sokolov, a higher-up in the Russian group that now controlled the gasoline industry in Long Island, Brooklyn and Queens, when learning English on his arrival in New York, read the story of the unwise frog and boiling water. Throw a frog into a frying pan of boiling water and he'll jump right out. But place the frog in cold water and slowly turn up the heat, and the frog will never know the moment he died in the boiling water. The Russians raised the prices of gasoline and services so slowly, the customers barely noticed, if at all. He mockingly referred to his American customers as *lyagushkas*, Russian for *frogs*. Never, however, to their face. He would never insult his customers directly, even if they were just Americans.

Chapter 18

The problem with being a criminal is that it is almost impossible to stop being one. How many times have documentaries ended by lamenting that the criminal mastermind, head of such a successful criminal empire, could have been just as successful had he applied his considerable talents to honest enterprise? It seems like such a shame and a waste of talent to lock this person up. If only he'd had a different environment to grow up in, he would have turned out differently, they say, casting the monster as the victim.

Victim? Perhaps, long ago. But choices were made, sides were taken, and wars were waged. Early on in the process, the heart hardens and darkens. The poison fruit of crime has dropped its roots deep in the soul. Alliances were forged, promises made and contracts formed. Contracts need not be written to be enforceable. Basically, all it takes is that consideration is exchanged. This could take the form of money or actions in reliance of the agreement. Just because illicit and illegal contracts cannot be enforced by a court of law, like before a judge and jury, they certainly are enforceable by the street law, or mob law. Russians had a very effective way of enforcing their contracts without the formalities of law. In a land where government laws are regularly unenforced, the law of the streets prevails.

In the 1990s, as Russia opened the emigration floodgates, allowing their citizens to migrate out, many left. But not all strings were cut. They still had contacts, friends, even family. Not everyone permitted to leave actually did. Family and cultural ties to the homeland were too strong, and the lure of wealth and materialism was not completely overpowering. For many, however, staying in a bankrupt country created new problems.

Since the exodus of the high-ranking government officials during the 1990s, the power positions in the government-run monopolies, military and police were vacated. The highly educated brain-drain was a harsh reality. As a result, organized crime began to surface in Russia like never before. Previously, graft and corruption had been managed by the government. The state's managers were the beneficiaries of the spoils. But now those individuals had emigrated and were never returning.

The streets became a dangerous place, and lawlessness in the mother country sprang up everywhere. Since personal ownership of guns was prohibited, the people were truly at the mercy of the criminal element. Several bands of ruthless crime organizations fought to control the black market, which included most everything, even food. However, the most lucrative market at the time was the drug trade.

The import, export, and distribution of illegal drugs, mostly ecstasy and cocaine, was bringing prosperity not only to the criminal element, but also the remaining police and customs officials in on the movement of the trade.

Back in their new home country, America, it was only a matter of time, and entirely logical, for the new owners of the Long Island gasoline network to figure out that there were non-Russians in their neighborhoods with a cash cow of their own. The Russians did not like this. No other group should be making money in their new neighborhoods, they reasoned. It did not take them very long to realize how easy it would be for them to control not only the gasoline market, but also the illicit drug trade inside their new neighborhoods.

Back in Russia, there were multitudes of lower-level managers, police and military who were not allowed to participate in the privatization wealth redistribution, or looting of the mother country. They were living day-to-day existences and affording no luxuries. For the new Russian-Americans, it was simply a matter of reaching out to find the right person with the right connection to the underworld back home. Soon, they had a steady stream of heroin from Turkey, and plenty of Columbian cocaine smuggled into Russia. They could easily turn that around to the unsuspecting ports in New York City.

Of course, there was the old Italian Mafia to contend with. The real Mafia with the Sicilian heritage, that is. These criminal enterprises were already in control of the drug trade in the immediately surrounding communities outside Manhattan. The Mafia already had their own deals worked out with the Caribbean cartels, including Jamaicans, Haitians, and Dominicans. But they had no idea how ruthless the average Russian criminal was. Bring them to America, the land of the free and home of the credit card, and their brutality and cruelty took on a whole new dimension. It was a good thing for them that the Russians didn't want Manhattan. Yet.

After several brief but brutal turf wars on key distribution areas on Long Island, the Italians were not in the mood for an all-out war with the Russians. They heard what they had done to the small drug networks and their families. The body counts of headless, handless and footless corpses showing up in the city morgues were proof that the Russians were willing to go to any extreme to take full control of their new neighborhood. This was not the time to get cross-wise with the new boys in town. They were much more focused on expanding in their truly lucrative areas all over Manhattan and into Jersey.

Once gas and drugs were under control, the next industry to conquer was going to be the most lucrative, and most fun, for the

Russians. At first, they didn't know it. They were doing so well with gasoline and drugs that they just couldn't see it right away. They only went to The Red Velvet strip club to relax, drink vodka, ogle naked women, and, if they tipped enough, hook up with one or more.

They started realizing they were spending so much money there, in drinks, food and private lap dances, that it started to annoy them. They would much rather get all that stuff for free and let others pay for it. Making the owner an offer he could not refuse, which included keeping himself and his family alive, as long as they moved out of state, they bought their very first strip club.

As nice as the American girls were, with their expensive boob jobs and plastic surgery, the new owners really did miss their own Russian girls. At least Eastern European girls. Amazingly, it was not at all difficult to have their Russian contacts recruit native Russian and formerly Eastern Bloc girls to come to America with the promise of good pay and a path to citizenship. With a horrible economy and an equally bleak future, and no real opportunities for women, almost any excuse to leave the Eastern Bloc would do.

Tragically, for these girl recruits, no due diligence was done by anybody over there. The internet was just beginning its rise to eventual worldwide coverage. The poor Eastern Bloc countries did not even have access to the internet. Even finding a computer was difficult. There were no employment agencies to vet the potential employers.

Frankly, the girls had no idea how to find whether the jobs offered were even real. Even so, imagine their surprise when the girls got to New York and found out that their new job was being a stripper or "escort," and worse, the price was two years' apprenticeship before they could even apply for citizenship. Otherwise, their new bosses would ship them back home to live in the hell they left.

Some of the girls actually thought they had a choice. After a few of them disappeared and were never heard from, the other girls readily agreed to the two-year option. It was called survival.

As it turned out, the local American customers liked the Russian girls too. Once the Russians saw the increase in patronage and profits, their appetite was whetted for more opportunities and ways to take over yet another industry.

Duh! Strip clubs.

They would even use the same entrepreneurial model they used for the gas business, since it worked so well.

Chapter 19

Ten years later, it was the end of February, and Vladimir had just returned from Miami Beach, hearing there was a very healthy Russian population there. In his boredom one night, he visited a decent-sized strip club in the Golden Triangle area of Miami off I-95. He was only mildly impressed. Actually, compared with their club in Long Island, the Miami club was really lacking.

On his return, Vladimir stopped by The Red Velvet Club for a couple vodka tonics and told his comrades they could really make a big splash in Miami. North Miami Beach, toward Surfside, was loaded with Russians. It was such a happening place but the strip clubs were just marginal. The more he told them about it, the more interested they became. Vladimir told them about the tropical breeze and the palm trees, and the cool vibe of Miami Beach. But he knew he had them convinced when their mouths and eyes gaped opened as he described the girls on the beach in their barely-there bikinis. Every day, sunup to sundown. Rollerblading, swimming, sun-bathing, beach volleyball, they were all over the place.

Within five years, he and his buddies, the Bratva, or Russian Mafia, from Long Island, acquired all the strip clubs in Miami. The new look for the girls was Russian and Eastern European. The quality of the upscale strip clubs around the Golden Triangle and Fort Lauderdale took a quantum leap skyward. Flush with drug money, the clubs expanded and remodeled to look like the Czars' castle in St. Petersburg. Limousine service was added to and from the hotels and clubs on Miami Beach. The cash flow from the drugs, alcohol, escort fees and cover charges was like they had tapped into an artesian well. There was no end to the water, or the cash.

The clubs they bought on the west side of Miami, for the most part, they kept the same. Those places drew a very familiar crowd of regulars, who spent plenty on the girls and drank like fish. There was no need to upgrade, at least for now.

However, the new money was in something else. The real money, that is. Even more off the books. They had conquered some pretty tough businesses already. Gasoline, drugs, and now strip clubs. The lure of the money, and especially that they weren't the ones making it, was irresistible for these strongmen. Their eyes had been opened to the sheer magnitude that could be theirs. Confidence oozed out of the pores of their thick Russian skin. They knew the time was right for their new venture. Their strip clubs were on the razor's edge dividing legal and criminal activity anyway. The next step was just another branch of the same tree. This branch was just loaded with fruit. It was time to cash in.

Human trafficking, Russian-style.

Chapter 20

Human trafficking has of course been around since the dawn of mankind. Until recently, it was called slavery. In recent times, offensive words are relabeled to protect the overly sensitive. Political correctness dictates by whom the subject may be discussed. Any voice outside that group is to be shunned and mocked. Slavery is one such word. In America, discussion of that horrible word and subject is only for a certain group of people whose ancestors of one hundred and seventy years ago were direct victims of it.

However, the word *slavery* can be applied to almost any ethnic group since the dawn of mankind.

The ancient civilizations even depicted slaves on cave walls, dating back many thousands of years B.C. Since that time, humans have been forced into involuntary servitude, building entire countries, laboring under the sun in every conceivable enterprise, fighting wars, and doing whatever else their masters required.

Astonishingly, it was just 1981 when the last country in the world officially abolished slavery in their country. In spite of the new law, the enslaved in the tiny African nation of Mauritania still number from 43,000 on the low side to 600,000 on the high end. Clearly, slavery still exists in that country.

International human trafficking takes on many different shapes and sizes, some more nefarious and sinister. In the Unites States for example, from the live-in domestics and nannies in Miami and Key Biscayne, Florida, to the Ukrainian and Russian pole dancers and "escorts" at the Russian-owned strip clubs and escort services in Miami, Fort Lauderdale, and Long Island, they all have this in common: Keep your mouth shut and do what they say or you will pay. At best, they could be sent back to their country, penniless, like the domestics of Key Biscayne face every day. At worst, they could lose their life, like the girls working the clubs or as high-end escorts.

They lack the same thing. Power.

It all gets down to power. Who has it and who doesn't.

On the idyllic island of Key Biscayne, just over the Rickenbacker Causeway from downtown Miami, about a dozen Latin American countries are well-represented, but the biggest demographic is Venezuelans. The wealthy Venezuelan families moved there decades ago, fleeing the country after the landslide socialist victory that brought Hugo Chavez to power. Their monopolistic elite, some of the richest people on the planet, were forced to recognize their country would never be the same, and quickly safeguarded their assets in other countries like the Caymans, Aruba, Switzerland, and of course, America. They then moved to the nearest, safest, Latin American city: Miami, Florida. Key Biscayne and Doral to be precise.

Doral is located on the far west side of Miami. Key Biscayne is on the farthest east side. More important to the new residents of the Key was that it was an island, with only one way in and one way out, unless you had a boat. They felt this fact made their homes, cars, children, and wives a little safer from the more dangerous and notorious neighborhoods in Miami. They were dead right. But not all of them could afford the Key. Instead, some moved into Doral. Hence, the Doral Venezuelans.

The new residents also brought their culture to the Key. Like most third-world countries, there was no middle class in Venezuela. Either you were very rich, or poor as dirt. Like everywhere else on the planet, the rich were not served by the fellow rich. With an endless supply of impoverished millions, the rich grew up alongside disposable humans. For any job imaginable. Domestic housecleaners, cooks, nannies, gardeners, builders, landscapers, all were cheap and plentiful. It was nothing to fire one of these for any reason. A hundred others were instantly ready to take their place, and maybe even do a better job. They had no rights or benefits, nor did they expect any. They'd never had any before, anyway.

The rich did not educate their children in how any of this worked. The children just absorbed it from infancy through childhood and into adulthood. They became what their parents were before them. The exact same is true of the poor. They knew their place and their purpose. If they were to eat, if they were to put clothes on their own babies, they would serve the rich in any way they could. If the mothers were domestics, their daughters would be also. If the men were landscapers, their sons would follow them.

Never in their entire lives would it occur to them to talk back or question their employers. They knew the instant they did, they would lose their job, as would their relatives in many cases.

Chavez's election victory caused the upper class to jolt awake, as if from a sweat-soaked, horrible nightmare. Like a terminal diagnosis of advanced pancreatic cancer causes a flurry of estate planning, the mobile rich sent their families to Miami on the first flights out of Caracas. Unlike pancreatic cancer, which is nearly impossible to detect in its early stages, Venezuela's decline into socialism and totalitarianism had many signs. They were just ignored. Generations of privilege and wealth had dulled the senses, blinded the eyes and shut the ears of the ruling party politicians as the middle class disappeared and the gap between rich and poor grew from a mere gulley to a Grand Canyon-size divide. The once-jailed but charismatic Colonel Chavez would finally succeed in an anemically low turnout election at what he failed to do in his military coup attempt. Take the presidency of the country.

The very wealthy had no idea how fast Chavez and his Socialists would shut down travel so they could fleece the wealthy of everything they had. With newfound terror, they envisioned a bloody takeover like Castro implemented in Cuba in 1959. They would stampede their families out of Caracas like they were escaping a burning house.

The difference was that Chavez was actually elected. He was not in a hurry to immediately and violently destroy his political opponents. He could take his time. Do it slowly. Chavez' experience being jailed forced him to learn patience. And planning.

With their families safely in Miami, the men would stay "in country" to run their businesses for now. There was just too much money at stake. They would stay as long as possible until Chavez eventually nationalized their companies or took their homes. Any business, any property, anytime, was under threat of being nationalized. The value to be paid was set by Chavez, and far less than its worth. Only the largest international companies could fight for higher compensation in the international courts. Individuals just had to take the paltry amount that was offered.

There was no challenge to the taking itself. And God knows, they either got out when they were told to, or were arrested for trespassing.

Now, under Maduro, it had only grown worse. Chavez and his death squads were kind and gentle compared to Maduro and his thugs.

The wealthy families hated to leave Caracas. This was not a choice they would make in a million years for a million reasons. The lifestyle they had there was god-like. The poor lived to serve them for almost nothing in return. Generations had come and gone like this, and family histories were the stuff of legend. From their luxurious estates in and around Caracas, they lived the life of privilege and pleasure. The businesses their grandfathers had built, they had managed well and passed them on to their own sons and families. Life was not just good, it was incredible.

The richest Venezuelans' second and third homes around the world were decent attempts at reproducing their home estates, although on a far smaller scale. It was much more expensive to build in countries with a middle class. Middle class folks simply would not work for nothing, and even had attitudes. There was truly no place like home, and nothing like the unlimited peasants who lived to serve them.

So, when they were forced to move to Miami on short notice, it was indeed a hardship.

For instance, their new Miami friends, especially their rare "gringa" friends, just had no idea how to act with their Venezuelan domestics and nannies. Worse still, however, even their own workers would forget their place. It must be something in the air in this new place, America. Perhaps the sweet scent of freedom in American air, like an addictive drug, was influencing them.

If the nannies spoke to the mother's friends, acting, heaven forbid, like a normal person, they would be shipped back to their life of poverty and oppression in a New York second. Equality and mutual respect were not to be tolerated in any form with their workers. The surprising thing was how ignorant their new friends were with their help. Unlike in their own country, at the birthday parties, the invited children's parents would actually talk to the nannies and domestics, almost as if the nannies were invited guests or part of the family. Especially if the workers spoke English.

The workers who understood their sudden predicament would quickly attempt to excuse themselves from the friendly questions from the ignorant guests.

"Ssssst, please," they would say as they touched their finger to their lips, slightly nodding toward their employer. "Ella nos verá!" "She will see us!" a worker would whisper to the clueless American mother, her whisper laden with fear and heavily accented English.

She would then quickly reengage in her work, tending to the children if she was the nanny, or striding to the kitchen if she was a domestic. The surprised guest would be sure to mention to her husband how odd that experience was.

And that would be the last time the gringa would ever speak to that mother's workers, as they would avoid her like she was a crack addict robber waving a gun. The clueless but friendly gringa would have no idea what a clear and present danger she was to the worker, who was probably under heightened scrutiny already just for speaking with her. One more slip-up and she would be gone. Sent back to the life she so desperately wanted never to return to.

In thousands of homes throughout greater Miami, on Key Biscayne, Doral, Coral Gables and Pinecrest, this form of human servitude played on. The supply of domestics and nannies was inexhaustible, almost like when they lived back home. Universally, the poor would use any excuse to leave their abject condition in their country. Maybe they could make enough money to send some home so their mothers, children and siblings could actually eat one spartan meal a day. With the "forbidden" American dollars, they could buy food on the black market, away from the government *grocerias*, which were empty anyway. Maybe they could save enough to pay the *coyotes* to bring their families to the US for a chance at a better life.

At least that's what they thought when they got here. After a month of being paid in room and board, but no money, they began to see just how this dream they had was almost worse than being back at home. At least there you didn't expect anything, and everyone was in the same poor situation. Living in clean, affluent Key Biscayne, with all the sunshine, beaches, luxury homes, condos, yachts and Italian and German supercars, the lowly, desperate state of their lives was even more glaring and cruel than it was at home.

For some, it made the longing to return home overpowering. It was much better than being surrounded by everything you could never have, not in your lifetime.

And yet this was the kindest, most generous form of human trafficking in existence. From this pinnacle, human trafficking's descent was like a train derailing on a bridge, heading straight down to the river a thousand feet below. The destruction of lives, if they survived such a fall, was devastating and real beyond imagination.

Unfortunately for the victims of mass human trafficking, the worst form of it was the most lucrative for the lions and wolves that ruled in this jungle.

Chapter 21

After eleven more months, seven days and seven hours, Rob was finally finished with his last tour, and his last day on active duty. Now 26, Rob had been an Army Ranger for the last five years.

It had been three days since he had his final dinner with his five other teammates on what had to be the most kick-ass year of his life. He was actually very pleased that the team had stuck together, even after Jim's crash that nearly ended his life. He made a mental note to call Jim to see how he was coming along in his long rehab. At least Jim was alive. How well he recovered depended on him.

More on that later.

A badly broken leg, arm and three cracked vertebrae were horrendous, but not as bad as getting maimed by an Afghan soldier you had just trained. Which is what happened right in front of Rob to his good friend and fellow Ranger, Combat Medic Stuart Ash, aka "Doc."

Reflecting back to over a year ago, on his last mission near Kabul, Afghanistan, Rob's mind rolled out the events that night that would alter his view on life forever.

••••••••••••••••••••••••

The US brass had resolved the only way they could leave Afghanistan was to train their Afghan allies in advanced warfare and hand-to-hand combat techniques. After two and a half months of this boot-camp-like training, where Rob and Stuart were two of the hand-picked Rangers to be mentors and instructors, they knew their trainees were now actual high-value and skilled soldiers. Too bad they could not train their hearts.

One inky black, moonless night, in the Herat Province of Afghanistan, a platoon from the 75th Ranger Battalion Alpha Unit and an equal number of Afghan Special Forces commandos were preparing for a joint pre-dawn raid. They divided into two groups, about one hundred yards apart, awaiting the arrival of two massive Chinook CH-47D transport choppers to take them to their drop point deep into a Taliban target stronghold. Each group consisted of 20 Rangers and 10 Afghan commandos plus an interpreter. At the last minute, Rob was switched to the second group, while Stuart stayed with the first.

As much as the Rangers had grown to like the Afghan commandos over the last couple months, he kept reminding himself of rule number one regarding his new Afghan comrades: "trust, but verify." Of course, he would never forget that his Dad had taken it a little further. As an Army veteran himself, he had seen enough and heard enough to add a little extra salt on this advice. On Rob's last visit home, after giving his mother a bear hug and tender kiss on the cheek, he turned to his father.

"Dad, I'll be home soon. Don't worry, I'll be careful," he reassured.

His Dad pulled him close in a hug, amazed at how strong his son had become. As Rob turned to go, his Dad put a hand on his shoulder.

"Son, one more thing," he started. "Look at me," he said as Rob turned to face him. Locking eyes with his son, through gritted teeth, he said, "Don't trust *any* of those bastards," referring to the Afghans. "Not one. You do *not* know them, no matter how much you think you do. Understand?"

Rob could see the intensity in his father's eyes, that his whole soul was behind those words.

"Dad, I hear ya, ok?" was the only thing he could think of saying. And then he was off.

....

Within minutes of the groups settling in, and without warning, two loud explosions erupted on the first group, a hundred yards away from Rob's group. Two bursts of automatic rifle fire pierced the air. Chaos followed. He heard screams coming from the other group. Someone was hit. No one knew what was going on, as they were "inside the wire" and this should not be happening.

Within seconds, however, they realized it was yet another dreaded and traitorous "blue on green" attack, from one of the Afghan commandos with them on the mission—one of the very same men they had just trained for two months.

Moving quickly next to the interpreter in his group, Rob learned it was his best friend Stuart who was hit. Instantly he got up and sprinted the hundred yards to the sounds of his friend screaming in pain. Throwing himself on Stuart, and putting his hand over his buddy's mouth, he said,

"Shut up, Stu! This fucker will hear you!"

Just as he said that, he looked up and saw the rogue commando walking toward them, shooting at him and Stuart. In one motion, Rob jump-rolled over Stuart, putting himself in between Stuart and the shooter, grabbed his M4 and squeezed off a dozen rounds, hitting the shooter with at least half the shots, putting him down instantly. Rob ran over, put two more rounds into the traitor to ensure the threat was over, then ran back to his friend.

"Stuart! Hang in there, buddy! You're gonna be fine, man!" Then he yelled, "Medic down! Medic down! I need another Medic!"

Stuart, or Doc, tried to tell Rob what to do to help him, but the wound from the round that hit his neck was making his words incomprehensible.

Rob did the best he could to stop the bleeding, putting QuikClot on the wound and applying pressure, and at the same time trying not to strangle Stuart. How ironic that a fully stocked combat medic bag was right next to Stuart but nearly useless without his expertise. However, Rob's efforts undoubtedly saved Stuart's life. Two endless minutes later, a combat medic from another Ranger platoon ran up and took over trying to save Stuart's life.

In all, the rogue commando inflicted eight casualties, including two fatalities. It was one thing for a soldier to die for his own country. There was a special pain caused by dying at the hands of a traitor.

Fortunately, this kind of death would not be Stuart's. After eight months and seven surgeries, he returned to his duties as a Ranger combat medic. It would take a lot more than a shot to the neck to keep that son of a bitch out of combat. Combat medics were made of different stuff than other humans. Like with steel spines and titanium wills.

Rob's extreme valor under fire did not go unnoticed, however. In recognition for his heroics, he was awarded his first Silver Star, the third highest award for gallantry in the US military.

....

Just as rapidly as the flashback had begun, Rob's mind returned to the current mission.

Much to his surprise, two weeks before their first full ski, wing suit and parachute run, he was able to persuade command center to let him hire the girl they rejected based on the flimsy domestic violence conviction. After several requests, the brass finally relented, for the success of the mission. But only as a technical assistant, and not as a skier. Not surprisingly, she accepted, even with the reduced role. Hell, it was still a paid gig, and the best job she had gotten since the conviction was a grocery store stocker in Denver, near the former Stapleton airport.

She really wondered how long she could hold out from stomping on this one fat slob's face. This clod, a produce stocker named Tyson, kept invading her personal space and lustily whispering propositions as he intentionally brushed against her every time he passed her in the public aisles and the back storerooms.

Since this was the "best" job she had since her conviction, she was determined to not make waves and call attention to herself. On the flip side, the tide had clearly swung in women's favor over sexual harassment issues. Companies were forced to deal with it more fairly. Even so, she was not ready to play that card, just yet.

But she was sure ready when Rob finally reached her in the middle of her shift. Recognizing his voice, she barely waited for him to say his name before blurting out, "I'm in!"

It was a good thing she was so eager to join Rob's mission. She was to report to Fort Carson in El Paso County, Colorado, in only two days. From there, she would get a transatlantic lift on one of the Army's cargo aircraft, landing in Camp Ederle in Vicenza, Italy, just 25 miles from the floating city of Venice.

It wasn't like she had to pack much anyway. Rob told her to pack her essentials, like she was on a short backpack trip to Europe. The Army would be providing everything else, including winter gear. Sam agreed to sign the NDA in Vicenza. Rob was very impressed with how enthusiastically the 173rd Airborne Brigade Combat Team, the "Sky Soldiers" were taking this mission. They had spared no expense in equipment and logistical support for all their jumps. Allowing a new member on the team was highly unusual, but the commander allowed it eventually. He let Rob know, in no uncertain terms, that if she screwed up it was all on him, not the commander.

Samantha "Sam" Ross would be a welcome addition to the group. Her knowledge of back country skiing and avalanche risks would be key to the continued success and safety of the mission. Sam would be strictly in a support role. Because she had not done any of the extensive dry-land training and intense skiing evaluations, she would not be allowed to do any of the actual runs. She would, however, be in the chopper, giving technical support that very few in the world could even contemplate.

If nothing else, this turn of events for Sam could change the trajectory of her life for the better. For that, Rob was pleased. For Sam, it was earth-shakingly awesome.

Newly empowered and sensing her new independence, she was on her way to the manager's office to immediately resign. As she cut through the back storerooms, Tyson the clod appeared directly in front of her, blocking her path.

Sneering, he asked, "Why're you so happy, Sammy? Thinking about giving me a blowjob?"

Highly unluckily for Tyson, he decided to push things a little further than other times, and he reached out his hand and put it on Sam's shoulder. With zero hesitation, Sam grabbed his hand and twisted him around in a perfect straight-arm twist move, immediately straightening his arm, forcing him to his knees squealing for mercy. Now behind him, Sam forced the arm up more, pushing him down flat on the floor, face-down. Then she bent his arm at the elbow, holding him down, nearly breaking his arm. She put her knee into his lower back, right into his kidneys, then bent down and quietly spoke into his ear.

"If you ever do that again to me or any other girl, anywhere, I will find you and cut your balls off and stuff them down your throat. Are we clear?"

"Yyyyyes!"

"I can't hear you," Sam said in a singsong way.

"Yes!" he rasped. "Please! No more!"

One more deep knee thrust into his kidneys, just for fun, and Sam released him. Tyson curled up on his side and just moaned, very lightly. He for sure didn't want anyone to hear him.

On her way out of the manager's office, Sam got all the girls together and told them what happened with Tyson.

"If he even looks at you wrong, just say my name," she said, smiling.

As she walked out the front door, the sun seemed to be shining a little more brightly, and even the drab early winter landscape seemed pretty.

Things were looking up for Sam.

....

The mission lasted another thirteen jumps. The last four were smack in the middle of April, after a "surprise" snowstorm that dumped four feet of fresh snow in the Italian and Swiss Alps. By this time, the group had all but perfected their technique and proven their ability to pinpoint their landings at the precise pre-planned targets. In fact, they did so well that the 173rd brass decided they did not need further testing in the Argentine and Chilean Andes.

The elite group of "alpha-testers" would be de-commissioned by the Army. They had accomplished what the Army wanted to know: A remote, winter, mountain assault could be successful under very narrow circumstances using covert ski, wing suit and parachute protocols. Although they would not have another group like Rob's in continuous training, they would add an elite segment dedicated to wing suit and parachute assault training.

At first, they were highly disappointed by that bit of news. Their mission would end in Europe. But as the week wore on, they were also relieved. It had been an exhausting and dangerous mission. They had gone through a rough patch near the beginning, in an accident that could have killed a friend and derailed the entire mission.

....

It happened in their third run. In the third week of the full ski, fly and chute segment, almost immediately after launching from their starting point, Jim skied over a hidden rock that tore the bottom of his ski out, instantly twisting his leg, breaking the tibia and fibula, causing him to fall awkwardly on his upper arm, also breaking the humerus. Hitting another rock as he catapulted down the nearly vertical slope, he cracked two vertebrae, and broke three ribs, puncturing his left lung. He was very lucky his head hadn't hit those rocks or he'd be dead. Had it been nearly anyone else, though, he probably would have been killed, but Jim was such a strong, thickly muscled guy that he escaped with his life.

With those injuries, however, he still was in imminent danger of dying, given the high altitude and freezing temperatures. They needed to get him to a hospital, stat.

The protocol for just this type of occurrence was thoroughly discussed and planned for each run. Using satellite GPS and topographical maps, they would designate several areas that the uninjured skiers would ski to in case one of them fell and was incapacitated. On the morning of the run, they would then helicopter over the proposed areas for the final decision on each area.

In the first several runs, they carried out exhaustive research, to plan for as many contingencies as they could imagine. Their thought was they would need to do this for the first half dozen or so runs, and then, having perfected their techniques, would scale back their detailed preparation. To cut costs, they would only do topographical and SAT GPS, but not pre-run aerial overflight. Sam was not shy in saying she did not like that proposal.

When Jim crashed, those plans were scrapped. When Jim screamed into the microphone embedded in his helmet, the guys knew he was hurt, and hurt bad. When seconds later, he screamed in pain again, they immediately began their diversion to one of the escape areas they had identified during their overflight hours before. It had been a high outcropping ridge just outside a bowl. The area resembled a Bundt cake baking pan, with the multiple ridges that give the cake its unique look, the thin ridges defining the thicker, rounded sections. They raced to one of the thin, narrow ridges, overlooking a huge bowl section.

And just in time, too. Just as they skied onto their ridge area, the bowl section they had just traversed simply collapsed into a massive avalanche, breaking from a section 200 yards higher than them. Had they been almost anywhere else, the boulder-size chunks of avalanching snow surely would have buried them. Instead, they were standing witness to this uncontrollable and destroying force of nature that swept past them a mere 20 yards away. The immense and powerful snow spray and ground shaking was enough to cause them to crouch and cover their faces with their forearms, barely able to keep from being knocked over.

Another nearly half mile above and to their left lay Jim, but the other guys couldn't see him. The avalanche had passed, but the snow cloud still hung heavily over the area.

"Holy shit!" and "God Almighty!" were said so much and so loudly that it sounded like a Pentecostal tent revival service getting out of hand.

In a few more seconds, their focus turned to Jim.

"Jim! Are you okay?" yelled Rob. "Jim! Come in! Jim!"

"I'm here," came the labored, hoarse reply. "Pretty banged up," he gasped, "Can't move much."

"Jimmy, glad you're alive, man," said Rob, and all the other guys chimed in simultaneously.

"Fuckin' A, Jim! You had me worried you som'bitch!" retorted Danny, his voice cracking, trying to control his emotions over nearly losing his best friend.

Each of the guys had a homing and tracking wristband, just in case they were actually buried in an avalanche. But they didn't want to find a body. They wanted their friend alive.

Rob had immediately radioed the chopper pilot as soon as he got to the designated stopping point. Fortunately, the 173rd's Bell 412 had not descended too far to turn around, but its waning fuel supply would cut any potential rescue effort extremely short. It would have been nearly impossible for the other skiers to attempt to hike up the nearly vertical slope to get to Jim, even if it was less than 200 yards. Now with the spent avalanche field between them and Jim, it was far too dangerous to traverse back and up to Jim, as another section higher above could easily break off and start roaring down on them, carrying certain death. All they could do now was watch and hope.

Having spotted Jim, the pilot brought the chopper to hover, and Sam was already lowering the medic on the bright orange stretcher cage to where Jim lay. Moments later, from their perch on the ridge, they could see the medic lifting Jim's leg, accompanied by Jim's screams of pain, to get it immobilized in a splint. Stopping for a moment, the medic gave Jim small doses of morphine, stabbing the morphine stick into his leg, back and upper arm to help him with the pain. There was no way else he could manipulate Jim's leg and arm into position, then roll him into the stretcher for the hoist up to the hovering chopper.

Time was not on their side. In 7 minutes, the pilot would have to leave or they would run out of fuel before getting down the mountain. After 6 minutes and some herculean effort by the medic, Jim was halfway up to the chopper. Sam grabbed and secured the litter with Jim in it, reattached the end with a sling contraption, and shot the cable down to the medic on the snow-field. Although the pilot was screaming that they had to leave now, he still hesitated, grudgingly agreeing to give the medic a few more seconds. Like a pro, the medic strapped the sling around himself, under him arms and through his legs in less than 10 seconds, grabbed the cable in front of him, looked up and waved his hand in a circle.

Immediately, Sam started the winch up, and the chopper pilot tilted downward, picking up speed going down the mountain to the quickest way back to base, and eventually to Landstuhl Regional Medical Center in Germany. As the chopper was headed full-speed to base, the medic was expertly hauled up and in by Sam. Jim would get the best care from American military surgeons that side of the Atlantic.

The guys realized then, had they not done their pre-run reconnaissance overflight, they would have picked a lower escape point, about a hundred yards below. Right in the line of the avalanche. That lower one looked like the best place, on paper. Sam had convinced them to change their minds on the overflight. Rob had decided the budget would not be trimmed by skipping that final safety measure after all.

It was time to get on with their run. Jim's catastrophic fall and the crazy avalanche would have shaken any other skiers to their core, making them unable to continue their dangerous run. But not these guys. Seasoned ski racers take these situations like race-car drivers take a crash at the Indy 500. It's just part of the job. Get the wreck out of the way and let's get on with it. I have a race to win and there's one fewer competitor to beat. I'll visit him in the hospital. Maybe.

Jump-turning and quickly accelerating to mind bending, face-flapping speeds, they hit their launch point, executed their equipment-shedding sequences, spread their arms and legs for wing suit flight, and headed straight for their target zone, flying in perfect formation. On Rob's count, two flyers cut 10 degrees left and the other two, 10 degrees right. In two seconds, Rob said, "Now!" and each pair cut back 20 degrees the opposite direction, one pair over, one pair under, instantly and perfectly reforming their formation going the same direction.

It truly looked like the Blue Angels in an insane close-call maneuver, only without the jets.

Although Rob was truly pleased by the near-perfect execution of his remaining team, he knew they had to do a better job scoping out their actual ski run, or this same situation could happen to another buddy. Although he knew there were no safety guarantees, especially in their crazy mission, he hoped he could think of something.

He knew one thing, though.

He was sure as hell glad Sam was here. If changing their escape point was all she ever did, it would still have been worth all the hassle to bring her in.

Chapter 22

Just this morning, Rob said goodbye to his team as everyone was going in different directions. His best friend, Mike, had decided to pick up his career in construction management and move back to Vegas. Ricky the same. He was headed back to Denver, where he had arranged an interview with Vail Associates. There's no better credibility boost to a ski school than to have a few Olympians running the show.

Since Steamboat already had Billy "The Kidd," they were not looking for another Olympian, even one from Steamboat. And Billy looked like he might go on for another 30 years, so Ricky had to look elsewhere to capitalize on his skiing prowess.

Danny announced this amazing experience had become his new passion in life. He was staying in Europe to join a premier Heli-skiing guide operation that would take excursions in the Italian and Swiss Alps. Danny would head the flying suit training phase in the summers, and lead the excursions in the winter.

In a somewhat surprising move, Sam would also stay and be employed by the same company as chief safety officer. Due to the technical proficiency Rob's group achieved, along with their impressive safety record, even including Jim's accident, another opportunity presented itself that practically guaranteed the company's initial success.

The Army's 173rd Air Brigade Combat Team committed to sending a minimum of 10 flying suit trainees per summer, and no fewer than 10 full runs each winter. This amount of business would cover all their fixed costs. Anything they made over that would be pure profit.

Lucky for Danny and Sam, they didn't have to fly back to the States, like Rob did. They were just contractors, not enlisted soldiers. The only commitment they had with the Army was their civilian contract, which had just ended. Rob had to fly back to the States and endure a week's worth of out-processing from the Army. That meant Fort Benning, Georgia, and multiple medical evaluations. That messed up his plans a bit. He wanted to stay in Europe for a while. Now he wondered when he'd ever get back to Europe.

Rob was especially not looking forward to his PDHA mental eval. The three tours to Afghanistan were bad enough to leave him with life-long mental scars. But Syria was a whole different ballgame altogether. As horrible as it was to be *in* those horrors, it was arguably worse to *relive* them. He had talked to no one about Syria, and Syria was over a year ago. But lately, the flashbacks had been waking him up in cold sweats, re-fighting the seven ISIS combatants each time. He was sure the evaluators would want to dive deeper into that particular PTSD much more than he thought necessary.

Aside from that, the 173rd was a little upset that Rob would not be joining the Heli-ski company in some field operation role, but Rob's heart was not in it. After his friend Stuart was so senselessly and traitorously attacked, Rob decided he would only follow his heart when his active duty days were up. Unfortunately, his request to be discharged overseas so he could remain and ski some Swiss ski resorts, was denied. The Army machine was not in the mood to make exceptions, especially for some flimsy excuse like that. Actually, it was never in the mood to make exceptions, but Rob gave it a shot.

Rob decided not to let them know his real reason—he wanted to find out if his Grandmother's stories were really true. They would laugh him out of the Army if he told them that.

In retrospect, maybe he should have told them the real reason. It couldn't have been much worse than what happened.

Just yesterday, at zero eight hundred sharp, he was called in by his base commander to be told the answers to his request, in person.

Entering the commander's office, Rob saluted and stood at attention, waiting for the "At ease" command. He didn't get one.

"No," Col. Jordan "Smitty" Smith said from behind his desk, not even looking up.

"Oh, excuse me. I mean, '*Fuck*, no.'"

Rob stood at full attention, eyes forward, hands lightly clenched at his side. This would not be a fun talk. Col. Smith continued his rant, slowly standing and bending over his desk, fists on the table, perversely enjoying every syllable. Lifting his gaze slowly, face red, eyes bulging and veins popping out on his temple and forehead, raising his voice to a yell, visibly spitting out each word.

"The *Army* will *not* make its *first* exception since *World War II* so *you* can stay here and *ski* a little more, and maybe catch some *snow* bunnies while you're at it." His words were dripping with sarcasm.

"*So*. I suggest you just *chill* out and be fucking *grateful* I'm not sending you *back* to *Syria* for your last four days of your commitment! Get me, Sergeant?"

"Yes, sir!" Rob chopped back, eyes forward, at full attention.

Bringing his tone down to just above room temperature, he finished his last command.

"Oh, and be ready to ship out to Fort Benning in four days at oh-five hundred! And you *will* report *immediately* for PDHA ME just like every other combat infantryman in the Army!"

"Yes, sir!" Rob retorted, respectfully.

"That will be all," Smitty concluded. "Dismissed!"

Rob immediately barked, "Yes, sir!" saluted, about-faced and marched to the Colonel's door. As he turned the handle, the Colonel stopped him.

"Ranger," he started calmly, pausing for a moment. Rob wheeled around, standing at attention.

"Sir!" Rob said, looking at the Colonel's forehead, like he was in boot camp getting yelled at by the drill sergeant.

"You've had a good run. I'm aware of your service and bravery." Now Smitty's tone was almost conversational.

"Like I said, you've got four days. If you want to waste those days skiing somewhere, this late in the season, that's your problem," he said matter-of-factly, looking down at his papers.

"You can use whatever ski gear you want. I'll let MWR storage know," Smitty was now shuffling papers.

"Thank you, sir!" Rob blurted out.

"Ranger," the Colonel continued, still shuffling papers. "If you are one minute past oh-five hundred on seven May, I will see that you get an other-than-honorable discharge. Is that understood?"

"Yes, Sir. Thank you, Sir!" Rob exclaimed.

"That will be all," the Colonel said.

Rob saluted, and the Colonel returned the salute with crisp formality. Although no one else was there to be a witness, the moment would be immortalized in both their minds. The soldier-to-soldier respect is something regular civilians could not easily understand, or even relate to. Rob's documented bravery, although not rare among the military *per se*, was exceptional. A combat officer like Smitty would recognize this, and show proper respect, whether a four-star general was there or just he and Rob.

As Rob left and the door shut, Smitty sat down. Chuckling a little bit while slightly shaking his head, he resumed attending to his grinding paperwork.

....

Rob's upcoming ship-out day, on May seventh, was somewhat emotional for him. That was the day his Grandmother had died, ten years prior. As he was packing up his stuff for the six-hour train trip to Zermatt, Switzerland, he knew now was the time to find out if her stories were true. How the hell he was going to do that, he wasn't sure—especially since he was shipping back to Benning in four days, and going to Switzerland instead of Germany his last four days in Europe. He needed to get some chill skiing time, like maybe some normal, fun skiing. Leading a high-probability fatal run, with four other lives hinging on his choices, was a thing of the past.

The train to Zermatt from Vicenza was beautiful, or at least that's what he'd heard. Once he got his gear stowed and his seat reclined, the train's motion put him right to sleep. It wasn't until the final small jolt as the train pulled into Milan Centrale, only an hour and a half trip, that Rob's eyes opened. He scrambled and got to his next train to Domodossola, the last stop in Italy, for another 90-minute high-speed ride. As soon as he got into his seat, he went right to sleep again. By the time he got to Brig, he was a little more rested, and even got to see a few mountains in the distance. Knowing he had only 11 minutes before his final train to Zermatt, he hustled his bags together and just made the last train. By the time he arrived at Zermatt, it was thirteen hundred hours, one p.m., and he was starving.

Quaint little restaurants were not hard to find in the picture-postcard alpine town. He ducked into the first pub that looked good and ordered up, and dieting wasn't on his mind. Eating was.

Blinking back to reality, Rob tilted his stein upward for the last swallow of Falken Lagerbier Hell, an independent brewery lager pleasing to both the palate and the nose, according to the menu. It was right. He nodded to the waitress in the nicely revealing blouse and lifted his mug for another round. She smiled and headed back to the bar. He focused in on his third Sankt-Galler Bratwurst, loaded with sauerkraut, pickled peppers and mustard, the kind with the seeds in it. He found he was a big fan of Swiss food, especially in this little town of Zermatt, where he'd arrived just a couple hours before.

As he washed down his last bite of bratwurst with his favorite new brew, he grabbed his bags, including the last issue of skis, ski boots and all the gear from his last run. Thanks to Smitty, he had picked out exactly what he wanted, except for the top-secret electronics, the flying suits, and the parachutes. That stuff could be reused for the next group. That stuff was not offered.

Hell, they were just going to throw out the ski stuff or put it in Army surplus. It's not like Smitty was being all that generous. But Rob appreciated the gesture anyway.

For now, he needed to find a place to stay for the night that wouldn't take all his limited cash. He was thinking there might be a youth hostel or something. First stop, the rather large barmaid, who kept refilling his mug and handing it to his buxom waitress for the last two hours.

She slightly laughed when she told him in her thick German-accented English, "*Yah, ober dair, three blocks zat vay and left two blocks*," she said, stabbing the air with her stubby forefinger. "*Hostel. Yah, bathroomz, too.*"

Rob hoisted his backpack on his shoulders and grabbed his ski gear bag, and walked the five blocks to what he hoped was his lodging for the next two nights. They did have an eight-person dorm room on the third floor, and no elevator. Rob was so used to little or no privacy after nine years in the military that he was fine with a dorm environment. There were ski lockers on the first floor, so he stashed his gear in one of them, and went up to check out his dorm room.

Once satisfied, he walked out on the street and down to a grocery store he had noticed on the walk over. Wanting to stock up on some protein bars and other snacks for his upcoming day of skiing, he was happy to find it so close to his hostel.

Just as he entered, he heard a scream come from one of the cashiers. A large, bearded man had grabbed the hair of the woman cashier and was pushing her head down on the counter. The free hand was grabbing the cash out of the register and stuffing it into a small sling knapsack the man had around his neck and shoulder.

Without hesitation, Rob sprinted over, jumped on the other register, and launched toward the big man at the same time he was cocking his fist back, then connected his clenched fist directly into the man's nose, instantly smashing it, causing a small eruption of blood. Immediately the man let go of the cashier and crashed backwards into a display shelf, sending all its contents everywhere. Rob jumped over the counter as the man was getting up, hand over his nose and his other arm outstretched, like a stiff arm, trying to keep Rob away. Rob grabbed his hand, twisting it down and backward, causing the big man to spin around like he was on a string, and forced him to his knees, his arm in a very awkward, very painful position.

"Stay down!" Rob ordered, "Or I break your arm."

"Anyone have any rope, or duct tape?" Rob asked the frightened onlookers.

Within 30 seconds, that same cashier came running back from the household goods aisle with a roll of thick gray duct tape, just like the stuff in the USA. Rob quickly and thoroughly taped the man's wrists behind his back and his ankles together. He wasn't going anywhere.

By that time a couple other store employees had come over, checked on their cashier, and positioned themselves in front of the now-subdued robber, who was groaning in pain from his broken nose. Rob knew they would be able to take it from there. He decided he would leave and not be a part of all the police reports and witness accounts. He just wanted to have a nice, relaxing couple of ski days in the Alps. He didn't want anything to complicate that, especially police. He was leaving.

Confirming the cashier was ok, he had just gotten outside the store when he heard directly behind him, "That was a very brave act, young man," in perfect English. He turned around to face a very attractive, roughly middle-aged woman, smartly dressed. She had raven black hair, but deep blue eyes.

"Well thank you, ma'am," Rob said. "I just did what anyone should do."

"Maybe so, but less than one in a million would. And less than one in *ten* million could," she said evenly, walking up to him. "He was twice your size," she observed.

She was right. The big man was probably six-five or six, easily two seventy. Rob was six feet, with his cowboy boots on, meaning he was more like five-ten or eleven. He weighed a good one seventy-five, nothing but muscle. Even so, Rob knew the second he saw him it wouldn't be a fair fight. Unless he had a gun and knew how to use it, the big man did not have a prayer against Rob, a highly trained Army Ranger, Special Forces.

"Aren't you going to stay for the police?" she asked politely. "You know, they give commendations for this type of thing, even though it is quite rare here," she added, seeing if she could pique his interest. "Sometimes, they even give a key to the city, which includes ski lift tickets," she added.

"That's fine, ma'am," Rob started. "They can give that to the cashier lady. She's the brave one. She ran and got me the tape, even after what she went through," Rob countered.

"How long are you here in Zermatt?" asked the woman.

"Just passing through. Trying to get a little skiing in, is all," Rob answered. "Maybe a couple days. I just got here this afternoon."

Police sirens could be heard, from not that far away, and getting closer.

"Then if you are not staying for the police, you will join my husband and me for dinner," the lady said, matter-of-factly. "We will be dining at the Alpine Gourmet Prato Borni at seven p.m. sharp. We will be expecting you. Please bring whoever you are traveling with."

At that, she turned and walked quickly away, not waiting for a response.

"Wait!" Rob said. "I don't even know your name!"

Without stopping, she turned slightly, just for a moment, and smiled.

"Rasha."

Rob watched her for a moment, then turned and started walking quickly away from the store. The shrill volume of the sirens meant the police were moments away.

"Rrrasha," Rob repeated, trying to imitate her rolling r's. "Rrrasha," he repeated. "Hmm. What the hell?" he muttered under his breath, deciding he just might do it.

Chapter 23

After a shave and a not-hot-enough shower, Rob scrounged his backpack for nice clothes. He hadn't brought any. Fact was, he'd been in Army gear since the last he could remember. His only other turtleneck and the same tactical pants would have to do for tonight. He wasn't about to go buy anything for this dinner.

The only reason he even had that thought was the reaction of the hostel clerk when he asked her how to get to Prato Borni.

"You're going to Prato Borni and staying here?" she asked incredulously. "Why are you staying here? It will cost you 10 times for dinner what you're paying to stay here. Besides, they have a strict dress code. Did you bring your suit?"

Rob didn't bother to explain the situation, and the clerk told him how to get there, looking at him curiously.

Rob walked out of the hostel at four thirty. This late in the season, the sun was still shining, but the afternoon shadows were shading big stretches of the beautiful town. Another hour, and darkness would cover the town. Like any other night, the soft street lights and glowing windows would create the feeling of warmth and safety, magical in itself. Rob wondered if the towns and cities he fought in inside Syria and Afghanistan had ever had that feel to them. He doubted it.

By the time Rob walked up to Prato Borni, he had made a complete circle of the city. It had been a good while since lunch, and all the walking had made him quite hungry and thirsty. Walking up the steps to the lobby of the Grand Hotel Zermatterhof, he knew he was seriously outclassed. Hotel guests were all wearing dinner jackets, like the white one that Roger Federer liked to "sport" immediately after crushing his latest victim at Wimbledon. Rob wondered if Roger had gotten the idea from here, or if they'd gotten it from Roger. Whatever.

For a moment, Rob thought he should turn around and just keep to himself while he was here in Zermatt. He could get a decent meal somewhere, and would not have to deal with all this pretentiousness. Ms. Rrrrasha would probably not really expect him to come anyway. Rob had a strong urge to not make a fool out of himself.

Then he thought, chuckling, if he could survive Afghanistan and Syria, jump off a frozen precipice, live through killer avalanches, and perfect the big triple: ski, glide, and parachute, and live to tell about it, he could do this.

Walking up to the hostess, Rob leaned over and asked if Ms. Rasha was there, trying his best to roll the r's the way she had.

"Oh, yes. They are expecting you. Right this way," she answered in flawless English. Walking past the other patrons clinking away at their dinner, the hostess led Rob to a private nook with its own table. A few heads turned, but basically people were into themselves and their own beautiful culinary delights created by the master chef and his staff.

"Herr Walther, Frau Walther, may I present your dinner guest," the hostess said, motioning with her hand to Rob.

"Peiter Walther." He stood up and reached out his hand, and Peiter and Rob exchanged a strong handshake. "It is a pleasure to meet you, young man. Please call me Peiter," he continued. "And I believe you met my wife, Rasha."

"Yes, briefly, sir," said Rob, shaking the hand that Rasha offered him. She smiled but did not stand.

"Thank you for the invitation to dinner," Rob started. "And my name is Rob. Rob Russell. It's very nice of you to invite me."

"Please. Have a seat," said Peiter, sitting down. "What will you have to drink, Rob? A glass of wine, or a beer, perhaps?"

"A beer sounds real good right now. I kind of like the Falken Lager," Rob volunteered.

"Good choice. I like it too," Peiter said as he motioned to the waiter, who immediately came over. "*Zwei Falken Lagers, bitte,*" Peiter said. The waiter hurried off.

Even though Peiter and Rasha already had a bottle of expensive Italian *Pinot Grigio* opened, they had not yet poured it, still letting it breathe a bit.

Inside of a minute, the waiter returned, pouring the beers into thick frozen mugs. Rob knew he would like this even better than the pub. Peiter motioned the waiter to pour him a taste of the wine, which he did while Rob waited. Satisfied the wine was good, he pointed to Rasha's wine glass and the waiter filled it halfway.

Raising his mug for a toast, Peiter smiled and said, "Long live the heroes in our midst!" Rasha smiled as they all clinked their drinks together. Rob checked himself to only one big pull on the glass. He didn't know how many beers he could order yet. Better make it last for now. Besides, he had an empty stomach, so the alcohol would affect him more.

"So, Rob," began Rasha, smiling slightly, "have you rescued any other damsels since we last spoke?" She was smooth and effortless in her words, more like singing than speaking. But there was no innuendo or sarcasm, only sincerity.

Laughing slightly, Rob answered, "Not since then, Ma'am. It was pretty routine after that. Up to now, that is. This place is anything but routine. Very beautiful."

"Well, we are so glad you decided to join us. We were hoping you would find your way over here," said Rasha. "Tell us please about yourself. Where are you from, what do you do? Things like that," she said, invitingly.

Just then the waiter arrived to take their dinner orders. Peiter ordered two appetizers for the table and motioned to Rasha. She ordered a salmon dish from memory, and Peiter ordered a special cut veal. Rob already knew he wanted pasta, given the higher altitude and for energy for skiing the next day. He saw what looked like some amazing dinners, but hesitated when he saw the insanely high prices. At that instant, Rasha interjected.

"Rob. You are our guest. Anything that looks good, please do not hesitate," she encouraged.

It was a good thing she said that. Noticing the absolute cheapest item he could order still cost a whopping 75 euros, but meant he had to order 12 separate items, he quickly decided to order the ravioli special. It was 115 euros, for God's sake. But he only had to order once. The rest of the items were already included. What a relief.

Once the waiter left—without taking any notes, of course—Rasha smiled and looked at Rob. "Please now tell us about yourself," she said lightly.

Rob already knew what he couldn't say.

He couldn't tell them about the most interesting thing in his life so far; the last nine months of the cutting-edge, death-defying, beyond-exhilarating radical mission he'd led with his old racing buddies. He couldn't tell them about Jim nearly dying on a mountain, with the incredibly daring helicopter rescue, immediately after the avalanche that nearly buried him and his team. He couldn't tell them about his top-secret Special Mission Unit assignment in Syria, being inserted deep within ISIS territory with 3 other combat-tested Rangers, 3 Green Berets, and 6 Delta Force operatives, basically free to do what was necessary to exterminate these vile human rodents. He couldn't tell them that 2 of the 12 didn't make it out alive, and that one of them, a fellow Ranger, died in Rob's arms. He couldn't tell them that in that particular deadly encounter he killed 7 ISIS rats in a raging and fierce hand-to-hand combat trying to protect his comrade, earning his second Silver Star and an extremely rare field promotion from corporal to sergeant. Nor could he tell them about his best buddy, Stuart Ash, and the traitor his very own Rangers trained who'd nearly killed him.

God love the incredible Navy SEALs, but Rangers and Delta Force were a different breed. Hell, the Army didn't even acknowledge the existence of Delta Force until very recently. And that was perfectly fine with them, and also with Rangers. Actually, it practically took a crowbar to pry even non-classified mission details out of Army Special Forces, especially when it looked like bragging. Navy SEALs, by contrast, who were publicly celebrated for their successful missions, were thrust into the limelight and forced to recount their exploits. Rob couldn't blame them for learning to enjoy that. But Rob didn't. And never would.

But Rob had to think of something to tell them. He definitely didn't want to be rude.

No, he would have to tell them about bland, normal crap everybody else talks about that doesn't mean shit and nobody cares about anyway. And he didn't want to have to keep saying, "I can't talk about that," over and over if they started asking him questions. Right in that split second, he decided how he would throw them off his military story and get them on a fun rabbit trail.

That was the exact instant that Providence kicked into overdrive.

"Well, my Grammaw was a full-blooded German who came with her parents to America before World War One," Rob began. "She used to tell me about the women in her family, who were like secret agents or something. Like her mom's sisters and her cousins," Rob said with a smile. "I'm here to find out if it's true."

Rasha coughed, apparently her sip of wine went down the wrong pipe, as they say. She carefully placed her glass on the table, naturally keeping her movements smooth, with no hint of trembling.

Rob smiled and grabbed his beer and took another drink. Peiter had frozen, not even breathing, looking straight at Rob, then at Rasha. Rasha dabbed her embroidered cloth napkin to her lips, and gracefully cleared her throat. Awkwardly, both started to say something, but Peiter instantly yielded to Rasha.

Smiling but with her eyes sharply focused, she looked at Rob and said, "My, my. Your grandmother had a wonderful imagination. She must have been so much fun. What was her name?"

"Well, uh, her maiden name was Mirium Weissen, but I believe she was talking about her mother's sisters and her daughters, who would have been Mirium's cousins," Rob answered. "*Her* last name was Nitschke. I'm not sure if I'm saying the name correctly."

Peiter looked at Rasha, mouth open. He was not quite as smooth as Rasha.

Rasha noticed it immediately, and said, "Peiter, my dear, tell Rob the story your grandfather used to tell you about your family. Remember when you later found the book in his library that was the identical story?" She stood up and subtly winked at him.

"If you'll both excuse me for a moment, I must freshen up," she said as she strode quickly away from the table toward the ladies' room.

....

As soon as she was out of sight, she called her cousin, who, along with three other family members, was on shift at Us headquarters, which was three blocks away but over one kilometer below the quaint old office building. The building was like many others in Zermatt, also known as the Matterhorn Village. A designated historical building, the owners could never alter the structure. They could only restore it.

Like many of the centuries-old buildings there, it was built like a castle. On the street level, there was a retail chocolate shop, with chocolates of all shapes and sizes, with many shaped like the imposing Matterhorn that dominated the small village.

The shop had been managed by a husband and wife duo for the last 30 years, who looked like they could easily do another decade or more. In their traditional Swiss outfits, they looked exactly like a Swiss postcard.

Unlike any of the other buildings there, it sat atop a secret shaft and elevator accessible from behind a false wall in the small side room in the back private area. The side room doubled as the mop-room, containing the deep tub-style sink used to clean the mops. When triggered—by turning the water faucet upward 180 degrees, then back down, twice—the false wall would actually move backward four inches, then completely move left, leaving all the various cleaning devices attached to the wall in place.

Now fully exposed was a modern-looking metal elevator door. A high-tech palm-print reader and eye scanner would call up the pneumatic elevator from far below. The centuries-old cable lift had been sufficient when Us relocated from Germany before WWI. The need to upgrade the elevator became exceedingly obvious during Hitler and the Nazi party's ascension to power and throughout the war. When Switzerland became one of the few nations on the European continent able to remain neutral during the ravages of World War II, it was faced with dire choices. At one point in the war, the Swiss government had given orders to reject any new Jewish refugees, perhaps to appease the Nazis. However, Rasha's mother Ana had a policy of not turning away any Jewish refugees whom brave Swiss individuals had smuggled into the country despite the government's ban. Taking on considerable risk of being discovered, Us secreted hundreds of fleeing Jews in their underground headquarters until they could be safely moved or smuggled out of Europe.

Although Us and its beautiful operatives' identities and operations remained secret, several of these same Jewish refugees became benefactors of the group. By the late 1950s, the cumulative contributions from these grateful refugees was a substantial amount. Technology in pneumatic elevators had significantly improved, and now they had the resources and money to make improvements. Us was able to take the new pneumatic designs to unimaginable levels, and created a suction-based tube that was able to carry three adults at a time, or fewer with equipment. The speed of the device was extraordinary. What used to take 20 minutes now took 25 seconds.

The headquarters at the bottom of the elevator shaft, nearly 1.5 kilometers below, had undergone a few nice improvements since the last war. The elevator opened up into a dark mine-shaft, where motion sensors would trigger soft LED lighting. After 15 yards, the shaft itself split in two directions. To the left was a quite large bank-vault type door, with another palm- and eye-scanner pad. Behind that door was a secret, cavernous, cathedral-like area, with a soaring ceiling, converted into an active covert command center, full of flat-screen monitors and computer equipment, all operating at a steady hum. If one didn't know better, he would easily mistake this for a full-service CIA command center, only with fewer people.

The shaft to the right went on for miles, meandering through the granite underground, searching for the elusive lodestar vein that was never located.

"Sarah," Rasha said quietly into her mobile phone, a secured and scrambled military-grade device. "It's me. I need you to run a complete profile on Robert Russell. He is American, and in the military. Probably in his late twenties or so. Get as much family history on him as possible," she said, hurrying and hushed. "I need this five minutes ago."

"I'll get right on it. I will send it to your phone," said Sarah.

It took all of Rasha's extensive training and composure to not give away her complete shock and surprise by the name Rob spoke a scant two minutes ago. *Nitschke.* That was her own great grandmother's maiden name. Up until this moment, it was thought that all ties were completely cut when Amy Nitschke's sister and her husband migrated to America.

In fact, all ties were cut. There had been no contact whatsoever between the ones who stayed in Germany and the Weissen family for 80 years. The way Rob was describing it, his grandmother was the daughter of the couple who emigrated from Germany. Rasha was not even born at the time they left.

Chapter 24

The rest of dinner was filled with light conversation. Rasha did not want to explore any further into Rob's family until she had a complete dossier on him. Eighty years of covert operations and no contact with their American family brought a certainty and security to their covert activities. With Peiter's career, they had a cover so tight it was bombproof. But Rob's seemingly innocent purpose for being in Europe made her begin to question how truly impenetrable their cover actually was.

Peiter's credentials as a tenured professor of economics at Swiss Federal Institute of Technology in Zurich were impeccable. He was one of the early believers in cryptocurrency, recognizing the disruptive impact this technology would have on global currencies and trade. Fortunately, he was also a very early investor in the company called Bitcoin. His thousand-franc investment back in 2011, which he never sold, was now worth over 20 million Swiss francs.

Peiter's sizeable portfolio contained many other positions, not all as wildly volatile or meteoric as Bitcoin, enabling him to have his buy and hold strategy. A nice professor's salary at the leading university in Switzerland didn't hurt either. Due to his teaching schedule in the fall and spring, Peiter would be gone from Rasha and his beautiful home in Zermatt for weeks at a time. It was the best cover he and his wife could have.

Peiter was also an accomplished skier, and naturally the conversation moved to the favorite topic for a visiting skier. The Matterhorn. Rob shared that he was here to ski the famous resort, and Peiter was able to tell him where to go for the best runs on the mountain.

Twenty minutes after Rasha called Sarah, her mobile phone vibrated. Sarah had sent a quick bullet point bio on Rob. He was 27, a US Army sergeant, and most interestingly, a Ranger who had served tours in Afghanistan and in Special Ops in Syria. He was an elite warrior. There was no information yet on his family, or more importantly, whether he had a great grandmother in common.

When Rob finally told them he was an Army Ranger, Rasha was of course properly impressed, but not shocked. She actually already knew, from 15 minutes prior. It was more interesting that he was getting out of the military next week.

"What are you planning to do once you get out of the Army, Rob?" asked Rasha, with genuine interest.

"I am really not sure, ma'am," mused Rob. "I wanted to stay here in Europe, but I have to be discharged stateside, at Fort Benning." The disappointment in his voice was easily detectable.

"Oh, where is that?" asked Rasha.

"That would be Lawson Army Airfield, in Fort Benning, Georgia," said Rob. "There are way worse places," he laughed.

It was getting late, and Rob was thinking about getting prepared for an early morning breakfast—and making sure he was on the first gondola up the mountain in the morning.

"Thank you all for your generous hospitality," Rob said as he stood to leave. "I plan to look for more damsels to rescue, and hope you will be there to witness it," he said, smiling as he shook Rasha's hand. Rasha smiled and remained seated, shaking Rob's hand. Peiter stood and held his hand out.

"Rob, you really are a hero," Peiter said, slightly clearing his throat. "We know what you did was no small thing, as much as you'd like to have us believe otherwise.

"It was a pleasure meeting you, and I truly hope our paths will cross again very soon. Best of fortune to you, young man." A short, strong handshake later, and Rob turned around and walked toward the exit, going to the hostel to catch some sleep.

Peiter and Rasha sat down and looked at each other for a full minute in complete silence.

Rasha finally spoke first. "Peiter, I have never been so taken off-guard before in my life. Of all the things I've seen and done, that tops the list," she finished in a hushed tone.

The waiter came by with their check. Peiter looked at it and gave him his black Centurion credit card.

"He's telling the truth, Rasha," Peiter said. "This young man is as genuine as my Rolex," he said as he glanced down at his black on black Submariner, a gift from his wife.

Although he could afford any watch he wanted, Peiter was a practical man. He wasn't greedy, or even materialistic. Since he was a scuba diver, he wanted a reliable and accurate timepiece for his dives in the Maldives and Caymans, his two favorite spots for his underwater adventures.

Even after his tour of the Rolex factory in Geneva, he would not change his mind. The stainless steel, rather understated but elegant Submariner would do just fine.

"You know, Peiter," Rasha finally whispered, "I don't believe in coincidences. Luck, yes. But not random chance." She thought a moment longer. "Wait until Lia hears this," she said, shaking her head. "It will shock her to her core."

"I wonder what else we will find out about *Sergeant* Russell," mused Rasha as they stood up.

At that, they gathered their coats and walked to their waiting and warm car at the front of the elegant hotel.

Chapter 25

Rob admitted to himself that he had pushed his luck. Getting back at three a.m. in Vicenza, with a 30-minute ride to the base, didn't leave him much margin for error. But it was just enough time to return the borrowed skis and equipment and salute his base commander before he boarded the C-141 troop carrier for the long ride home.

Virgin Atlantic it was not, but he wasn't complaining. And no one was shooting at him.

After 10 hours, he was back on US soil. After a quick touchdown at McGuire Air Force Base in New Jersey, they lifted off for the final leg to Benning. He knew he really wasn't ready for the normal life yet. He had seen and done so much. He still was a warrior, and in many ways, still fighting. Especially in his mind. Especially over the guys he lost, due to some bureaucrat's decision from a cushy chair thousands of miles away, ignoring the advice from the eyes on the field of battle. Rob wasn't sure he would ever get over that, frankly.

The week of out-processing from the Army started as soon as they landed at Benning. Rob's PDHA evals were every bit as bad as he thought they would be. It took almost no time in the interview to establish that Rob's case of PTSD was real and not insubstantial. It was nothing the evaluators hadn't seen before. In fact, with the kind of extreme combat experience Rob had, they would be more concerned if he didn't have PTSD. Rob had it, but was not disabled by it, at least at this time. He was told to get evaluated every quarter for the first year at his local VA hospital, wherever it was that he ended up. He could, however, come in at any time to have a session with a medical health professional.

On his last day at Benning, Rob stopped by the SRP building to pick up his DD Form 214 honorable discharge document. As he turned to leave, honorable discharge documents in hand, the clerk said,

"Oh, Sergeant Russell?"

"Yes, Ma'am?"

"This was delivered here this morning for you."

The clerk handed him a DHL overnight express envelope from Switzerland.

"Thank you, Ma'am," said Rob, as he turned around and headed for the door of the SRP building. As he heard the door close behind him, he felt a bit unusual. A piece of the enormity of his decision to leave the Army registered inside him like a slot machine as it landed on the last magic 7. He had definitely closed that chapter in his life. He would not be dressing up in camo and doing night raids and going on dangerous missions anymore. Aside from his recurring nightmares, he was physically intact. Unlike so many unfortunate brothers and sisters in uniform, he returned home with all his limbs. That blessing could not be overstated. His heart would always ache for his disabled fellow vets. He was done shooting at humans.

He might do some hunting, he thought. But none of those animals would shoot back, he was pretty certain.

Or was he done after all?

With all his belongings in his duffle bag, and the overnight package under his arm, Rob's last stop at Benning was the finance office in Building 35, where he could put in for travel pay and put a little cash in his pocket. Since his home of record was Steamboat Springs, Colorado, and he was paid on a mileage basis, it was a nice chunk of change. Instead of a plane ticket, Rob had asked for bus fare. He needed the cash. He wasn't sure yet if he would go directly home. In fact, he was practically sure he wouldn't.

Not quite ready for a trendy and expensive Starbucks, he located a diner near the base and ducked in for a coffee, black. That's all he'd had in the last four years anyway. Somehow, the powdered creamer and sugar just made the bitter MRE instant coffee worse. He'd just gotten used to the hot, black liquid. He looked down at the DHL package, having no idea what this might be. "What the hell?" he thought. "Open the damn thing."

Tearing it open, he reached in and brought out two envelopes. He opened one, and pulled out a round-trip ticket from Columbus, Georgia to Geneva, Switzerland. He opened the other and pulled out a letter and a check for five thousand US dollars, made out to him. As he unfolded the letter, his mouth dropped and he blinked rapidly five or six times, trying to focus. He started reading.

"Dear Rob,

Rasha and I greatly enjoyed meeting you last week. Congratulations on your very successful military career. Enclosed please find a round-trip ticket to Geneva, an EU Rail Pass, and a bit of expense money to get around Europe for a small amount of time. Perhaps you will even have time to search out your family roots. We only ask that you begin your adventure here in Zermatt for a few days. Perhaps we could show you some things most explorers of our small country could never appreciate. We hope you will accept our offer, and be in Geneva in two days. Call when you land. We will have our driver pick you up. We have a room reserved for you at the Zermatterhof, the hotel where we dined together a short while ago.

Cheers,

Peiter Walther, President

Walther Economic Solutions, LLP."

Rob involuntarily dropped the letter on the little table and rubbed his eyes, squinting hard. He then picked it up again and reread it two more times. He held up the check to the light, then quickly put it down. "What am I looking for? A forgery? It's a damn check, not cash!" he thought, laughing out loud a little.

"What in the effing hell is this?" he thought. In his mind, he quickly recounted his 'little' act of heroism. He knew the second he saw the big guy that he was unarmed. He instantly knew the idiot wouldn't expect a physical challenge from him or anybody. He instantly realized his best option was a complete, full-on aggressive attack which would catch him by surprise. When he got within three feet of the thug, albeit in midair, he already knew it was over for the guy. A done deal. Threat neutralized. Simply routine.

"So, what's the big effin' deal?" he thought. "But, shit! They want to give me a paid vacation over it, that's fine with me!" he concluded. "Hell, yes. I'm going!"

"Shit. Mom and Dad will be disappointed," he instantly thought, calming his enthusiasm for a moment. "But I'm still not ready to be 'normal' yet."

He had a day before he left. That would be more than enough time for Rob to call his Mom and Dad and explain what he was doing. The welcome-back parties would have to wait.

He was going to be on that plane and that was that.

The hand of Providence was moving again.

Chapter 26

"Rob, why did you enlist in the Army?" Rasha asked him, between sips of piping hot coffee.

The morning after he arrived at Geneva, at 7:45 a.m. sharp, Rob was sitting with Rasha and Peiter at the indoor patio at the Zermatterhof Hotel, watching the sunrise slowly lighting up the massive Matterhorn looming above them. He had just taken his first bite of pancakes so loaded with nuts and whole grains, topped off with whipped butter, fresh blueberries and pure maple syrup, it could have also been his lunch. On the side were two poached eggs, and two links of thick Swiss sausages. Black coffee was steaming from its cup next to him. Life didn't get much better.

Putting his fork down quickly and bringing his cloth napkin to his lips, he looked up at the mountain for a moment in reflection. He also didn't want to hurry his tasty mouthful of pancakes.

"Well," he started, "adventure. Joining the best military in human history, no offense to the Swiss Army," he added quickly, smiling. "Proving myself..." Rob paused and took a sip of coffee.

"I also wanted to go after the bad guys. The freakin' terrorists. The ones who hated America and anyone else that didn't believe in their brand of religion. The cowards and punks that chopped heads off and put it on YouTube to recruit other crazy idiots. I wanted to personally deliver them to their 72 virgins."

"Did you accomplish all that?" Rasha gently probed.

Rob shoveled another forkful of pancakes dripping syrup into his mouth. He put a finger to his lips, doing his best to keep from talking with his mouth packed.

"Yes, ma'am," he said, swallowing. "Sometimes, yes. Sometimes, no," he said, frowning a little. "I think politics got in the way. I mean, *damn straight* politics got in the way sometimes. Cost lives. American lives," he said, disgust clearly visible in his face.

Rob knew he couldn't divulge too much, but he was out now. Out of the Army. Not even in the Reserve. He had fulfilled his original four-year commitment, and two more, all active duty.

"Why did you leave the military?" Rasha asked next, sensing the answer already.

"Politics," he spat out without hesitation. "If it weren't for that, I'd still be in," he said, continuing to attack his breakfast.

"What if you could continue to go after the bad guys, without the politics?" Rasha asked, then sipped her coffee. "You know, it's not just terrorists that are bad guys," she added. "Take human trafficking, for instance. It's modern-day slavery. Sex trafficking, same thing." She paused for a moment, letting it sink in. "Terrorists chop off heads. But sometimes they buy slaves. The traffickers for the most part, are under the radar. Governments are busy chasing terrorists. Rightly so. But they have let the slave trade grow in the meantime. Now, it's big money—like drug cartel-magnitude money.

"And just like the cartels did with drug money, the traffickers do with slave money. Corruption has gone to the highest levels in some governments, and private businessmen, and I mean the super-rich, are involved." Rasha took a breath, and another sip of coffee.

She was clearly passionate about this. Peiter sat there, sipping his coffee and watching the exchange between Rasha and Rob. He was silent for the most part, only grunting his agreement and nodding his head at key moments.

"So, what can you do about that?" asked Rob.

"You find out who they are, and you take them down, by any means necessary," Rasha said evenly.

"Oh, I'd love to be a part of that," Rob said in a low, serious tone. "There's meat on them bones, as we like to say," referring to his Ranger buddies.

"Well," said Rasha, "perhaps you could be. It might interfere with your immediate vacation plans, though."

"Peiter. Rasha," Rob said quietly, leaning over for emphasis, "this is exactly what I'm looking to do. I need to go after the bad guys. Without all the bullshit. Vacation is nice, but hell, I can do that some other time. What are we talking about here?"

Rob was inwardly surprised how cautiously interested he was. Hell, he had just gotten out of the freakin' Army, for God's sake. In one piece. But his warrior spirit was clearly lit and excited by what he was hearing. Was this just a theoretical mental exercise by these two nice people? He was thirsty for more information.

Rasha looked over at Peiter. He met her gaze evenly, and almost unnoticeably nodded.

"First things first, Rob," Rasha said, smiling, lifting the intensity of the moment.

"First, we'll pick you up here at four p.m. sharp," she said, standing up. "Until then, enjoy your vacation," she said as both she and Peiter turned to go.

Rob shook Peiter's hand, again noticing the strong grip. Rasha's handshake was also purposeful and very firm, and Rob was careful to only match her strength, not overpower it. Rasha held his hand for a moment longer, getting his full attention, and smiled, flashing her extraordinary teeth.

"There's a family we'd like you to meet." Rasha let go of his hand, turned and walked away, arm in arm, with Peiter.

Sitting back down, Rob watched them until they disappeared into the hotel. He looked down at his half-eaten breakfast. He was still hungry so he wolfed down the rest of it. A couple hours later, he'd go to the gym for a workout and get an hour-long massage.

For Rob, that would be all the vacation he wanted right now. Four p.m. couldn't come soon enough.

Chapter 27

As they walked off the patio leaving Rob at the table, Rasha leaned in to Peiter, putting her lips near his ear.

"Are you sure, Peiter? How do we know we can trust him?"

"I'm sure, my Rasha," Peiter said quietly. "Everything checked out. He is the real thing, and you know it." He paused now that they were inside and out of Rob's view. Turning her gently to face him, he lifted both her hands in his, their eyes meeting.

"He is one of *you*."

It was true. Through their discreet private investigators, they had been able to compile a very complete and expedited dossier on Robert Russell. Actually, they had done this within 24 hours of their last meeting with him, which was dinner at this very hotel, less than a week ago.

The family connection was there without question. Rob was the great grandson of Amy Nitschke, the sister of Rasha's great grandmother. There was no denying it. He was a distant cousin, somewhere in the fourth level or more. In terms of DNA, that's slightly more related than the random European person on the street. But he was in the family tree, and that was special.

Rob's military career and commendations were impressive, to say the least. Just achieving the elite warrior status of Ranger would be enough, all by itself. But to earn two Silver Stars, and do tours in both Afghanistan and Syria, put Rob in a unique category. His close-combat skills were simply astounding. His recorded encounter in Syria proved this beyond any doubt. Not only was he one of the toughest, he was one of the bravest. Even Rob's last mission, about which surprisingly they were able to find out, though with some difficulty, was just shocking. Having deep contacts in the Swiss Army proved once again to be invaluable. That mission, with its unique scope, level of difficulty and technical expertise was breathtaking.

Even though they weren't being shot at in this last mission, the level of danger was beyond measure.

Rob would be perfect for Us's latest mission in South America. *Perfect.* Like he was made for it. It was almost like the US Army had asked Us, "How exactly do you want us to train someone for you?" And they did it with Rob.

Us needed Rob on the last leg of the mission. Before Rob arrived, Us knew the extraction phase was their weakest link of the mission. Given the timing of Gui's completing his deal, Us would have no choice but to proceed with a less than ideal plan, all on foot. Then Rob showed up. His exact skill set was the last piece of the puzzle for the complex mission currently underway in South America. Both Peiter and Rasha knew they could not have planned for someone like Rob to show up when he did. The only thing they could think of was that Someone must be looking out for them. They were right.

Providence.

Chapter 28

Across the great USA, the scourge of human trafficking rears its ugly head and occasionally its hideousness is exposed for a few brief seconds. Sadly, there are different grades of trafficking. All are present in America. There is the poor Filipina woman working consecutive 24-hour shifts for the San Diego, California private senior-care home for two dollars an hour. Then there are the young Central and South American girls who are brought to work in the Florida Gold Coast mansions as a gateway to a new life in the most prosperous country in the world.

Like the Filipina woman, they quickly find the wage they were promised is being used to pay their debt for the cost of the trip to the States, and for their food, care and basic needs. The few dollars their employers let them have beyond the monthly debt payments are not enough to buy anything for themselves. What little they make, they send back home to their destitute parents and siblings. At least they're not starving here. But at one or two dollars an hour, they'll never pay back the debt.

In Miami, unless she becomes a favorite with the wife, the domestic will return home in about a year, maybe two. The cycle repeats itself so often that the only real cost to the rich is the employee's round-trip travel cost to her home country.

This type of human trafficking is very difficult to stop. For one, it is so fragmented throughout the country. It could be in hundreds if not thousands of cities. The new senior-care private group homes are sprouting up in many cities, but mostly the sunshine states. Florida and California seniors have embraced these new alternatives to large nursing homes and assisted living facilities. Even lawyers and CPAs get in on it. A new cottage industry has popped up, with seminars in swanky hotels offering professional and legal help, exposing loopholes in labor laws to legally overwork employees and screw them out of benefits.

Some of the owners don't care about the labor laws. Ignoring the costly seminars, they couldn't give two shits for following the law. They just pay a fraction of the federal minimum wage and if they lose a lawsuit, they'll just declare bankruptcy. They can transfer the assets to other family members, and the poor employees and their lawyers can collect their judgment from an empty corporate shell. That is if they can't intimidate their employees before they file a lawsuit. Sadly, threats to blackball the poor and powerless tend to work very effectively. In real life, there are very few Davids to go against a Goliath. People need to eat or they die.

In the human and sex trafficking world, there are only a few events that have a promise of a massive payday. The events have such a lucrative one-time bonus, that it brings out the big guns. The money to be made is staggering. The small money in this game is in the millions. The total money for the big event, split amongst the elite underworld, is in the hundreds of millions. The global players in the human trafficking world come out to play. These are the ones who only show up for the big games.

There is no doubt these global players ground it out in the small stuff, working their way up, over years and years. They cultivate many key contacts, in unusually familiar but of course unknown places. This year and next year, however, are special. Two of the best events right here in Florida, in consecutive years.

The Super Bowl. Miami, 2020. Tampa, 2021. In past Super Bowls, law enforcement made a big deal out of busting human trafficking rings, netting a hundred or more johns and a couple dozen small-scale traffickers, better known as pimps. These sting-ops rightly touted their cyber-efforts to fool and legally entrap the perpetrators, exposing them to public shame and potential incarceration.

But the real money, the most egregious trafficking, was not executed by such crude methods. The most lucrative transactions in this dirty business were done at the highest levels of society, but only by word of mouth among the world's elite. Money and privilege at these levels use an intricate web of enterprise. The fact that this occurs outside the purview of the FBI's efforts is understandable. The elite do not rely on the web, even the dark web, for their business. This business takes place on private jets, from Learjets to the Boeing 777 and everything in between. And that the highest known levels of trafficking activity peaks during the most watched macho sporting event on the planet, is not lost on those who occupy this malignant orbit.

Guilherme "Gui" Rodrigues was at the right place at the right time to take advantage of this logistical dream.

But with so much money to be made, other lions would join in the hunt. Russian lions, arguably the most ruthless predators in the jungle, were also in the hunt. The Russians didn't just kill for food, or even sport. They killed for pride. They killed in such a way that no one could ever forget who was being messed with. After they were done extinguishing their prey, slowly, agonizingly, and horrifically, they went after as many relatives as they could find. One by one, or a dozen at a time. It didn't matter. The message to any and all, especially the police, was clear. If you messed with us, you faced the consequences. Not just you, but your entire family.

In Long Island, Brooklyn and Queens, more than a few cops on the beat, detectives, and even police brass found it much more appealing to take a little under the table than the alternative. A little more longevity too. For the Russians, bribery was nothing more than the cost of doing business. Hell, official corruption in Russia made Mexico look like a convent run by nuns. Business owners in Russia only started getting uncomfortable when bribes took over 50 percent of their profits. Anything less than that was cause for celebration.

In their new home, America, by contrast, they could not believe their bribery payroll was less than 10 percent of profits. Even in their illegitimate businesses. Even better, the corrupt police, judges, county officials and politicians couldn't believe how generous the Russians were. It had the appearances of a marriage made in heaven. Trouble was, these Russians didn't believe in heaven. Or hell. Or God. Or right and wrong. The bribe-*takers* knew they would be going to hell for their sins. But hell could wait; as long as they weren't caught breaking the law, they could enjoy this life with a little more non-taxable cash. And who knew, maybe God would change His mind if they did some good things later on.

Too bad for them, going to the dark side never seems to work out in the long run. And sometimes even in the short run.

Chapter 29

As he was an only child, the family fortune instantly passed to him upon the tragic death of both parents when he was in his late twenties. By that time, Gui Rodrigues had already graduated from the finest engineering school on the planet, Massachusetts Institute of Technology. MIT. He spent the first two years of college at Brazil's second home for engineering students, the University of Florida. Ever since World War II and the USA's dire need for Brazilian rubber for the war effort, UF had opened its doors, and became the school of choice for Brazilians studying abroad, even employing Brazilian professors. Brazilian freshmen felt very comfortable hearing as much Portuguese being spoken as English.

But for Gui's father, Humberto "Tico" Rodrigues, UF was not the right school for the future engineer. After his sophomore year, at his father's insistence and aided by his considerably influential contacts at Oderhoffen and other firms he "helped," Gui was admitted as a transfer student to MIT in his third year. The stipulation was that he had to repeat his sophomore year. He didn't mind that one bit. Although extremely rigorous, most of the material was very familiar, and he was able to achieve high marks, which made him a minor celebrity in his class. It also gave him the flexibility to seek out the night life in Boston, and even meet people involved in some very profitable activities, squarely positioned in the gray area of legality. Activities which dealt with some very beautiful, international girls. It didn't matter to him that they didn't speak any language he knew. They knew more than enough without speaking at all.

He did not realize it then, as he was having much too much fun, but those contacts would become much closer after he graduated and moved back to his native land.

His wealth origins were not unlike many of the richest families in the resource-rich South American nation. In South America, politics equals power and wealth follows. In every country, there are those who abuse their political position for their own wealth. In the United States, except for perhaps Chicago, Miami and New Orleans, corruption is the exception rather than the rule. And when it is exposed in such a way that it makes front page news, at least the federal safeguards kick in and the corrupt official is exposed, prosecuted and jailed, even in those three great cities. But not without exceptions, depending on the individual's power and clout.

However, in Latin America, corruption is deeply ingrained in the culture. It's simply the cost of doing business. As long as the right people in the accountability or enforcement chain are properly and well-paid-off, or bribed, the corruption continues. Sometimes for generations. Even when good, untainted, moral people win elections promising to finally root out graft, the corrupt system is so rooted, the machine is so well-oiled, that only token successes are possible.

To stay in power, the corrupt and wealthy class know when to sacrifice one of their own. Usually the sacrifice, if you want to call it that, is to a prison that has amenities and luxuries more like a five-star resort in Vegas. Also included is access to constant and varied female companionship, well, more like conjugal visits, or more precisely, orgies. Fine food is prepared fresh daily, good liquor flows freely, and Cuban cigars, Cohibas, arrive weekly directly from Habanos S.A. Obviously, the bribing did not stop when the poor sacrificial lamb was sent to jail. That's just where it intensifies and concentrates. The prison wardens love it when one of these guys comes to their prison. Talk about winning the lottery.

And in Latin America, men control everything. Exceptions rarely occur, such as the rise of Dilma Rousseff, the corrupt former president of Brazil. Women are rarely more than trophies and mistresses, depending on their family status. Bribes are just a line-item cost of doing business. The corrupt ruling class, from their billions in illicit funds, pay with pocket change of millions to the right people in control of the prisons to properly care for one of their own. It's amazing how easy it is to spend money they knew they shouldn't have. It is just as easy to kill for it too.

In Gui's father's day, as it is now, there was a vast difference between the local corrupt officials and the national corrupt ones. The most glaring difference was the amount of wealth. The wealthiest were the families in control of key government positions on the national level. There, the biggest, most lucrative deals were for roads and infrastructure, like the new freeways and huge hydroelectric dams. With the contract being in the billions of dollars, it was much easier to funnel off millions without being detected. With the right public official in place, the winning bids already contained the padding to pay off the officials once the public money was distributed to the company.

In city politics, the payout might be smaller, but still very significant. One reality was that the bribes were always baked into the bids, and public officials would be paid off. Everyone in the right places knew it, condoned it, and facilitated it. Why? Because they too were being splashed by the river of wealth that was flowing by. As long as the splashes were frequent enough, those in government didn't care that most of the wealth flowed right past them.

And this is exactly what happened in Gui's family.

Born and raised in Sao Paulo, his father, Tico Rodriguez, was a well-connected, influential city councilman. Which of course meant that he was in the right position to make the most of his position personally, and for others in important positions. In exchange for discreetly placed bearer shares in offshore trust accounts as bribes from the Oderhoffen Company, his father was able to open doors for the fledgling company.

The company would have been sure to fail had it not been for his father's "help." Sr. Rodrigues' influence, and bribe-taking, resulted in new jobs and opportunities, bringing his city, and country, for that matter, into the twenty-first century. The poor and uneducated got free schools. New roads, parks, and libraries were built. Even public transportation was improved. All because Humberto made sure the new company got the county projects. Why should only the Oderhoffen family benefit from this?

They were not the only ones who did. When the company later became a multinational, multi-billion-dollar empire, those initial shares became worth millions of dollars.

Even though several politicians were murderously envious of Tico, as he was affectionately called by the poor working class of Sao Paulo, no one would or could stop him. As long as residents were benefiting in such large ways, no opponent would dare stand up to him. He was constantly in the news dedicating a new park, school or road, and would invite the whole neighborhood in for a free feast. No one could touch him.

One of the last moves Tico made before his untimely death, was to cash out of the Oderhoffen shares by selling the entire stake. While the Oderhoffen family was not pleased that Tico would sell his shares to an outsider, they refused to pay the price the hedge fund had offered for the old shares. As was typical of closely held family companies, the owners were incapable of paying more than what they felt their shares were worth. Having to actually buy back your own shares was hard enough. To overpay for them was just inconceivable. With the hedge fund offering *five times* the family's top offer, all cash up front, Tico pulled the trigger and sold the shares.

In 1981, when Tico sold his shares, Oderhoffen had just purchased a company in Europe, immediately expanding and diversifying their revenues and expanding their business into non-engineering ventures. That the family could not overcome their emotions and pay the then-obscene purchase price the hedge fund was willing to pay, would cost them in many ways. When the family finally did buy the shares held by the hedge fund, two decades later, they would pay nearly 20 times more than the "obscene" price they could have paid Tico for it.

Tico, for his part, again showed his shrewdness in investing. With beautiful Sao Paulo just beginning to attract new residents and businesses, Tico invested most all the money in the downtown sector, starting with three vacant city blocks, as well as one of the prominent city office buildings. In those days, banks did not care where money came from, they just wanted it in their vault. Tico had the multi-million-dollar proceeds wired to three banks, into shell companies the banks could never connect to him. Tico's attorneys always dealt with the bankers. The clueless bankers never even knew that their customer, Councilman Tico, was the real owner of these massive accounts.

Over the next two decades, Tico was able to watch his investments grow from 50 million dollars to over 500 million. He was one of the wealthiest individuals in Brazil, but thanks to the shell companies, no one but his attorneys knew about it.

When Tico and his wife were killed in the tragic car accident, Gui had no idea what his father was worth. Gui was enjoying his successful engineering career with Oderhoffen, often taking part in the most high-profile projects throughout the world. He knew his parents lived comfortably and did not lack for anything, but they were not extravagant or showing off excessive wealth with expensive cars, yachts or jewelry.

So, a week after the large and exhausting funeral, a massive, city-funded affair attended by thousands, he met with his father's lawyers to open his father's and mother's estate. After the first five minutes, he nearly fell out of his chair from shock. The last three weeks of abject grief and deep anguish over the news of their death and all the funeral plans was like being forced to sit in a rollercoaster in its initial straight-up climb to the very top. Time had moved like thick sludge through a straw. Everything had seemed difficult and time-consuming.

Five minutes into the attorney's explanation of his father's enormous holdings, Gui was feeling lightheaded. He couldn't grasp exactly what the attorney was describing.

"My father owned all this?" Gui asked incredulously. The next sentence from the attorney put Gui's mind into a state of freefall weightlessness.

"Yes. And it's all yours now. You are the sole heir," stated the silver-haired attorney.

The feeling Gui had right then was identical to the heart-stopping moment just as the rollercoaster hits the peak height, slowly rolls over, and instantly becomes a freefalling, free-floating projectile you are trapped in and have no way out. Gui's head was spinning, his mind reeling. His stomach was in his throat. He couldn't breathe. He wanted so bad to scream like a scared little girl, puncturing eardrums of anyone nearby, and cover his face with his hands. Outwardly, however, his face was frozen, mouth open and his unfocused eyes just stared at the attorney. He couldn't speak, let alone move.

"Gui, are you ok?" asked the attorney. "Would you like some water?

"Gui?"

Gui blinked a couple times, closed his mouth, cleared his throat, and looked again at the attorney.

"Gui," began the attorney. "We are here to help you in any way you need. We set up the entities with your father many years ago," he continued. "We can bring you up to speed on how your father managed all his assets." He paused for a moment. "Do you understand?"

Gui managed to nod in the affirmative. The attorney continued. "Gui, given the vast size and scope of your father's estate, I recommend that you contact your employer and let them know you will need a 90-day leave of absence. Let them know there are more details than you could imagine with both parents being killed simultaneously. One month prior to the end of your leave, submit your resignation. Let them know you have re-examined your life since your parents' death and have decided to change course.

"Under no circumstances should you tell them of your new wealth, or of that of your father's estate. In our estate planning meetings, your father instructed us, actually threatened he would return from the grave to haunt us, if we did not impress upon you that this anonymity of wealth is the primary key to keeping it.

"And the way things have been set up, no one can possibly find out you are the owner of your father's holdings, unless you yourself tell them. The offshore trusts and shell companies we created for your father ensure that fact.

"Do you understand, Gui?" finished the attorney, looking at a slightly recovered and present Gui. He punched his intercom key and spat out to his secretary in the next room, "Bring a glass of ice-water to Mr. Rodrigues, please, right away."

"Right away, sir," came the prompt reply.

He looked at Gui again, who had sat up, rubbed his legs twice, looked up at his new *abogado,* attorney, and nodded quickly and slightly several times.

With a light knock, the secretary opened the door a crack as the attorney waved her in. Gui gave her a weak smile of gratitude as he took a sip of the ice-cold drink. As soon as the secretary closed the door as she hurried out of the room, Gui said, almost in a whisper, "I can't believe it. I just can't believe it." He paused for a second.

"How could my father keep this from me my whole life?" he wondered aloud, disbelievingly. "I take it my mother never knew," he stated matter-of-factly, looking at the attorney.

"Your father was old-school," said the attorney. "The last thing he wanted was to burden your mother with too much information. He felt she was too sensitive and pure to deal with all this business and enterprise. Probably more to the point, he did not want to answer all the questions she would have. It also prevented her from asking for things, no doubt."

At this, Gui managed a slight smile, with a little "Hmmhmmhm," and nodded in agreement with the attorney.

Again able to speak, but not yet fully recovered, Gui said quietly, "I think your recommendation is good." He paused as he looked up and met the attorney's eyes. Finding a little more strength in his voice, he continued. "I would like to start my learning as soon as possible, starting tomorrow morning."

Although still feeling the shock of the news, the dizzying roller coaster feeling had dwindled, and he stood up slowly, as did the attorney.

"Perhaps you could drop by at ten tomorrow morning? We could set you up in the conference room, and I and my staff will begin to walk you through things. By the end of next week, you should have a good grasp of all the operations and management. We also have transfer paperwork and various items that need to be addressed. Does that sound acceptable?" asked the attorney.

Shaking the man's hand, Gui said, "That will be fine. Thank you."

As Gui walked through the door and out into the afternoon sunshine, he suddenly realized his life would never be the same. He would never again answer to an employer. From now on, everyone would answer to him. The very people he worked for just yesterday might someday be working on a project of his.

As he got behind the wheel of his three-year-old Ford Expedition, it felt much older than it had just hours prior when he arrived at the attorney's office. Without hesitation, he drove straight to the local Toyota dealer in Sao Paulo. After a couple hours of price wrangling, Gui drove off the lot in his brand-new Landcruiser, with all the options, literally the car of his dreams.

"It's not like I went out and bought a helicopter, for God's sake," Gui thought. He doubted anyone would even think twice about it.

He rightly thought people would realize he probably got a little money when his parents died, since he was the only child. No one would accuse him of extravagance. Engineers were known to love these amazing vehicles anyway. Besides, give the grieving son a break. He just lost both parents.

What they didn't know was that Gui had permanently and instantly transitioned from the grieving son. He was now the ecstatic and celebrating heir. The challenge, and Gui knew this, was not to celebrate too ecstatically.

Chapter 30

The beauty of being the middleman, just bringing the parties together, is underappreciated. It's actually the best job in the world. Neither party knows the other, and never will. A tidy 25 percent commission makes the world go around, and clearly is the safest and most humane thing to do for these unfortunates.

But Gui was nobody's fool. He did not get as wealthy as he was, even with his significant head start, by burying his head in the sand.

On the contrary, like many of the uber-rich, Gui had his ways to be informed on almost everything in his enterprise. Given the incredible risk in the dark side of his profit-making machine, he wanted to ensure his payments were secure. Through meticulous research, and at great personal cost, in the millions of dollars, Gui learned about the four largest brokers in global human trafficking.

There was the Eastern European group, run by former USSR middle and upper managers, who'd left the country shortly after its breakup and Boris Yelstin's privatization. He knew many now lived in New York and Miami, and were in the business of gasoline distribution and strip club ownership. They were the Russians. He knew them from his fun first year at MIT, the year he had to repeat to be admitted, thanks to his Papá. Gui had spent many a night at the bars and strip clubs, and had become acquainted with all types. He actually had hit it off pretty well with a young Russian named Vladimir, Vlad for short.

Vlad liked the fact that Gui was at MIT, and smart enough to get good grades and still party pretty hard. Vlad was hanging out in Boston on his quest to get to know his new country. Boston was one of the first cities he wanted to explore. He had always heard of Harvard and MIT growing up, as so many prominent men and women had gone there. Also, his new citizenship classes told him that the United States began in this area. So, he wanted to check it out, and see if any of the greatness would rub off on him. That's when he met Gui at one of the local watering holes, known to attract a good number of the student-elites.

Gui and Vlad had a few things in common, which helped cement their relationship. Love of beautiful women, good Vodka, and a distaste for their American hosts. "Such bigshots," Vlad would say. "They think they're so great *becauz vall* came down in Berlin," he spat out in his thick Russian accent. "They are all corrupt and *stoopid*," he would laugh. "Without Reagan they are *no-thingk*," he would conclude. "*Ve vait. Ve* are patient."

Vlad told Gui probably much more than he should have. He let his guard down since Gui was a Brazilian, not an American. Gui was pretty talented at talking and getting Vlad to open up, as much as a street-smart Russian would allow. When Vlad would boast that he "could *bringk* whole roomful of fresh Ukrainian *vimen* better than all these *girlz*," Gui took special notice.

"How could anyone say that? What the hell is he tied into?" Gui thought.

It didn't take Gui very long to glean that Vlad seemed to be able to bring in gorgeous girls from the poor areas of Russia and the former Eastern Bloc nations.

But back in those days, the term "human trafficking" was not really on anyone's radar. Bringing groups of people into America to start a better life was admired and not closely questioned or monitored for illegality, even though it often resulted in human servitude. That bleak era of human history didn't exist anymore, or so most Americans believed. Rather, they believed those ethnic groups chose their occupations, whether they were domestics, nannies or strippers. It was just their way of pursuing the American Dream.

Besides, these were Russians, who barely spoke English, and they looked every part the Russian boogey-man they grew up believing they were. They stayed in their own area, spoke only Russian, and went to their own parties. The police were never called for domestic disturbances, and their tight neighborhoods had no crime to speak of. All the murders, drugs and frequent shootings were in the nearby Black and Latino slums. Hell, these Russians were model citizens, the police thought. The police could now focus on the more crime-ridden areas, and leave the Russian neighborhoods alone. That was fine with them. And more than fine for the Russians.

Vlad knew better. He and the Long Island Russians had been enjoying free labor for years now in The Red Velvet Club. Well, at least the strippers were free "labor." Room and board were small prices to pay for all the very tangible benefits they so frequently enjoyed.

It was not long into their new friendship before Vlad invited Gui to The Red Velvet to prove to his Brazilian friend that he was not just a lying braggard.

"Gui, my friend," he said in a low, hushed tone, three quarters done with his own bottle of Beluga Vodka in an ice-filled carafe, his go-to brand if he couldn't get his favorite, Baikal. Vlad knew the trick of sprinkling some table salt on the ice to get the vodka even colder. Leaning forward and lowering his head slightly as he looked up past his cocked, bushy eyebrows, he said through a crooked grin, "Come with me for a weekend. Two nights. *Eef* you have, how do you say? The *energiya*. The stamina. I *veel* show you paradise."

A quick weekend trip to Long Island and The Red Velvet opened Gui's eyes to a whole new world, full of endless worldly pleasures.

This was a world devoid of sunlight, inky, oily and black as a coal mine, but garishly lit with neon, track and spotlights strategically commanding one to look in a certain direction. Red velvet was indeed the only thing this place could be named. Every chair, every couch, barstool, doorframe and curtain was covered by it. The floor was a dark laminate hardwood tile.

All the tables, chairs and couches were bolted to the floor. The Russians had learned quickly that things you couldn't pick up and throw in a drunken fight did not need replacing very often, and that knowledge and practice kept costs down. No need to clean the dirty, grimy corners that no customer would ever see. Unless, of course, the customer got carried away and touched one of the girls, and quickly found his nose thrust directly into that corner. Thickly muscled Russian bouncers were not known for their gentle ways.

Throughout all the years since, Gui and Vladimir had remained friends, calling each other once every other month or so. Gui traveled to Miami fairly often, meeting with the mayor and county commissioners to close construction deals with a personal touch. The personal touch included, of course, the anonymous, numbered Swiss bank account where the most recent "contribution" was deposited.

It had been fairly easy to recruit this kind of cooperation from the local politicians. Not too surprisingly, some of the male politicians were intrigued by the VIP invitation from Gui to visit one of his Russian friend's gentlemen's clubs in Fort Lauderdale, the next county north. After all, it was an invitation for a steak dinner curated and prepared by their new executive chef, direct from France, who for the past 15 years, was head chef at Le Pre Catelan, one of only nine Paris restaurants rated the highest three stars by the Michelin Red Guide. This was the perfect excuse, for any commissioners of dubious morality, to just slightly get off the fence, and experience what their political position entitled them to. Especially since "the experience" was in another county.

This invitation, of course, did not include the spouses, nor was it in writing. Rather, it was a personal phone call from Gui himself, whose driver would drop by at three p.m. outside the commissioner's office and take him up to the club. He would leave it up to the commissioners to make their own excuses to their wives. He rightly assumed they were pretty good at credible deception with their wives, or they would never have made it this far in public office.

If things got a little out of control, as Gui hoped they would, and a little too much alcohol was enjoyed, they could always stay in a local hotel. Gui already had rooms booked for these events well in advance, as past experience told him he would always need at least one room. The commissioners, safely out of their own county, left most of their inhibitions behind even before they started drinking. The odds of being seen by one of their constituents, or other Miami-Dade residents, was very low. About one in a hundred.

Except for the stills and video, that is.

Once the commissioner was seated and served by very beautiful, foreign, young women—hell, each one looked like a fashion model—his guard went down a little further. Maybe it was the amazing cuisine, so expertly prepared and exquisitely seasoned. Or maybe it was the server, whose blouse opened up revealing much more than his imagination every time she leaned over and asked if he wanted more wine, another appetizer, or an *entrée*, always with an inviting smile.

At the end of the main meal, there was simply no objection or hesitation when Gui announced that dessert would be served in the adjacent, private room. Dessert had the added perquisite of being served by those very same servers from dinner, this time wearing only a smile, high heels and a "why-is-it-even-there" thong. From there, the rest of the evening was, from Gui's standpoint, perfect. He would have all the compromising video and photographs he would ever need, in full high-definition quality. Gui typically opted for the classic black and white video and photos. Those gave things a more "criminal" feel.

Gui would store these photos away and most likely would never use them. He didn't really care that Vladimir and the Russians would do the same. Once these commissioners tacitly accepted the anonymous, numbered account, their phone call to Switzerland to verify the balance was all they needed to begin steering Gui the jobs. They would start with small jobs at the new Miami International Airport. When Gui's company did a great job, no one would be overly suspicious when another contract was awarded to them.

Vladimir especially enjoyed reading in the Miami Herald about Gui's company scoring yet another county project worth millions. Vlad knew he and Gui had a special bond, formed when they were both young—in their early twenties in Boston. Aside from his Russian comrades and family, Gui was really one of the few men he trusted. He respected the fact that Gui obtained these "insurance" videos and photos on the corrupt Miami politicians, but to his knowledge, never used them. He was pleased that Gui had been so wildly successful in his international engineering business, and correctly guessed that his net worth was north of 500 million. He of course would never directly ask his friend for this information. He had been in the USA long enough to know that *Forbes* magazine would let him know when he became one of the most elite and rare ones on the planet, a billionaire.

After all, *Forbes* had rightly tagged his fellow countryman Alexander Berezofsky as one, almost immediately after the collapse of the Soviet Union. They were even surprisingly accurate on criminal billionaires. How they got this information was a mystery to him, although he suspected there were insiders selling *Forbes* this information.

Vlad felt the time was right to approach Gui with a joint venture, one that would add substantially to both of their bottom lines. The surge in profits would benefit Vlad very nicely, but not directly. Vladimir was just a cog in the massive wheel of the Russian Mob. He was not the top nor even one of the most powerful. He would never be. He was just the son of a well-liked middle manager in the government-owned Russian lumber industry that was allowed to participate in the privatization under Yeltsin. Upper management, extremely well-connected and powerful, were the biggest benefactors of Yeltsin's folly. They were the new bosses in Long Island and Miami.

Vladimir would be very well-compensated and amply rewarded, but those upper positions were occupied, and vacancies would be filled by their own, from their class, not Vladimir's.

But the enormous profits from this venture would go directly to Gui's bottom line. An alliance between the South American and Russian human trafficking network would be worth hundreds of millions of dollars in profit, for each party. There was no reason the two groups could not work together, rather than getting in each other's way and hurting business.

Up to this point, the competing networks had never had the desire to explore any opportunities with each other. On the contrary, they often bumped into each other with their shipments of "product," real live humans, with at best a lost sale and at worst, a shootout with both killed comrades and killed product. It was one thing to lose product, which affected the bottom line. It was entirely another to lose fellow Russians. Vlad had worked very hard to convince his bosses that a joint venture and huge profits were preferable to an all-out war and business disruption.

Vladimir said he had a plan in mind, and it could come together in less than six months. He told them he had the right connections in South America to make this happen.

With the blessing of his bosses, he booked the next first-class ticket to Sao Paulo, Brazil on his favorite airline: American, of course. Gui would be a little surprised to see him there, as he was in Miami only three weeks before, and they had met for a quick drink at the Black Diamond Club near the Golden Glades interchange. He would wait a couple days, actually as long as it took, at the swanky and luxurious Emiliano Hotel in Sao Paulo for a face-to-face with Gui.

There was no reason to skimp on his digs, as he was not paying for it anyway. The organization, the notorious and brutal Bratva, had plenty of cash, and his ideas had directly produced a big chunk of it. The cash flow from the Miami strip clubs was off the charts, and was projected to grow at 30 percent per year. Had Vlad not given them the idea to take over Miami, none of that would be coming to the organization.

So, Vlad was not at all unhappy when he found that Gui would be arriving in five days. He would sip cold vodka by the pools, catch a good suntan, and maybe even bag a few lucky ladies. He knew there were plenty with no natural defenses against a deep Russian accent.

After five days, Gui flew back home and dropped by the Emiliano for dinner with Vlad. As Vlad suspected, Gui was not only all in, he actually knew more than a little bit about the business. He marveled how lucrative it had gotten in the last half dozen years. With all his contacts, loosely translated as bribe-takers, in the police and other government agencies, he knew the major focus was on illegal drugs and murders in the city slums. Even on the national scale. The emphasis was on cleaning out the barrios, the neighborhood slums, with their child gangs of thieves and the drug gangs. The bad publicity was affecting the mega-profit tourist trade.

They were not even thinking about human trafficking. Gui could taste the profits to be made, and thanked his patron saints for letting him meet up with Vlad two decades ago. So much for chance, or random, accidental meetings. "No way," thought Gui. "God has his hand in everything in life," he continued. "I just have to release myself to the universe and expect great things."

"The *vay ve* do it, my good friend," started Vlad, his accent perhaps a little smoother around the edges after all these years in the USA, "is clean and simple. You *vill* be our *nocpeahnk*, how you say? Broker, intermediary. *Zat* is all, for us," said Vlad. "For the South Americans, you *vill* be their intermediary too, yes?" asked Vlad, in the standard end-of-sentence question mark used by all Russians.

"Keeping us from *keeling* them and them from *keeling* us *vill* pay you a very handsome amount. Do you see? Yes?"

Gui knew nothing was ever as easy as it seemed on the surface, but for a twenty-five-million-dollar payday, twelve-five mil from each, it was worth the risk. It sure did seem easy. Gui knew he could locate the traffickers in his domain, South America, through one of his father's old acquaintances. He'd stayed in touch with him over the years since his parents were killed.

If he could broker this non-compete and mutual cooperation agreement, which he was certain he could, the human trafficking lanes would open wide the profits for each side. With advanced satellite technology at their ready use, their movements would be virtually invisible to any police or government that could muster up an effort to bust a sophisticated trafficking ring. That Russians were working with South Americans would be beyond any legitimate government's imagination.

Gui was just going to love this.

Gui and Vlad agreed to never discuss this over the phone in the inception phase. They would meet in three weeks at the brand-new resort in Georgetown, Grand Cayman. The Seafire. Vlad would do some scuba diving and Gui would buy an original *Guy Harvey* painting at Harvey's Downtown Gallery and Gift Shop. They would then take a private deep-sea charter and see if they could hook up a marlin. There would be plenty of time to talk and plan.

In a couple weeks, Gui's research would reveal the other major traffickers. Besides Vlad and the Russians, another group of traffickers came from Southeast Asia, controlled by a very vicious group out of Hong Kong. From this group came all the North Koreans, North Vietnamese, Filipinos, and Malaysians. They occasionally dealt in Indians and Pakistanis. Gui referred to them as the "Chinks." "Asians" would be a more politically correct term, but Gui was not planning to write a book about it, so he didn't care.

A third group operated from the Congo, Uganda and Kenya in the middle of Africa. Their market was almost exclusively sold to the Middle East. Iran, Saudi Arabia, Lebanon, Tunisia, Oman, Bahrain, Egypt and the United Arab Emirates, mostly. Being closed societies, keeping victims hidden was much easier than say, in Western Europe and the West, with their free press. This particular trafficking group was experiencing a boom in product availability due to the chaos in Somalia. It was not too much of a diversion to pick up a shipment on the way to their Middle East clients. He called this group the "Jungle," which was not nearly as offensive as the Asian group's name.

It was a wonder how the foreign press largely dismissed the idea that the slave auction block was happening in the open square in some of the poorest areas of Uganda. To civilized societies, it was inconceivable that the auction block was alive and well, although illegally, in any country on the planet. In the USA, there was only obscure, back-page coverage of this scourge currently happening in Uganda.

Back in the USA, the only news about slavery was how much cash reparations should be paid to descendants of former slaves from a couple centuries prior. To the world just outside this cabal of presidential candidates, it looked like nothing more than a pandering bidding war for votes of a certain color. That a civil war to end slavery at the cost of more American lives than all other wars including World War II, combined, was not enough "reparations," remained a mystery to most Americans and a source of derision for America to the world.

The fourth group was from Gui's own hemisphere, Central and South America. With Venezuela being the worst on the South American continent, Honduras and Nicaragua ran close behind on the international human trafficking lists. Just like Southeast Asia, the "product" was practically inexhaustible. Gui understood that buyers were able to be very specific in their demands. Height and weight were fairly easy to accommodate. But hair and eye color specifications were not as easily met. The humans coming from this hemisphere were primarily of indigenous and Afro-Caribbean stock. Dark hair and eyes and brown skin were the vast majority. The rare lighter eye and hair color would fetch a premium price.

As Gui's thoughts returned to present day, his mind continued its rationalization. Unlike the Russian and Hong Kong traffickers, Gui's conscience had not yet been scorched into oblivion. Thanks to his dear mother, it was still alive inside, ghastly sick but still breathing, needing to be dealt with. The stronger side, without the conscience, could unfortunately easily talk over the whispers and gasps from the dying part of humanity that still lived in him.

"Without my help," Gui's strong side told him, "God knows these unwanted souls would end up in truly oppressive, despicable hands. I am actually helping these people! And the commission is untraceable, thanks to bitcoin, the greatest invention since electricity, and just as revolutionary.

"And I get to work with such amazing people," he thought. "Take Maya. Brilliant, hardworking, beautiful, and young. I can even see a future with her, perhaps being one of my favorite affairs," he said to himself.

Maya had been introduced recently as his contact for the South American trafficking group. She was the one who would make all the arrangements for the final transaction, cementing the two groups, the Russians and the South Americans, into their alliance. He could not be more pleased with this development. She was both seductively beautiful and smart, and without a doubt knew what she was doing. Gui marveled at how professional this group was.

Continuing his smug thoughts about Maya, "Not my only mistress, of course. No man of my stature and wealth has only one affair with just one woman at a time," he laughed to himself.

"Rules and laws are written for the masses. Not for us, the truly rich. The powerful. With such great wealth comes power. And power enables favors, and favors, permission, and permission, anything. Rules do not apply." Gui's strong side had his weak conscience pinned down hard on his mental wrestling mat. With one final kick to his fully defeated weak conscience, he was fully committed to his despicable business of trafficking humans like they were sheep. His strong side, now fully inflated with pride, thought, “How could any country impose their individual laws on a global citizen like me?”

Ironically, he was right. Governments had their hands full with wars and rumors of wars. The current war on terrorism was nearly all-consuming for America. Throw in the containment of Russia, Iran and North Korea, and America’s plate was full if not overflowing. Also, dictatorships had huge conflicts of interest regarding human trafficking. How could they pretend to care about human trafficking when they literally enslaved their own people? That most of the victims came from their countries was another matter as well.

The elected politicians in democratic governments, although officially against human trafficking, had their own local issues to deal with. They knew that focusing too much on human trafficking while in office would mean they would not be in office for long. It wasn’t like the illicit drug trade, where dead young American bodies were piling up from fentanyl and crack cocaine overdoses.

Given that reality, somebody or something else had to step up to stop this insanity.

Inconceivable to Gui, or anyone else for that matter, he just might get his ass handed to him by a bunch of women, unaffiliated with any country or government.

Chapter 31

Gui was overthinking it again. But as soon as his conscience pricked him, he was mentally ready to fight back. Instantly gaining the higher ground, he began his familiar rationalizations. Vladimir's proposition and promise of pure sizeable profit, based on his minor involvement in these negotiations, overrode any hesitation on his part.

He thought back to the time when his father's attorney first explained to him the origins of his father's wealth. After the first week of meetings, reviewing and learning about his father's enterprise, Gui started asking the attorney questions.

"How did my father put all this together?" Gui asked, at first just to himself. After the first two weeks of meetings, when he had read the last profile of one of his father's properties, he asked for a private meeting with the attorney.

"Your office has done an amazing job bringing me up to speed on all the matters that my father was involved in," started Gui. "I am shocked at what he put together, and amazed he could keep it from me my whole life.

"I mean, I knew he had a small apartment complex, of eight units. But that was just the tip of the iceberg," Gui continued. "He obviously had others running everything, including his office building and his stock holdings," he stated. "You?" asked Gui.

The attorney nodded. "Yes, Gui. I helped your father with all his businesses, and had specialists and experts help in certain areas. None of them knew they were dealing with your father. It was all done in the strictest confidence," the attorney stated, with no hint of a smile.

"Why?" Gui blurted out. "Why was it so confidential? Why didn't my father tell me and ask me to work for him? What was the big deal about all this confidentiality? Why couldn't he just tell me what was going on? I mean, what in the hell was this all about?" he asked, completely exasperated.

"Gui," the attorney stated, softly but firmly. "Your father couldn't tell you. And no one else could know, either. Except me."

Gui just looked at him, nothing but confused questions going through his mind at a hundred miles an hour.

"And no one can know now, Gui," said the attorney, as he came around his desk and sat next to Gui, bent forward and looked directly at him.

Gui looked directly back at the attorney and said, "I believe you're about to tell me something I really don't want to hear, aren't you?"

Attorney Rangel nodded slightly, stood up, patted Gui's shoulder, and started walking toward a secret compartment in his bookshelf against the side wall.

"Gui," said the silver-haired *abogado*, "what I am about to tell you requires something truly special. I have been saving a bottle of Novo Fogo, already aged seven years, for such a time as this. Care for a glass?" The attorney loved his aged cachacas, considering it Brazil's favorite spirit, much like Jim Beam was America's favorite bourbon. They would need a good sipping drink, as this would take the rest of the afternoon.

With that, after swearing Gui to secrecy on his mother's fresh grave, Sr. Rangel took Gui through his father's entire history of bribes and politics, including from Oderhoffen, Gui's recent employer.

Three hours later, Gui's perspective on life had changed again almost as dramatically as it had after their meeting two weeks ago, when he found he was now one of the richest men in the world.

Now, nearly 20 years later and with much success under his belt, and perhaps never being caught, Gui's perspective had indeed ripened even further. The fact that his father's wealth came from bribes caused him to re-evaluate his perceptions of right and wrong.

His concept of morality came under fire, and was almost incinerated. It was as if a suicide bomber had blown himself up in the church of morality. When the dust settled, nothing was the same as before. As Gui's mind began to pick up the pieces, his new concept of morality resembled a broken-looking Frankenstein's monster rather than an angelic Mother Teresa, his own mother's favorite saint.

His new morality completely changed his views on bribery. Especially on the new government crackdown. With all the good gained from such progress, the recent bribery laws were so overreaching, so obstructive. None of the good things would happen. It may have been the law, but it was clearly meant to be broken, or carefully evaded. And if cleverly evaded, only the good happens. And he has to provide for his family, no? He would never take drug money; those men were beasts. Even his new morality condemned the illegal drug trade. He would only accept clean shares of stock from real businesses to his offshore bearer shares trust.

Everyone does it. Everyone takes bribes, as they officially call it. But some are so greedy, and stupid. They deserve to be caught and should be punished. For their stupidity. Gui was trying to remember if he ever got a government contract without well-placed bribes. He actually couldn't remember one instance of a purely clean, merit-based contract award.

He knew that when his Papá was alive, there was no such industry as human trafficking, at least in the western hemisphere. Now that there was, with such enormous profits, it was just another way to gain wealth that could be spread around for good.

And really, thought Gui, Papá would of course agree that human trafficking was just another vice on this planet, to be taken advantage of by the smart, the clever. His profits could cause good things to be done. For Sao Paulo. For the children. The poor and downtrodden. It was time to lift them up and give them a chance at a better life.

The trafficked humans were unwanted even in their own country. Mostly, they were nameless, parentless, helpless sheep. They are already being robbed, sheared, maimed, raped, and sold anyway, if not killed, after one or all of the former.

"At least I sell them into organized and safe groups. At least they're not being raped. Or killed," thought Gui. "When good money is transferred, the value is established. The investment must be protected, is protected, and cared for. My contacts assure me of this, and I trust them."

"These people are actually better off because of my involvement. Of course, I never see the inventory," Gui continued to himself.

There can be no payments or records between me and the parties. The parties to the transaction will never know each other. They are anonymous. The companies are all shell companies. The exchange is by bitcoin, the greatest invention of the twenty-first century by far. The anonymity enjoyed by all parties is an incalculable blessing. A whole new era of commerce is now achievable outside the chokehold of the "Yanqui's" Federal Reserve, Department of the Treasury.

Gui continued his perfect reasoning to himself. "Criminals could do just about anything they wanted before bitcoin with international wire transfers. American banks and their clueless compliance departments." He spat in disgust as he thought it. "If they only knew how much they facilitate criminal ventures and terrorism. How easy it is to move funds for any purpose, and how much pure profit has been made with so much bloodshed. These fools have hundreds of thousands of peoples' innocent blood on their hands and they don't even have a clue. These big banks and their big names and community service PR stunts. Wells Fargo, Bank of America, JP

Morgan/Chase, HSBC, Banco Espiritu Santo. Hah! They have no shame as they turn a blind eye to all of it so long as they make their fees and commissions."

Many times, though, it is not just stupidity, it's outright criminal. A small but consistent bribe is all that is necessary to slightly turn a well-placed and underpaid compliance puke's eye from any particular wire transfer. Of course, all prophylactic protocols would be done to ensure textbook compliance was followed. No rules would be broken. Past the first two levels, further investigation would be squelched. It would be nearly impossible to prove any crime had ever been committed.

The monthly payoffs were ingenious, he had to admit. Few places arouse less suspicion than a doctor's office. Very few of the older generation of doctors, particularly family doctors, were not embittered about the drastically reduced rate insurance companies would pay for office visits of sick patients. They openly complained to each other, but eventually would tire from preaching to the choir. They then complained to anyone who would listen.

"How can they justify paying thirty dollars for an office visit?" the doctor lamented. "That took me all of my residency to be able to diagnose someone! If I do something wrong, or miss something, the patient and her lawyers could turn around and sue me for everything I've ever worked for. And for God's sake, I can't afford malpractice insurance. That's a hundred thou' per year! How could I afford to pay that with these pathetic payouts?"

Complain loudly and often enough, and somebody's bound to listen. But sometimes it may be the wrong person. Although it may take some time, when a doctor begins to act out like this, remembering the good old days of insanely high insurance payouts, streamlined paperwork, and prompt monthly payments, they expose their vulnerability to compromise. It doesn't take a psychiatrist to figure that out. Lack of money is their problem. A lifestyle built on past largesse and high insurance payouts has become unaffordable.

To bridge the gap, some people, including some doctors, would do whatever it takes to make a bit more.

As people in Gui's shadow businesses knew, this problem can be solved for the good doctor with a nice supplemental income. Something that doesn't make them lose concentration in the main practice. Something easy. Something like a legitimate patient who comes by for a checkup on a chronic condition. Where all that has to be done is to document the visit and give him his prescription, along with an envelope of samples, including another envelope of cash. The doctor only knew that the patient worked for Wells Fargo. The good doctor would never know he was in operations approving illicit wire transfers. Money laundering even.

Sadly, the doctor wouldn't care even if he found out. His regular payment would also be there, making up very nicely for the amount the insurance companies had stolen from him in the last 20 years. With only a couple more years before he could retire, the good doctor was banking that his plausible deniability would never be exposed.

This very last thought of the doctor was like an unknown cut on the bottom of a diabetic's foot. If left untreated for too long, it may be too late to save the patient's life, even after amputating the leg. The "cut" to the doctor was when he started complaining in the first place, years earlier. By the time he accepted his new "job," the gangrene had already spread up past his knee, making its way to claiming his heart.

The wire transfers would be fairly infrequent, and only through the busiest international wire departments, like Miami. True of any too-large-to-fail bank in the United States, more international wires were processed each month in Miami than in a year everywhere else, combined. Using all different sizes of transactions, from less than $3,000.00 to six and seven figures, wires would flow. It was a random pattern.

The criminals were smart. Much smarter than the compliance departments of banks, judging from the number of legit-looking criminal wires that got through. But the banks were getting smarter, he had to admit. Ever since 9/11. Then the Patriot Act. Then the new Anti-Money Laundering Act, the "AML," laws and regulations. It was starting to get annoying. It had the potential to seriously cut into profits, and worse, expose criminal activity.

Enter bitcoin. It had the potential to be far superior to using the Federal Reserve's system. There were literally no regulations. The "coin" was not the property of any country. It was not recognized by any government in the world. Yet real business and real commerce were consummated thousands of times every day on this exchange.

It is said that "nature abhors a vacuum." *Crime* despises it. Whether or not created for this purpose, bitcoin instantly became the international criminals' favorite method of transacting in illegal business. Similar to the way pornography was by far the greatest engine for advances in the internet, cryptocurrency is currently being perfected by profit from illicit yet undetectable transactions. Bitcoin is to cryptocurrency like porn was to the internet. Well, actually, porn still is the main driver and money-maker on the internet.

Far from perfect, bitcoin is king in the new international cryptocurrency game. It is yet to be determined what or who will be the next Google or Amazon of cryptocurrency to dethrone bitcoin and thrust it into obscurity, like Netscape and Yahoo. It may very well be Google or Amazon, for that matter. With the number of users in the billions, even Facebook is taking a run at cryptocurrency. The potential profits are simply too compelling to ignore.

But for now, bitcoin was entirely useful.

Chapter 32

"That completes our transaction, and now we can celebrate!" gushed Gui Rodrigues in Portuguese, to Amelia, cover name Maya Casanovo.

Maya, dark brown hair matching her flashing black eyes, answered in perfect Portuguese, "Only eight months since we first spoke, Gui," calling him by his nickname, pronounced "Gee" with the same hard g in "go," which he insisted Maya use.

As he walked through the doors of his penthouse office to the rooftop helipad, his waiting Eurocopter EC130 sat idling, blades motionless. About to board the luxuriously customized helicopter, which he liked to use for relatively short trips, Gui felt the giddy excitement in the pit of his stomach—the giddiness that accompanied another closed deal. This one brought his net worth to just over one billion American dollars. Not that he would ever tell anyone. He remembered his father's warning that his attorney gave him years ago. Anonymity is the key to keeping your wealth.

But today, even if only he knew, he finally belonged at the "cool" table, with the big boys, the movers and shakers, actual world-shapers. He made decisions that moved countries in a direction of his choosing and for his benefit. He could speak and move the stock market, for God's sake, if he so chose.

Gui smiled at Maya as they settled into their lux seats on the EC130. His mind was racing to what he planned to do with her when they arrived at his chalet in the vast national park in the southern corner of Brazil, in one of the last remaining coastal rainforests. His body was already giving it away. Perhaps she noticed it too. He hoped she did. It was nearly 4:30 p.m. in July, and nighttime still came early during this time of year in Brazil, but he had just enough time to get to their destination before darkness set in.

Power is the apex aphrodisiac, and for several years he didn't have to work at bringing out the wild tiger in any woman he wanted, and he wanted it now. Maya would be no different, despite the 25-year age gap.

Gui's chalet was just one of his many homes around the world, but one of his favorites in the western hemisphere. Built by his late father before the surrounding virgin Atlantic Forest became Guaricana National Park, the hidden gem on the mountainside was a few helicopter hours south from Sao Paulo. Isolated by thousands of acres of pristine forest on all sides, it could not fail to impress his new young guest. When Gui inherited his father's estate, he immediately began to remodel the remote hideaway. No expense had been spared. With two master bedroom suites with vaulted ceilings, private whirlpool spas, showers and baths, and four regular bedrooms, six other bathrooms, a private movie theater, a 10-foot-deep ornate blue-tiled infinity pool, and of course the helipad, it was extraordinary. The living room and kitchen were masterpieces of architecture and visual effect. With the hardwood beams soaring thirty feet high, separated by special non-glare, bullet proof glass, one felt as if they were literally inside the rainforest. Gui had a cloaking device installed inside the glass, in which one could see to the outside perfectly, but impossible for one to peer inside the home. The canopy of the trees completely obscured the home from above and below. Gui also had a tower installed that looked like a natural tree. Once at the top, the view was a sensational 360 degrees, with the coastline and ocean in full view 20 miles away. Their next three days together would be something close to perfection. He looked forward to fulfilling his most ambitious fantasies with this exquisite creature seated next to him.

Damn the fact there were two other men, his bodyguards, in the helicopter with them, one up front with the pilot and one in the back with him and Maya. Confirming his most adventurous amorous fantasy, Maya's eyes locked on his and she smiled, just enough to expose some of her flawless teeth, only accentuating her full red lips.

After just over an hour of flying, with Gui pointing out notable scenery, Maya leaned in to him and smiled.

Gui was a pro at reading people, especially women, and he knew that Maya Casanovo would soon be owned by him in a hundred more ways than the illegals were now owned by his contacts. He kept her eyes just long enough to set the hook in her, and then he chose to turn to his left and look out the window, continuing his vision of sexual fantasy. Quickly noticing the bodyguard was absorbed in his novel, Maya extracted a hidden retainer from her mouth, in a movement obscured with a slight cough.

Once the retainer was out, Maya immediately pierced its side with a hairpin that had been holding her hair in a bun. Instantly, a fast-acting nerve agent released into the passenger air cabin. Within seconds, the three other passengers scratched furiously at their noses and throats before slumping unconscious in their seats.

The pilot looked back and yelled, "What is going …?" before he, too began clawing at his nose and throat, inadvertently hitting the stick, causing the chopper to fly erratically. The flailing pilot's other hand hit the autopilot button on the HeliSAS panel, turning it off. Now they were in deep trouble. Simultaneously affording herself a half-second of relief that her nerve agent antidote had worked, Maya had already snapped open her seat belt to reach into the pilot's area, but was thrown against the limp, unconscious Gui. Instantly thrown against the opposite seat, she slammed her shoulder into the stomach and ribs of one of the unconscious bodyguards, that absorbed the impact for her but broke a few of his ribs. She would have to thank him for that, maybe in another life.

With autopilot off, the chopper continued banking sharply to the left and rapidly descending. The chopper's warning sirens were screaming. Maya knew she had mere seconds to get ahold of the cyclic stick if she had any hope to avoid a crash and certain death. Leveraging her feet into the seat and straining herself to the front, just before the chopper's banking was 90 degrees, Maya reached forward with all her strength and got hold of the cyclic, righting and then elevating the aircraft, with just 500 feet above the closest trees in the deep mountain forest below. As an expert in both roto-craft and fixed wing airplanes, Maya increased the chopper's elevation to just under 4,000 feet and hit the auto-pilot button, resuming their flight plan for what came next.

••••••••••••••••••••••••

Ironically, Gui's own obsessive due diligence made him the ideal takedown target for "Maya" and her ultra-covert organization. Nearly nine months earlier, as Us was monitoring all web traffic regarding human trafficking activity, particularly on the dark web, they were able to identify a significant spike in web search activity coming from South America. Suspecting this might indicate some major trafficking event, Us concentrated its highly sophisticated surveillance technology, which exceeded even America's ultra-sophisticated NSA technology, into revealing the source.

Combining the sophisticated technology and downright old-fashioned sleuthing, they were able to narrow the searches down to Sao Paulo, Brazil. Another week and they had uncovered the complicated ownership of the building in which Gui had his office. As they dug deeper still, they traced the actual computer to a company that listed Gui as its CEO. From there, they pieced together the life of this most interesting scion of a deceased councilman named Humberto "Tico" Rodrigues.

Apparently, Attorney Rangel had not been as thorough as he thought.

Gui was supremely confident that all the firewalls and protections he had on his laptops and phones would make him invisible to any hacker. After all, he had paid over a million American dollars for the most advanced firewalls and VPN, or Virtual Private Network, that existed on the planet.

What he couldn't be aware of, was that Us had recently conducted an ultra-secret operation in Bulgaria on a Soviet-sponsored hacker outfit, and had stolen a working copy of the world's most sophisticated hacking software, so far completely undetectable by even the most advanced global powers.

With that advantage, they were able to advance the profile of Maya Casanovo, embedding her in the South American human trafficking group, without that group even being aware. Given her native-like fluency in multiple languages, particularly Russian and Spanish, Maya became the primary negotiator for the South American trafficking group. Gui was the middleman between them and the Russians. However, Gui would only meet in person. He refused to speak over the phone or electronically. Fortunately for Lia and Us, the Russians and South American groups were not as disciplined. Unknown to either group was that Us had covertly hacked into the communication flow of the Bratva and the South American group.

On more than one occasion, this intel directly saved Lia's cover, and more to the point, her life. At the beginning of the operation, when Lia was first inserted as Maya Casanovo, Us intercepted a secure call made by Ramon, the Venezuelan colonel coordinating a load of human cargo being shipped to Iran.

The primary buyers of South American stock were from Iran, Belarus, and Russia. Seriously, they could not get enough of the product, and the younger the better. As was typical of the importers, the desired product mix was about 80 percent female. In the load leaving the next morning, there were nine boys under 12, the youngest being 9, and 41 girls, all 13 and younger, the youngest girl also 9.

To prove to the South American group she was the real deal from the source of the product, in Guyana, Ramon put a gun to her head and asked her for the exact number and makeup of the cargo. If she was who she claimed to be, an insider sent to facilitate all further product concerns, she would know the exact details of the shipment. If it hadn't been for the intercepted communication, Us would have lost one of their best ever field operatives, not to mention the daughter of the current leader, Rasha.

Chapter 33

In the true certain-death moment, your life flashes before your eyes. Time is relative. A second in time is a year in pure, unrestrained, uninterrupted total and complete brain engagement. It's a beautiful thing, those moments in the human mind. It is where reality meets eternity, where mankind meets his true self, and touches the finger of God.

It is therefore the most terrifying place to be in the universe, and why it can only last mere ticks on the clock. To extend this time would be to never return again sane. This is not to be confused with the often-abused insanity defense that shameless lawyers plead for truly evil clients accused of heinous crimes. Rather, this may be the "insane" person who refuses to acknowledge reality, and therefore cannot function or survive in human society anywhere on Earth. If they were not locked up and monitored twenty-four-seven, they would die.

But, as many have experienced, when their lives flashed before their eyes in a certain-death situation but they miraculously survived, sane, they marveled at how amazing that moment was. How incredibly detailed and vivid the memories, emotions and thoughts were. How many minute details in their lives had come into full high-definition color. The smell of a distinct perfume, the heat and humidity of the day, feeling hot and sweaty in this memory flash, then cold and shivering in the next.

Crystal clear. Clarity. Purity… Truth. Not just one memory was clear. Their entire life. Things that were unclear, didn't make sense, now were clear. Understanding the why. Knowing what you did, now knowing how to fix the brokenness. Of a relationship.

And then it's over. And it's been exactly three seconds.

For a split second more, Maya wondered how many temporary geniuses had perished in the final seconds before the Titanic sank below the liquid freezer of the ink-black Atlantic.

It had been said that under normal conditions, people use only 10 percent of the brain. The theory is, therefore, that if we could only figure out how to kick in the other 90 percent, the human race could achieve so much more. The higher the Intelligence Quotient, IQ, the larger percentage of brain is engaged. The geniuses in history, like Einstein, da Vinci, Michelangelo, Bell, Tesla, Algorithmi, Newton, Plato, Orville Wright, and others, perhaps accessed much more, like 20 or 30 percent of their brain.

At 100 percent, humans approach god-like awareness.

The discoveries these men made, all considered geniuses, and the changes they caused in human thought, profoundly and immediately advanced the human race in formerly unimaginable ways. The genius of these men and their discoveries bypassed and obliterated racial, religious and national boundaries. These were universal truths, oblivious to human divides.

The use of these discoveries started an avalanche of new thought and application to old ideas and methods. Like an avalanche, which often starts with the break and fall of one small rock or chunk of snow, cracked and loosed by the expansion of water as it turns to ice, and then melts again. It starts small and turns quickly into a monstrosity, engulfing and destroying everything in its wake as it recreates the landscape.

Old ideas, experts, leaders, whole institutions, even countries and governments, disappear as a new order is created. It is called Disruption.

World history is a study of disruption. Think of the Ice Age, Iron Age, the Renaissance, the Industrial Age, Atomic Age, and now the Information Age coinciding with the Technological Age.

Each of these ages was immediately preceded by a new and incredible human discovery. These discoveries came from one or just a few geniuses. Without exceptions, those in power, until recent history, were royals or dictators, decidedly not geniuses, just ruthless and violent men in their quest for and retention of power. They used the discoveries to exert their military might over less-informed nations. Wars were fought and won with newer, more powerful weapons, based on new applications of discoveries.

One blazing example in recent history is the controlled splitting of the tiny atom, the smallest particle known to exist on the planet. Used for peace, the atom can be harnessed and used to power entire cities without any pollution, keeping warm in winter and in cool air conditioning in the summer. Used for war, or terrorism, it can obliterate the same cities and all who live there in a split second, scarring, searing and poisoning the unfortunate land for many decades.

Had the USA and Allies paused in their furious march to Berlin at the end of World War II, even when Nazi defeat was by all military accounts inevitable, the victory could have evaporated into crushing and horrific defeat. As was feared by the US War Department, Nazi physicists could not have been far from perfecting an atom bomb, fully capable of destroying the entire advancing Allied militaries.

Truly chilling were the discovered Nazi plans to use the new bomb on London and other Allied cities simultaneously with destroying the Allied militaries.

Upon being fully apprised of the most guarded secret in US history, the Manhattan Project, and the suspected fact that the Nazis could not be too far behind, President Roosevelt ordered nothing less than immediate and unrelenting advance and defeat of the Nazis, including the complete destruction of Berlin and other major German cities. He just hoped and prayed that he would disrupt the last potential Nazi threat; that some of Hitler's newest bombs would hit the Allies' final advance on Berlin.

How ironic for the Nazis that their defeat was sealed in part by the very person Nazi policies forced to flee Europe, one who, mere years before, was a German citizen. The genius, Albert Einstein, the Jew. Without his urgent letter to President Roosevelt to beat Germany in developing a nuclear bomb, the world be a much different place right now. Also ironic is that the leader of the Manhattan Project, the brilliant American physicist, Dr. J. Robert Oppenheimer, was Jewish, and had obtained his PhD in Germany.

Einstein arranged for his brain to be donated for scientific study. Curiously, his brain was found to be no different than any other normal, healthy human brain. The leading neurologists, before and after Einstein's death, could not show any significant differences between his brain and that of any other person.

When asked why he was so much smarter than other people, all Einstein could come up with was that he "just spent more time on a problem than others." In other words, Focus. Einstein and the other geniuses had incredible focus, and thereby changed the world. In some cases, they even saved the world.

The Manhattan Project's research, analysis, successes, failures, progress, setbacks, and delays all took place over many months and into years, and countless hours, in a remote, isolated compound in New Mexico. There is no doubt their brains were focused as much as humanly possible.

Elite athletes describe it as being "in the Zone." After years of practice, conditioning, fighting through fatigue, boredom, repetition, strength training, drills, injury, bad coaching, bad teammates, it happens. One day, everything comes together for them. A big game is on the line. Everything clicks.

Outside of the game, the play, the point, the ball, and the move, there is nothing. You are aware of nothing else. The crowd, the noise, the yelling, barely registers on your consciousness. You see everything better. All things, opponents and the ball seem to go more slowly than normal. You seem to be faster than usual. You're making plays, getting impossible shots, making impossible blocks, tackles, catches, throws. It seems so easy for you, although to everyone else it is nothing short of amazing. You are in "the Zone." You have just hit a new level in your performance, and you are feeling it bigtime.

Until the next game. And you can't even catch a ball hitting both hands, or make an elementary block or tackle, or throw, or dig. What happened to you?

You are clearly not in the Zone. The amazing heights you just had last week seem like a made-up story, or a dream fantasy, or maybe it was someone else entirely.

It happens in every human endeavor.

But when you're in the Zone, whether you are a scientist, athlete, surgeon, lawyer, software engineer or soldier, there is no place like it. It is so good, and at the same time seems so normal yet terrifying on a certain level. It is now the place we long for. Where we know we should be, can be, want to be.

But there is a place even higher than the Zone. Even better. More clarity, more certainty. Compared with those fleeting seconds between life and certain death, as good as it is, being in the Zone is like just waking up from a deep, fuzzy sleep, with the senses as dull as a butter knife. It is so rare, there is no name for it.

Amelia—Maya—and her group called it "Zeno." Short for Zenith, and easier to say.

When the brain knows all bets are off, the end is here and this is it, it throws all caution to the wind and releases a near-fatal dose of adrenalin and dopamine into itself. It's like the fight or flight response, only a hundred times stronger. It is the brain's final attempt at survival.

The trouble is, with mankind's vast and incredible advances in technology and machinery, the likelihood of fatality in these moments nowadays is extremely high, like 99 percent. Why? Trains, planes and automobiles, frankly. That's where the vast majority of these moments occur in modern times. But there are survivors who attempt to describe it. Their stories are sometimes so fantastical, they are just not believed. But they are very real.

Why haven't scientists discovered the exact dosages and combinations of enzymes and hormones the brain releases at this moment? It is safe to say that people who experience this phenomenon were not prepared with the proper equipment and monitors to detect and measure the precise components and the timing of their release. It is also safe to assume that these same people are not too willing to repeat this situation under clinical conditions; that is, to be scared to death, literally, is not a voluntary thing.

Roller coasters, parachute jumps, bungee jumping, or any other similar thrilling activity does not even come close to fooling the brain. Apparently, voluntary death-defying thrills may cause extreme fear and great discomfort, but the acknowledgement of near-certain death? The human mind can differentiate between the real event, and fake news. Now if there were a malfunction, like a mechanical or equipment failure, then the event would trigger the response. Why? Because it is real, and the brain knows it.

Another good question is: Why can't the military conduct these experiments on their servicemembers? Sadly, they have tried, with disastrous results. Some "volunteers" have literally died being frightened so badly. Even then, the results were inconclusive at best.

The cover-ups of these failed experiments were awkward and potentially career-ending, or worse, outright crimes, implicating powerful and connected people. So, the testing abruptly stopped. All reports were buried in the most top-secret vaults in existence.

Technology was simply not advanced enough to justify the risks. Not the risk to the volunteers, of course, but to the powerful. Enlisted men were by no means scarce. Before they were even approached, the soldier's record and history would be thoroughly scrutinized. Any soldier with important persons in his record was immediately excluded. The ideal soldier was single, no ties, and a true nobody. No rich or important people in their family, if they even had family. As every civilization known to mankind has proven, it is not the little people, the poor or powerless anyone cares about, it's only the rich and powerful who care about themselves.

But that was about to change, and Maya and Us would be the catalyst.

At least in terms of human trafficking.

Chapter 34

Now flying smoothly at 4,000 feet, Maya quickly located the parachutes Gui had stowed under their seats in the EC130. Although Gui had tried to convince Maya that the Eurocopter's auto-rotator function in the event of an engine failure was better and safer than any parachute, Maya had refused to fly in Gui's chopper without two. She'd tearfully convinced him of her fear of flying in helicopters, and flatly refused to board before two chutes were stowed in the cabin under the seats. Gui never imagined how Maya intended to use the chutes. He'd nodded to his two bodyguards, thinking, "If this is the only way to get her to my chalet, then so be it."

Before strapping on the chutes, Maya had a little operation to perform. She reached over and took the knife out of the security guard's leg-sheath, then grabbed Gui's limp right hand, and cut the tip of his pinky finger off at the first knuckle. She stabbed the severed finger with the knife like it was a chicken leg wing and stuffed it into the seat. Then she opened the fully stocked emergency kit and used WoundSeal, bandages and tape to tightly wrap Gui's fresh wound. He didn't even stir.

With no time to waste, she then strapped the first parachute on Gui, and used the second chute to strap around her and click onto the O-rings on Gui's chute, preparing for a tandem jump. It was far from the perfect setup for a tandem jump, she knew, but it would have to do. She quickly but meticulously checked all her straps and cords, seeing they were secure, then opened the door of the cabin and pulled, straining with the immense task of moving an unconscious 180-pound man and herself into a ready position. Hanging both his legs out and then hers out of the chopper door, it looked absurd at best, and was incredibly awkward. Lastly, she leaned back, straining and reaching around the pilot, with just enough reach to push the autopilot button to "Off." Without autopilot, and an unconscious pilot, in less than 20 seconds the EC130 would begin a death-spiral that would end in a violent crash into the jungle below.

Turning back and grabbing the sides of the open cabin door, with one more big pull, they both fell out. Gui first and Maya stuck to his back. As Maya wrapped her legs around Gui as an extra precaution, she counted off "one thousand one," and pulled her ripcord, praying it would deploy. In another 500 feet of freefall, the chute opened, and she gained control of the descent, making it a fast but smooth ride down.

The unconscious Gui would never know that one of his fantasies had just come true. The beautiful Maya had her very strong, sexy legs wrapped tightly around him, holding him in perfect position. It was just as well he didn't know, since that was probably not the way he envisioned it anyway.

She was not at all remorseful about the three in the chopper. They were willing participants in human trafficking, conscripting thousands of innocent women and children, and some men, into slavery. Most men were simply killed. They were too risky and hard to control. With less than half of the nearly 1,000 pounds of fuel consumed, she knew the ensuing, fiery crash would obliterate the chopper and incinerate most of the human remains inside.

However, as a precaution, Maya, that is, Amelia, had been able to plant enough DNA of Maya Casanovo and now Gui's pinky finger that it would appear all five were killed in the crash. For now, that would suit her purpose.

As Amelia and Gui glided to the forest and swamp below in the Mandira Extractive Reserve, an hour north (by helicopter) of Gui's chalet in the Guaricana National Park, she reached over and pressed all three of the buttons on her watch, activating a secure beacon. Rob and his extraction team would be on their way to take her and her captive to the fishing trawler, just outside the Brazilian national boundary.

Once there, Gui would tell who and where all his filthy contacts were, and her group "Us" could then systematically go after them. He would have no choice. He was not a trained soldier or spy. He was just a very rich, spoiled, greedy person who up until now, had always gotten his way. She wondered just how high up this would lead Us into the realms of the Earth's power elite. Like most things in life, it would not be what was expected.

Now at 2,500 feet and closing, Lia expertly guided herself and her unconscious baggage to the forest floor below. As she glided lower, she reached behind her head, grabbing her beautiful brown hair, pulling off the wig that had hidden her long blond hair, now flowing in the wind like a national flag. The dark brown contacts covering her luminous, hazel-green tiger's eyes could stay until she was picked up by her extraction team, who was now tracking her descent to the forest floor, less than 2,000 feet below.

With Gui's "help," the Us organization was going to create a serious dent in the wheels of the worldwide human trafficking machine.

It just remained to be seen how outsiders, like Interpol, would also play a role in their war on trafficking. Once the strongman is dealt with, mistakes and blunders are made and an organization begins to crumble. When that happens, the local police are able to pick up the obvious signals of illegal activity. They may even stumble upon an active trafficking operation, if properly tipped off.

Lia and her group would provide anonymous tips at opportune times, thanks to the information that Gui would tell them, whether he wanted to or not. In a twist of fate that would surprise even the most ardent believer in karma, Gui would become, with his amazing wealth, with hundreds of millions squirreled away in numbered Swiss bank accounts, the world's largest private supporter of the fight against human trafficking.

Much was in store for Gui. In the final seconds before their landing in the dense Brazilian forest, Lia couldn't help but smile at her unconscious captive, and his amazing future life of doing good, whether he liked it or not.

Chapter 35

She then flashed back to meeting Rob, whom she hadn't seen in the last three months of the operation. She knew there was something there, between them. In the last seconds before landing, her mind still had time to process things. From the time she got on the chopper with Gui, her mind had been firmly in Zeno-zone. It had been less than 60 minutes since they took off from the rooftop of Gui's office building, 30 stories high.

In Zeno, with her mind working as fast as the speed of light, the last seconds stretched out as if time stood still. She reflected on their first meeting in her home village in Switzerland. Rob's story checked out. He was a distant relative, the great grandson of her own great grandmother's sister. Lia knew they were several generations past any marriage taboos, even though they really were cousins.

Lia thought Rob was obviously adjusting well to his new adventure. As the only male ever allowed into an Us operation, he was keenly aware of the new purpose in his life. Clearly jaded by his experience in Syria and Afghanistan, he was finished with his life as a soldier. He knew too well how politics would hijack *doing the right thing* so many times it was nearly a given.

Lia remembered well how Rob's whole persona began to change as her mother, Rasha, confirmed Rob's grandmother's stories. Rob was spellbound by all the other stories and operations the group had accomplished over the years. When Rasha showed him the files of operations, with worldwide headlines, video clips, and operative facts that could be known only by those actually in the operations, Rob was astounded.

Lia smiled thinking about when Rob said he "had to be a part of this." Of course, that was exactly what Rasha and the group wanted. Rob's experience as an Army Ranger, with his demonstrated acts of bravery and leadership under fire, could be very useful to the group, particularly the operation, code named "Freedom Sword," to apprehend Gui.

The fact that Rob was actually a relative of theirs, who was in Europe trying to find them, was truly providential and a big part of the decision. Actually, had it not been for the relative part, Lia was certain he never would have been invited in.

As for any feelings she may or may not have for Rob, that would have to be put on hold for now. They still had to get Gui out of the country.

Seconds later, she and her human cargo made a bumpy but surprisingly safe landing through the trees and onto the forest floor of a remote part of the Sebui Ecological Reserve, in the neighboring state of Parana. Gui would be unconscious for at least another hour, giving her plenty of time to securely bind, blindfold and gag him.

Rob's logistical and technical expertise, particularly from his epic last mission as a Ranger, proved invaluable. From the moment he became a part of Us, he began devising the extraction plan. He was beyond awed when the capabilities of the Us command center were revealed to him in real time. Once he saw the planning and intelligence power of their systems, he started to believe that Us could achieve some real success in their mission, or any mission they chose. As the power and reach of their surveillance became more and more evident, even into global military operations, Rob had a distinct jarring moment of clarity and a realization. He looked around at the Us group, his eyes misting up with emotion, and thanked God, or Providence, or whatever, that this power was in the hands of Us, to use against Evil, instead of the other way around.

Lia, who had been watching him closely from the moment her parents, Rasha and Peiter, introduced them, far below their little chocolate shop in Zermatt, was the first to notice. She had been the most skeptical about bringing Rob in, exposing their 80-year-old family secret, their well-oiled evil-fighting machine, to an outsider, even if he was "family." Even after she read every word of his dossier, she was still troubled.

First of all, he was a *man*. Us did not have *men* inside. Husbands were only in an advisory role, if that. This caused inconvenience, to be sure. Particularly in the all-important technology roles. Unfortunately, more boys than girls were drawn to the highly technical side of software and code-writing. Boys were the overwhelming majority of video-gamers on the planet. Boys could turn into older males, in their twenties and beyond, and the only real relationships they had were online with other gamers. Girls just weren't made for that. They needed real, personal relationships to survive.

Fortunately, there were some girls who didn't fit the pattern. They were exceptions to the stereotypical girl-aversion to software and code creation. They tended to be on the cutting edge of the smartest code writers, some clearly so. Probably because they still possessed the female need to have real relationships. No, they were not "normal," like other girls. Being extreme "geeks" meant they eschewed the girly girl things, for the most part. Much of that was purely cultural or perhaps slight personality disorder type stuff, like assertion of a female pecking order. The geek-girls did not need that. They would never even notice it, unless it was occasionally directed at them in a mocking sort of way. Us was adept at finding these girls and creating an opportunity for them beyond any other they could imagine.

When he was awarded his professorship, Peiter's role in Us took on a very important component. Through Peiter's contacts at the University, the technology professors often spoke of their exceptional students. Peiter's company, run by Rasha, would eventually interview them for a position in his economic research firm, Walther Global Economics, LLP. The firm provided white papers on global trends, macro and micro, and Peiter spoke at important conferences, like the annual conferences in nearby Davos, Switzerland and Jackson Hole, Wyoming.

At 62, Peiter was amazingly still young enough, expert enough, and most importantly, daring enough to include a few tries down Jackson Hole's Corbet's Couloir, but only if there was ample fresh powder. Known for its initial 30-meter drop-off, it was the most difficult in-bounds run in North America, and certainly in the top five worldwide. Even for Peiter, a former ski racer from Zermatt, the run was a great challenge.

If the new hires in her husband's financial firm showed real promise, Rasha would begin the process of assessing their likelihood of making a successful transition into the world of Us, just like her mother and grandmother had done. It had to be one of the most highly selective and exclusive jobs on the planet. Only seven such girls had ever been selected to join Us. Six were still working for Us. Only one had 'retired' from the technology aspect of the business, some 30 years earlier. She and her husband, however, were still around. They were the cute older Swiss couple who managed the chocolate store far above them. The husband managed the chocolate shop, but the wife still helped with Us, having grown into several more specialized roles.

Lia reserved the term "men" for those boys who had grown up, gotten off their special game-console chairs and elaborate joysticks, and could actually have an interesting, face-to-face conversation for more than five minutes. Oh, and they didn't live with or off their parents. Not that she was looking for any relationship now anyway.

She was doing exactly what she had always wanted, and didn't see that changing anytime soon.

Then Rob appeared. He clearly was an elite warrior. He was brave, decisive, and battle-tested. Not to mention fearless. Without being prideful, she had to admit he was a lot like her. With those qualities at least. He of course did not have the covert training, or language skills like her (although he was marginally conversant in Arabic and Pashto, from his Ranger training), but not many did. Maybe there was a strain of mettle that ran through the bloodline that both she and Rob inherited, where others didn't. It was hard to imagine that was possible, given that they were about as closely related as she was to any other German man outside her family tree.

"Rob, are you ok?" Lia asked. Rob blinked quickly, nodding his head and smiling, looking down. Peiter and Rasha both looked up and stopped what they were doing, and looked at Rob.

"Yeah. Yes, I'm fine," Rob answered, now looking up at Lia. Standing up and facing her directly, but far from confrontationally, he said, "Yeah. I just can't believe it's all true, is all. That you guys exist. That you have all this," he said, opening his hand, motioning at the computers, flat-screen monitors, and the underground cathedral they were in. "Most of all, that you're fighting bad shit, excuse me," he smiled, "I mean 'evil'. It all just hit me for a second. I mean, it's awesome. And now I'm part of it. Have to admit, it made me wish I could tell my Grandmom. I have a feeling she'd be pretty shocked it was all true, too," he finished.

"I can imagine your surprise, Rob." Lia smiled, pausing for just a beat. "But we still have a lot of work to do so this will not become our last mission, you know?" The last part was not sharp or unfeeling, but just enough steel to ease Rob out of any overt nostalgic feelings.

Rob immediately snapped back to the mission. "Right. Got it," he noted, turning his head to his notepad. "Ok. We can pull all these sites and study them. We need likely extraction routes and possible equipment needs. Lia, we need to do some parachute training. We need a helicopter simulator to plan a tandem jump, and for you to hone your helicopter skills, specifically on this bastard's chopper." Rob was referring to Gui and his EC130 chopper. "When was the last time you parachuted?" he asked Lia.

For the next week, they pored over the terrain maps around Sao Paulo and Rio de Janeiro. They didn't know in which city this whole deal would go down. They had a ton of planning to do, including how best to meet up with Lia, who would be in deep cover. There also was the parachute training.

Rob played the part of an unconscious person whom Lia would have to eventually harness to herself. It was serious business, but certainly not boring. Rob typically didn't get bored around beautiful women, and Lia was no doubt one of the prettiest he'd ever met. That is, as in pretty damn smart, pretty damn tough, and yes, pretty damn gorgeous. He actually had the thought that he wouldn't want to ever fight her and find out she could kick his ass, with one hand tied behind her back. But there was something else, too. He just couldn't put his finger on it.

It was too much to do in one week, especially the parachute training. But that was all they had. Lia had to return to Colombia, to rejoin her group before they became suspicious of her absence. She had the perfect cover, and Us continued its communications surveillance, and nothing had been said, either electronically or by voice communications that would make them think Lia's cover was being questioned. But still, they knew she had to get back. Face-to-face ops were the only way.

Over the next week, using GPS positioning and mapping, Rob and Us had meticulously studied each and every possible point on which Lia could land. From each point, he constructed detailed extraction plans, listing the equipment needs, including sea, air and land machines needed. Rob was a Ranger, not a SEAL, but being the student of warfare that he was, he had made good use of his downtime on all his missions, continuing his own training by himself, using the many resources the military made available in their training manuals and videos on military websites. Aside from this mission, Rob knew this extra training had saved his life on more than one occasion.

Rob and a small group from Us would be landing nearby from their wing suited, parachute drop from 20,000 feet, homing in on Lia's transmitter. Securing the now-conscious Gui between Rob and Lia, they would hike out to the Mar Pequeño, Small Sea, actually a massive river leading out to the Atlantic Ocean for a waiting military spec Zodiac F470® inflatable. Using darkness as a cover, and electronic interference on the satellite far overhead, they would take a fast boat-ride to the waiting trawler, just outside the international boundary. Immediately after boarding, they would start the slow transatlantic voyage home.

In between getting to know everything that Gui wanted or didn't want to tell them—it didn't matter which—about the trafficking network alliance, Lia and Rob would have a chance to get better acquainted.

Lia was ambivalent for now, not investing her emotions either way. She didn't know where Rob's head was, or if he was even interested.

Rob knew one thing for certain. He had never met a girl like Lia. Not even in his dreams.

Chapter 36

Unknown to Gui or the South American-Russian Alliance, the two trafficking cartels were in for a few more surprises besides Gui's "death." The moment Lia activated her tracking device when she boarded Gui's helicopter, a number of events were immediately triggered. An anonymous tip was phoned in to Homeland Security and the FBI. Precise descriptions and locations were provided of ships due to dock in the next 10 to 12 days in their respective ports. Each of these ships contained secret holding areas filled with human cargo. All were women and girls from 16 to 21 years old. Each holding area had guards and older women in their forties and fifties to keep the girls comfortable. Some of the girls were actually excited about beginning their new lives. Their naïve belief in their recruiters' lies was soon to be mercilessly crushed.

They had no idea they were about to be separated and groomed for the big event next year, the Super Bowl in Tampa, 2021. The deals for the "product" had been struck long in advance, on the private jets in face-to-face meetings. These girls were going to fill the best positions. Their useful work-life was three to four years at the elite levels. After that, they would be sold to local rings, or pimps, for the highest dollar. Or, they would be shipped back to where they came from. Or, they would just disappear, like so many before them.

But not these girls.

They were going to be the lucky ones. American law enforcement, even with its own corruption to deal with, was a hundred times cleaner than any country south of the border. Sadly, that was why the port police in Callao, Peru or Odessa, Ukraine could not be notified. Faced with rampant bribery and official corruption in South and Central American ports, or any Balkan nation's ports, a tip-off there would almost certainly result in the perpetrators' escape, or the victims' disappearance, only to reappear somewhere else, undetected this time.

Upon arrival at the American ports, these girls would be rescued and taken to a warehouse near the respective ports, set up to receive and process the victims, providing any needed medical attention, food and clothing. There, these frightened girls would be informed of the real intent of their supposed benefactors. The shock to some of the girls would cause them to be physically sick. From the warehouse, the girls would be assigned to secured women's shelters. The shelters understood that the girls would be severely emotionally traumatized by the information. They would have psychologists to help the girls come to grips with how close they came to a life they would never have chosen. Where they would literally become someone else's property.

In time, most of the women and girls would be returned to their own countries. The shelters did not want to simply dump the girls in their own country with no assistance, however. In many cases, the shelters had sister shelters in the home country. These NGOs, Non-Governmental Organizations, would do their best to ensure the girls would not again fall victim to the despicable traffickers. These girls, as traumatic as it was, were getting off easy.

These were the shipments made by the South American group.

The Russian shipments, sourced from the Ukraine and the Balkans, destined for the same event in 2021 in Tampa, were not so lucky. The Bratva, the Russian Mafia's worst international crime organization, had a different way of doing things than the rest of the criminal world. Unlike the way Vlad and his group did things 20 years earlier when they bought The Red Velvet near Coney Island, the pigs had evolved and were using different methods. Actually, evolving typically involves a movement upward, like to a more resilient, or smart adaptation of a species. With the Bratva, it was a rapid decline into brutality, coldly efficient and amoral.

Instead of surprising their recruits once they arrived on the shores of the Land of Opportunity, America, with the news that they were now either strippers or escorts, they started the process much earlier. The poor Ukrainian and former Soviet Bloc recruits would arrive at the holding areas, or staging centers in the port of Odessa, Ukraine. They would think this was the first stop on their way to their new and hopeful lives.

Then the Working Unit men, comprised of lower-level Bratva thugs, would methodically begin "breaking in" the girls, like they were captured animals. By the time they got to their new "homes" in the States, they would have no fight left in them. They would get right to work for their new masters. They would even be ready for the Superbowl in Miami in 2020.

For this group, the initial destination from Odessa, Ukraine, was to the Port of Callao, Peru. Due to the new Alliance, the united traffickers had enough cash and contacts to bribe the local port officials, politicians, and police into a dream arrangement, even by Russian standards.

Each month a different dedicated berth would be made available for the exclusive use of any designated Alliance cargo vessel. This berth had a special inspection police force that would certify all cargo without question. The Alliance negotiators claimed all goods were of course legal. They also supplied the necessary cash to convince the officials of their honest intent. In fact, no searches would actually be made by this special inspection force. Only official government documents would be issued. Ignorance of any crimes would guard the consciences of the bribe-takers, in case they had one.

The bribe amounts were on a level of Oderhoffen magnitude; into the millions.

From there, it was a 10-day voyage to the Port of New York and New Jersey, which was not all that far from the Bratva's base in Brooklyn. The anonymous tip to Homeland Security included all the intel for these ships, too. They and the FBI were ready when the ship came in.

The Bratva hated it when they lost a shipment, which was highly irregular. Someone would pay for this, in blood. Their family's blood, too.

The girls, however, had already paid a high price. In their current state, they were emotionally and physically broken. The secured women's shelters in Newark for trafficking victims would be working overtime to help these women regain themselves. This European group would face great difficulties. Going home to their countries would probably not be an option, for safety's sake. Most would now need to file for asylum in the US. This would take a battery of volunteer attorneys and a great deal of time.

But they were still lucky. Even in their broken state, they were rescued and removed from a life none had imagined even in their darkest nightmares. They still had a chance at a real life. Also, there were charitable-minded lawyers who would take asylum cases like these for nothing more than donations, if anything.

Some of the bad guys would even be caught at this time. The challenge to Us was to keep following the crumbs to the top of the food chain. That was the sweet spot for Us. Where that would lead and to whom, Us didn't know. Or care. Us could go where no government could. All would pay a similar, dear price. Perhaps word would get out in the trafficking underworld that their kind was finally paying the piper for their crimes.

Rob was all in. He finally had a cause that he could really be proud of. Even if nobody knew except Us. Of course, Lia had already beaten him to it. In fact, she had been born into it. But she did have a choice. Her mother had not forced or manipulated her into this life. That would never have worked in the long run, for Lia or Us. Lia had taken to all the training, physical and educational, better and more naturally than even her own mother, Rasha.

At 16, Lia's physical stamina, coordination and fighting skills had been beyond amazing. She was a second-degree blackbelt in four martial arts disciplines, and an expert marksman in handguns and small arms. She simply loved every bit of it. She had never done this for the glory. Most importantly, Lia possessed the key ingredient, without which all the other accomplishments were nice, but useless.

She had the killer instinct.

Us was ignited and moving like the Swiss Chocolate Train of Montreux in their covert war against human traffickers. Only there was nothing sweet about it if you were a trafficker, and you'd never suspect that Us was run by the most highly trained and skilled women assassins on the planet. With the new addition of one very special man, that is.

Chapter 37

The mission was over. At least for Lia and Rob, that is. After nearly a year undercover, Lia had dealt with the entire spectrum of characters, mostly men. From the most evil, cold, dead-eyed killers to the smoothest, richest playboys, she had seen it all. In a world this dark, men were not the only inhabitants. Women walked and operated in this shadowland as well. But only one human trafficking ring in the world was led by a woman; a plump, raven-haired Mexican, twice as ruthless as any male leader. But Lia did not cross paths with her in this mission.

She was dealing directly with the South Americans, and with Gui's unknowing help, the Russian Bratva. The South Americans were a craven group. Ironically though, they were quite religious. Like the Italian Mafia, they were Catholics. They were also Santeria; an animal-sacrificing offshoot of Catholicism mixed in with some Caribbean Voodoo, which rounded out their whole spiritual experience. Inside their twisted religious rituals and beliefs, they were able to find justification and acceptance for any depraved actions necessary to carry out their nefarious trade in humans, for whatever purpose, devoid of conscience.

The relief that Lia was feeling on this warm, subtropical evening could not be exaggerated. All the planning, the surveillance, the intelligence-gathering, the timing, the dual life she had to lead, was over. At least for this part of the mission. Among the many twists and turns of the mission, that Rob had basically dropped from the sky and become an integral part of the mission was completely unexpected. His entire package of competence, core skills, bravery and tactical warfare skills added an element to Us they didn't even realize was missing. Not only did they share ancestors, however remotely, but they shared a purpose, a meaning, a desire to dedicate their lives to attacking and destroying evil, wherever on the planet it arose.

And he was hot. Very hot. For a moment, in her mind, she thought she should say he was very attractive. Manly. Strong. Protector. A knight. All those were true, but those descriptors didn't do justice to how she *felt.* She was just slightly afraid, a feeling she had rarely felt in her entire life, that she was falling for him. That her heart was giving itself away in inches. In reality, they had not dated, *per se.* There were no candlelit dinners, with wine flowing, silly stories, easy laughter, whispered nothings. Hell, they were in the middle of a high-stakes global mission against two cartels engaged in one of the most illegal and dangerous trades on the planet, with the real possibility that one or both of them would not live to tell about it.

But it was in the off-moments in training, planning, detailing and outfitting when Lia would look up and catch Rob looking at her, then he would smile quickly and get back to his business. After the first time, she would meet his gaze for a moment and smile back.

Once, when they were eating a meal together, Rob asked, "Are you planning to do this forever?"

"What do you mean?" she answered a little defensively.

"I mean, dontcha wanna have kids someday? Raise a family? Go on vacations?"

"Well, that implies I have someone to do that with. The kid part, anyway," she quipped. "And I can't think of anyone for that right now."

Rob tossed his head back and gave a good laugh.

"Is that so? Well, you never know how things will work out, huh? Who knows? It may just be someone you've already met!"

That exchange had happened just before Lia left to go back undercover, two months ago.

Girls, women, however, do nothing without collaboration. Discussion. Debate. Argument. Endless scenarios. Multiple speculations of motives, meanings, intent. Contradictory conclusions abound, based upon multi-layered possibilities. Particularly regarding the opposite sex. Or more accurately, especially regarding a potential suitor.

The only thing is, they can't talk to the man about this. Not ever. They don't want to tip their hand, expose their feelings, their thoughts, their fears. To do this before a man's heart is in their hands to do with what they like, is catastrophic. For a woman, the worst nightmare is not fear of missing out, known as "FOMO," it is fear of chasing away, or "FOCHA." They may not even like the guy, but they sure don't want to chase him away before they know that.

Oddly enough, this uniquely female trait is one reason women make such good spies. They think through *everything*. In just about every case, the operation fits precisely into one of the scenarios that had been exhaustively debated. The problem was, however, in failed missions, it was not the scenario for which they planned. Even then, with such a highly skilled operative like Lia, a mission could succeed on the sheer improvisation skill and quick thinking she possessed. It was like she was a cat with nine lives.

Unbeknownst to Rob, every little exchange with Lia, every look, every smile, every blush, every touch, no matter how insignificant to him, was analyzed, debated, evaluated and judged by Lia and Rasha, with Peiter listening in occasionally, until he could take it no longer and had to move to another room.

It was concluded that this long boat ride home would answer many questions regarding Rob: what kind of man is he? Is he decisive? Is he romantic? Is he even into women? Is he just a good friend and trusted new member of Us? Is he interested in Lia, *in that way?* Can he handle a woman like Lia? Is he afraid of her? Is he intimidated by how amazing she is?

With so many unanswered questions, Lia and her mother decided one thing. If Rob didn't make a move, a decisive move, on Lia on this boat ride home, then he clearly was not the right one for her, and they would just forget about him and move on.

....

That evening, dinner was to be served at six p.m. sharp. It was not too elaborate, but it was a splendid, at-sea dinner. The fare was choice Kobe *petit filet mignon*, Maine lobster with melted butter, scalloped potatoes *au gratin*, and a wedge of iceberg lettuce with cut tomatoes and warm blue-cheese dressing. Fine Italian wines were served along with Fuji water, and dessert was a decadent triple-layer dark chocolate cake with chocolate frosting.

The conversation was excited and congratulatory. It had been a highly sophisticated and difficult mission, and was very successful. Us had taken no casualties, and their new best friend Gui, under close guard, was singing like a bird freed from a cage. But Gui was quite literally in a cage, in one of the holds two floors below the main deck. From Gui's rich confessions, Us was in the process of charting out the names and businesses, and some governments and government officials, making up the vast global chain of command in human trafficking in the two cartels involved in this operation.

Lia was toasted the most. Peiter explained some details of her undercover work that Rob had not yet been privy to. It blew him away how talented a field operator she was.

Peiter and Rasha were the first to push away from the table, followed immediately by the older couple, Gerty and Hans. Hans retired to his cabin, and Gerty spent a bit more time making Gui feel uncomfortable and highly motivated to cooperate. She showed Gui the charts of his entire empire, and how Us could systematically destroy his wealth. Gui had not met Peiter, Rasha, Lia nor Rob. He only knew Lia's cover, Maya.

All the interrogating would be done by little ole Gerty. After Gerty's retirement from field operations, she conducted all interrogations, very effectively extracting information from both cooperating and non-cooperating subjects. To be across the table from Gerty, one had to be a very special person, but for all the wrong reasons. One thing could be assured: it would not be high tea. The other thing was that Gerty would get what she needed. It was just a matter of time.

All in the pursuit of peace. Peace for innocent people, though assuredly not for the subjects of the interrogation. They were not sadists by any stretch. They were experts in logic, manipulation, and the judicious application of chemicals that had never failed to convert a reluctant subject into a wholehearted corroborator.

Rob and Lia were left at the table. Lia got up first. She reached her arms out in front of her and stretched.

"My God, that was good! But it has made me pretty tired. I think I'm going to call it a day."

Rob got up. "How about we take a little walk around the deck? Get a little fresh air."

Lia paused just long enough. "Well, ok. A little fresh air wouldn't hurt, especially after that dessert," she said, smiling.

"And I don't think the owners will care if I take this here bottle of Italian grape juice with us, will they? And a couple glasses maybe?" Rob really wasn't asking, as he smiled and grabbed a nearly full bottle of *pinot grigio* and two wine glasses.

It was a calm and balmy night on the open ocean. They were underway at about 33 effortless knots with flat seas, making for an ultra-smooth sail. The moon was cut just under half, allowing the stars to shine their glory as well. The deck had enough light for them to easily see where they were going. No one else was in sight. If ever there was a romantic setting, this was it. Cutting through the still, night air at the ship's speed did make it a little chilly. Rob was about to look for a cabin door to escape the breeze, but the ideal solution caught his eye.

"Ahhhh," said Rob, touching her shoulder and pointing. "Look at that. A nice couch, just up ahead. Maybe we could rest from our strenuous walk up there."

"Oh yes, I can barely take another step," laughed Lia.

When they sat down, Rob didn't ask, he just poured a glass of wine. The couch was indented into the ship's structure, shielded from the direct breeze. It was perfect.

"Here you go." He smiled and handed the glass to her. She smiled and took it. Rob tore his eyes away from her smile.

"One for you, and one for me," he said, pouring himself a glass.

Raising his glass to Lia, Rob said, "Here's to another successful mission, by the great Us, and its extraordinary women, present company very much included."

"And its extraordinary men, present company very much included," said Lia.

They clinked their glasses, sipped from them, and set them down. They were both still looking at each other. Neither broke the other's gaze. Like iron to a magnet, Rob moved toward Lia, resisting but not resisting. Just feeling the pull. Lia was feeling it too, leaning forward as Rob reached up his left hand to her cheek, then to the back of her head, running his hands through her long blond hair, pulling her close as their lips met, now eyes closed, taking each other in their arms as the kiss continued, soft at first but then more intense. After another moment, they slowly released, pulling back, opening their eyes, each looking intently at the other.

"Damn!" Rob whispered. "That was by far the most awesome kiss I have ever had!" He smiled widely.

Lia, herself feeling it from head to toe and especially everywhere it mattered, grinned back at him.

"You're a pretty good kisser, Sergeant Russell."

"Just pretty good?" he joked back with mock hurt.

"Well," she paused and looked down, "I may need more samples," she said, looking up at him, lips parted slightly.

"Anything you say, ma'am," he said as he took her face in his hands, pulling her to his waiting lips.

Time stood still. It seemed like they kissed forever. They both took in this moment and didn't want it to end. It would have gone on much longer than the last 20 minutes had it not been for the crew member making a quick walk around the deck, slowing down then quickly passing by without stopping.

"I have to go, Rob."

"I don't want you to go."

"I'll see you tomorrow, ok? It's a long boat ride, you know?" Lia said as she started to stand, patting the wrinkles out of her blouse.

"I'll walk you to your room."

"No, that's all right. I'll get there by myself. But thank you."

With that, she leaned over and gave Rob a kiss on the lips, lingering just a second longer, then straightened up, and walked quickly away. He sat there, watching her walk on the deck, her effortless glide, her amazing curves. As she got to a hallway door, she looked back briefly and smiled, and then she was gone.

Rob sat there. He knew he had fallen for this girl. Bigtime. He looked up into the sky, where the stars were shining brightly. He smiled at the irony of being more nervous before this first kiss than before any mission in Syria and Afghanistan. He really wondered Who was pulling all the strings up there. Why all this was happening.

From random to precise. He planned to just think it out for a little bit before he turned in for a well-needed rest. Another couple minutes would do. Then he could drag himself to his stateroom and fall unconscious within minutes – well –maybe after a cold shower.

Lia, who was also very tired, knew she had some girl-processing to do before she could ever get to sleep. She had to wake up her mom, if she was even asleep. There was no way she could think this through on her own. A tiny knock on her mom and dad's door was more than enough to get her mom up and opening the door. Their rooms were adjoining, so she could have just gone into her own room, but decided to take one fewer step.

"Come in, come in!" Rasha hurriedly whispered.

Lia came in and her mother shut the door behind her. Peiter's steady breathing told her he was fast asleep and wouldn't be waking up until morning.

"Oh, mom!" Lia paused, thinking for a moment. "Everything's *good.* I mean *really* good." Her luminous green eyes flashed as she smiled broadly.

"Oh, you mean I'll have to take back everything I was saying about him tonight with your father?" Rasha said, laughing.

"Oh yeah," Lia said with a smile, "everything." Her eyes danced.

And for the next hour and a half, even though she was still exhausted from the mission, Lia gave the minute-by-minute playback, multiple times, of the breakthrough with Rob. Rasha needed several playbacks to savor some of the most blissful moments Lia was sharing.

Although Rasha got up the next morning at her customary time of 5 a.m., Lia would not rise until well after 11 a.m., only to get back in bed with her journal, so she could write everything down.

She guessed the rest of the voyage could be pretty nice. She might not tell her mother *everything.*

The ultra-secret Us knew they had to keep moving, keep fighting like their very souls depended on it. Every day, lives were being lost or ruined. Now, with Gui's "cooperation," they would target high-value traffickers even more proficiently. They could potentially crack into the near-impenetrable sphere of the world's elite, the untouchables.

But the boat ride home was slow and steady. The interrogation of Gui was going better than expected. Gui was spilling his guts to save his miserable ass. It appeared he was truly looking for redemption. If that was true, and with his nearly unimaginable wealth, Gui could perhaps find his way back into the light, in large part by generous donations to fund the fight against the scourge of human and sex trafficking.

On the other hand, Lia and Us had enough incriminating evidence, including video, audio and financial transactions, that Gui could look forward to life behind bars, on any of at least three continents. When one country had made him pay for his crimes, they could always send him to another.

But it would be so much nicer if Gui actually wanted to do the right thing. The crucible of time would test his true motivations.

Maybe Lia and Rob could get to know each other a little better on the week-long transatlantic voyage home. Lia now had a pretty good idea that Rob was counting on it. They had a pretty good start tonight.

How coincidental.

And looking down from wherever He was, Providence smiled.

Chapter 38

Vladimir hoped he didn't show the overwhelming surge of giddiness when he spotted the Magalon's navigation lights as it first came into view on the Hudson River from the mouth of the Upper Bay. He had already heard from his spotters on Brighton Beach that the ship was making its way through the Lower Bay, guided of course by the Sandy Hook Harbor Pilot. Sitting shotgun in the black Cadillac Escalade with black-out tinted windows, Vlad looked through his Baigish 20x50 Russian binoculars, a gift from the *brigadier*, and that had reportedly belonged to Yaponchik Ivankov himself. Ivankov was the Bratva chief who had taken over the Brighton Beach Bratva until he was arrested and convicted for an extortion scheme. It was Ivankov who'd loved Vlad's idea to expand into the Miami strip club scene, and eventually monopolize it. Even a leader with the stature of Ivankov was not immune from the sniper's rifle, and he died a lingering, painful death after taking a shot in the stomach. When a jealous internal rival sees a threat to his power inside the Bratva, death is inevitable, such as it was with Ivankov.

But tonight, Vlad would rise in the ranks. It was he who had arranged this lucrative international bonanza. Because of his efforts, millions upon millions of dollars would flow to his organization every year. His elevation could not be denied. No longer did he belong as a member of a low-level working unit. No, he would surely ascend to *brigadier*, a man over four working units, and report to a *pakhan*, or boss.

Twelve and a half million dollars, in cryptocurrency, the Bratva's share of Gui's "brokerage" fee, would return ten times that in less than five years. Vladimir himself would start his own bitcoin account, with a million dollars' worth of bitcoins, as his "incentive" payment as soon as the money from the "product" paid back the Bratva's initial investment. This was the ultimate win-win. Everyone would win here, even his good friend Gui.

"*Oy, blyat!*" "Oh, shit!" thought Vlad, snapping back to reality. "Gui just died in a helicopter crash!" Vladimir would have to find the perfect spot for his favorite picture of himself with his former friend. His thoughts propelled him further.

Vlad knew the perfect place to set up his personal R&R pad. Smack in the middle of Sunny Isles Beach, adjoining Miami Beach, there were plenty of dedicated proletarian restaurants, no English spoken. Russian ex-pats everywhere. It didn't matter that he hated communism. It was just nice to be around his kinfolk. It felt like home.

Better yet, the high-rise condo on the beach had some one-bedroom suites that he could now afford, overlooking the Atlantic. The main attraction, at least for Vlad, was that the girls at the pool were decidedly European in their cultural mores. Why they even brought their tops to the pool was a mystery to him. They never wore them. Vlad knew from experience that he would never sleep alone unless *he* wanted to.

With all these lofty thoughts swirling in his mind, Vlad failed to notice the unmarked cars arriving at the port. His eyes were trained on the Magalon. His driver was looking in the same direction. The tractor-trailer truck and extra men from the working units were waiting at an all-night coffee shop about a mile from the cargo entry at the port. Vlad had already gotten their IDs and arranged for their entry with some well-placed *obochek*, bribes, with the local union boss on the CWA Local 1032. Getting their truck on port property, loading and leaving, should not be a problem.

Two hours later, the Magalon was docked and the unloading was well underway. These ports were amazingly efficient. They would be done unloading in just over three hours. Only six hours prior, the girls on board had loaded up from their ship's quarters into specially modified "reefers," a refrigerated unit normally used for fresh fruit transport, now converted into a fresh human transport.

Every forty-foot container had a unique ID number, which was automatically scanned, located, and placed directly on a truck. The container with the girls was in a group of five from the same company. This was of course done to eliminate suspicion. Each of the other containers was a reefer, and each contained fresh fruit that required refrigeration. If the bay door was opened on any container, the only thing seen would be carefully stacked crates of fresh fruit. It was a foolproof operation.

As Vladimir was watching his flawless operation unfold perfectly, and the trucks were nearly out of the port, he saw with horror about twenty blackened SUVs speeding toward the five trucks, blue lights flashing, surrounding and stopping the small convoy. Men in full SWAT gear, armed to the hilt, were pointing their assault rifles at the truck drivers and ordering them out and face-down on the ground. Now visibly shaking, Vladimir watched as the officers opened each container. They weren't just looking, they were *unloading* the crates.

With sweat pouring from Vladimir's head like he had just sprinted a mile, and with his heart pounding just as fast as if he had, he saw a girl come out, then another, and another, until he could see at least twenty. That was less than half the number.

....

Vladimir was actually surprised at how well the *brigadier* took the news. He reassured Vlad that in this kind of business, losses happened. Sometimes, things went very wrong. It was all part of the game they were in. He reminded Vlad that he had done many good things for the Bratva, including the strip joints in Miami. As a matter of fact, he encouraged Vlad to take a flight to Miami right now, just in case there was any heat or other fallout from the bust. They did not think there was any potential connection with the girls and the Bratva, but who knew for sure? They would summon Vladimir when things cooled off.

Miami was hot. It was unseasonably humid for a January in South Florida. Vlad had been there for almost two weeks. Tonight, he was finishing off his fifth vodka tonic at his new favorite strip club. He was impressed with how much better the clubs were than ten years ago when he first came down to Miami. But then again, the Bratva had good product, especially the Eastern European girls.

Vladimir was proud of his perfect record of keeping the Thieves' Code. Especially in his ability to handle copious amounts of alcohol consumption. Tonight was no different, at least until his fifth shot of his favorite vodka. To his mild surprise, he recognized two of his Brighton Beach comrades, unit brothers, when they walked up to the bar and sat next to him.

"Vladimir, kak, chert voz'mi, ty?" "Vladimir, how the fuck are you?"

Sergei was not a big fan of Vladimir. Sergei's family roots in Russia were relatively high-level. His father was even a mid-level bureaucrat in the Glasnost era in food distribution. Vladimir came from much more humble stock. Sergei was resentful anytime he saw that Vlad was getting recognition from the *brigadier*. Ever since Vlad had returned from Miami a decade ago and pitched the strip club ideas, Sergei had much to resent. Then came the trafficking ring project, when Vlad was back and forth to Brazil, Miami and NYC. This low-class

Russian peasant was clearly outpacing Sergei in the Bratva. He bristled anytime Vladimir had the audacity to ask him to do anything. Most times, he would just tell him to fuck off, and busy himself in lighting a new cigarette. When the *brigadier* was around, though, he would glare and scowl and finally, with a grand gesture of largesse, agree to do the thing requested, but always with a personal twist, and accomplished in a different way, just to show that Vlad's way was stupid and he was still able to do the thing, the smarter way.

So, when the order on Vladimir came down from the *convocation* to interrogate, then dispose, Sergei, feigning sadness, volunteered to take the assignment. He would reluctantly do his duty to carry out the punishment decided upon for Vladimir, the poor bastard. He was only mildly surprised that the penalty was one of the harshest. At least for Vladimir, none of his family members would be killed, unless they were directly involved. Not that any of the Bratva had anything to do with their families, since none had wives or children, but most had brothers, sisters, mothers and fathers. And as much as they had forsaken their immediate family to join the organization, none wanted to see their family members murdered as they watched, just before they themselves were executed.

When Vladimir turned to Sergei and tried to answer, he could not speak any words. Sergei just looked at him and smiled.

"Vlad, my friend, are you not feeling well?"

Vladimir was beginning to slump forward, as the Rohypnol, "roofies," were quickly beginning to impair not only his speech, but his ability to keep from falling on the floor.

"*Ve vill help Vladimir get home. He 'ees a good friend of ourz,*" Sergei said to the bartender, who, in fact, had poured the liquid into Vladimir's last shot of vodka. Unknown to Vlad, Sergei and Boris had been in town for nearly a week, doing surveillance on their comrade. They had scoped out the clubs where they thought he might be hanging out for drinks. Sergei had spoken with the bartenders and knew the precise times when Vlad might show up. A couple of nights ago, he gave the vial of Rohypnol to the bartender with instructions on when to pour it.

There was no concern about secrecy with the bartender. He would tell no one. Not his fellow bartenders, or his girlfriend, or the police, and especially not Vladimir. It was not just the ten $100 bills that kept his lips sealed. It was the very real fear that this Russian dude would just as soon cut a hole in his stomach and reach in with his bare hand and rip his heart out, or have him pour another drink. Either one was fine. And he wouldn't ask any questions. He seriously didn't want to know things. The money here was good. Beyond good. It was amazing, and getting this gig had been no easy thing. Every bartender in town wanted this job. There weren't many bartending jobs in Miami where you could make a thousand on weeknights and two grand on weekends. And the view from the bar wasn't bad, either. His current girlfriend was one of the new girls from a couple of months ago, from the Ukraine. She was still working on her English, but he didn't mind. He wasn't exactly looking for conversations.

Sergei nodded for Boris to get on the other side of Vladimir. With both his arms draped over their shoulders, they started walking him to the door.

....

Two weeks later, on the back pages of the *Miami Herald*, the small news story read: "Unidentified body discovered in mangroves on Key Biscayne, just past Bear's Cut. Anyone with information please call 1-866-471-TIPS." What they didn't write was that the body was found headless, handless and footless, and the arms, torso and back had the skin removed, which may have been to remove tattoo markings.

Word got back to the *brigadier* that the South Americans did not take the loss as lightly as the Bratva. The report stated that an entire village was massacred, over fifty poor souls with their tongues cut out.

The monsters were not as concerned with police finding the victims' identities.

The Bratva decided that someone had to pay with blood for the loss of millions of dollars on the busted shipment. Although the sodium pentothal-facilitated interrogation did not produce anything concrete regarding Vladimir's potential deceit of the organization, they had already decided that his life would be required for the failure, lest others begin to think failure was acceptable. At least the alliance between the Bratva and the South Americans was intact. They would make up for their losses in the next shipment. Regardless, Sergei was more than willing to carry out the sentence, even though the interrogation would take over a week. Or perhaps, especially for that reason.

Almost sounded like a fitting end for all human traffickers.

Lia, *Us*, and their newest warrior, Rob, were already working on speeding up that fate, to whomever and wherever it may lead.

Fact Versus Fiction in the Book:

Human trafficking is no fiction. It is a tragic fact that even today, slavery exists, both outright and in more subtle ways. Countless lives are lost in this terrible scourge on humanity. Countless others suffer under exploitive masters. Profits into the billions are estimated from the worldwide trade. There are recognized nations whose governments turn a blind eye toward the trade, or even partake in it, sharing in the illicit profits.

It is real.

This novel truly only scratches at the surface of the problem. Extreme poverty in many countries of the world provides victims for the perpetrators of the trade. It is a worldwide problem. But it is as close as your own neighborhood, too.

Be proactive. Vigilant. If you suspect potential human trafficking, call the National Human Trafficking Hotline, toll-free, at 1-888-373-7888, or text them at 233733. In so doing, you can help turn the tide and end this scourge.

For more information and other hotlines, please visit https://www.state.gov/domestic-trafficking-hotlines/

Made in United States
North Haven, CT
03 September 2022

23382207R00146